DAY OF THE DAEMON

A COUNTDOWN TO destruction and hatred has
begun!

The first exciting instalment in this brand
new trilogy, set in the dark and gothic
Warhammer world, is packed with action and
adventure. *Day of the Daemon* follows the journey of archaeologist Alaric and his assistant
Dietz as they return to the war-blighted city of
Middenheim. The recent war against the dark
forces of Chaos has corrupted the souls of
many mortal men and there is now no short-
age willing to do the bidding of the Dark
Gods. As the clock ticks down, the day of the
daemon approaches and it falls to those few
men who have remained true to the Empire to
stop it!

More Warhammer from the Black Library

A WARHAMMER NOVEL

BOOK ONE OF THE
DAEMON GATES TRILOGY

DAY OF THE DAEMON

AARON ROSENBERG

For Jenifer, Adara and Arthur who protect me from my own inner daemons.

A Black Library Publication

First published in Great Britain in 2006 by
BL Publishing,
Games Workshop Ltd.,
Willow Road, Nottingham,
NG7 2WS, UK

10 9 8 7 6 5 4 3 2 1

Cover illustration by Max Bertolini.
Map by Nuala Kinrade.

A CIP record for this book is available from the British Library.

ISBN 13: 978 1 84416 366 3
ISBN 10: 1 84416 366 0

Distributed in the US by Simon & Schuster
1230 Avenue of the Americas, New York, NY 10020.

Printed and bound in Great Britain by
Bookmarque, Surrey, UK.

See the Black Library on the Internet at
www.blacklibrary.com

Find out more about Games Workshop
and the world of Warhammer at
www.games-workshop.com

THIS IS A DARK age, a bloody age, an age of daemons
and of sorcery. It is an age of battle and death, and of the
world's ending. Amidst all of the fire, flame and fury
it is a time, too, of mighty heroes, of bold deeds
and great courage.

AT THE HEART of the Old World sprawls the Empire, the
largest and most powerful of the human realms. Known
for its engineers, sorcerers, traders and soldiers, it is
a land of great mountains, mighty rivers, dark forests
and vast cities. And from his throne in Altdorf reigns
the Emperor Karl-Franz, sacred descendant of the
founder of these lands, Sigmar, and wielder
of his magical warhammer.

BUT THESE ARE far from civilised times. Across the
length and breadth of the Old World, from the knightly
palaces of Bretonnia to ice-bound Kislev in the far north,
come rumblings of war. In the towering World's Edge
Mountains, the orc tribes are gathering for another assault.
Bandits and renegades harry the wild southern lands of
the Border Princes. There are rumours of rat-things, the
skaven, emerging from the sewers and swamps across the
land. And from the northern wildernesses there is the
ever-present threat of Chaos, of daemons and beastmen
corrupted by the foul powers of the Dark Gods.
As the time of battle draws ever nearer,
the Empire needs heroes
like never before.

PROLOGUE

DIETRICH 'DIETZ' FROEBEL flattened himself against the wall, the rough stone digging into his back through his sweat-soaked shirt and vest. 'If I make it out of here,' he muttered to himself, 'I swear I'll never look at cats the same way again.'

Just past him, an arched doorway broke the wall, and by craning his neck Dietz could see several tall, husky figures prowling down the hall beyond. He had seen beastmen before, of course – mostly when their bodies had been dragged back to Middenheim by bounty hunters and bored guardsmen. He'd even fought a few since enlisting in that madman Alaric's service. When he thought of beastmen he pictured those creatures: animals that walked upright, bestial men with strangely distorted features and scraps of leather and cloth for makeshift clothes. Some had crude armour they'd clearly ripped from their victims and pieced back together. Weapons were the same way, crude or stolen and poorly tended.

Not these, however. The creatures stalking past were built like men, except for their long lashing tails, but moved with the grace of cats, as well they should. Their bodies were covered in striped orange and black fur, their heads those of tigers, but with more intelligent eyes, their hands tipped with claws, but able to grasp weapons easily. These beastmen were nothing like he'd imagined. Their armour was clearly handmade, little more than tooled leather straps holding flat discs of metal and stone in strategic locations, but handsome and effective. Their weapons were hatchets and short swords, and spears with blades of glittering black stone and hafts of gleaming wood, far finer than Dietz had imagined beastmen capable of creating.

Everything about Ind had come as a surprise. Of course, that made sense. They were several thousand miles from the Empire, after all. If it were all like home, what would be the point in travelling? Some of the surprises, like the lush landscape, were actually pleasant; shame this wasn't one of them.

He ducked back and pressed himself even harder against the wall when one of the beastmen paused and snarled something. Hoping they hadn't heard him – or smelled him – Dietz held his breath. He heard a soft padding sound and knew at least one was approaching. His right hand crept to the long knife at his belt, though he knew he could only take one down before the others jumped him. Just as he was sliding the blade from its sheath he heard a loud, musical clang that echoed through the chamber, shaking the floor and setting his teeth vibrating. At last!

The padding stopped, then resumed again, but moving away, and Dietz slowly let out his breath. A moment later the hall was silent and he risked another glance. They had gone.

He and Alaric had watched the temple for several days before attempting to enter and had quickly seen the pattern. Every day, as the sun hit its height, a gong sounded from the temple's peak. All the beastmen stopped what they were doing and funnelled indoors. Whether it was the mid-day meal or group worship did not matter. The important thing was that all of the beastmen were occupied, which would leave the halls clear. Dietz had wanted to wait until the gong to enter, but Alaric had pointed out the temple's sheer size. 'You'll never get to the centre in time if you wait that long,' he'd explained. 'You'll have to start sooner so the gong can clear the final passages for you.'

And he'd been right, damn him. Dietz was only halfway through the maze of corridors, though the rest of his progress would be quicker without having to duck along side passages. He hated it when Alaric was right. Not that his employer would even notice. And where was he, while Dietz was doing all the hard work? Probably still staring at that tablet by the entrance, he thought.

'FASCINATING!' ALARIC VON Jungfreud brushed some dirt from the flat panel embedded in the temple wall before him and traced the rune he'd revealed. Then he copied it down in his notebook. 'Not an honorific at all. That's definitely a warning of some sort, or an admonition – perhaps a conditional? Coupled with this other mark here...'

His blond head bent over his notebook, Alaric barely registered the gong's vibrations. Nor did it occur to him to wonder where Dietz was, or whether the other man was in any danger. Or to worry about crouching by the temple's entrance, in easy view of anyone approaching or stepping out onto one of the balconies above. All Alaric thought of was the tablet and the words inscribed upon it. Dietz would be fine. He always was.

'SIGMAR'S BEARD!'

Though he kept his voice low, the words still echoed through the small chamber. Dietz had made his way down the corridors, trading stealth for speed now that the gong had cleared the halls of occupants. He had finally reached a door, the only one he had seen – every other portal had been an open archway. This archway held a slab of stone polished to silky smoothness, its glossy black surface providing a perfect reflection of Dietz and the hall behind him. The door had no lock he could find, but from its centre protruded a tiger's head of red marble, a massive ring clutched in its jaws. A sharp tug on the ring and the door had slid open silently. He had stepped quickly inside and the sight beyond was the cause of his sudden outburst.

This was the heart of the temple. It had to be. It was a small chamber, barely twenty feet across, with strange angled corners and walls that curved up to form a vaulted ceiling. A second smaller door stood to one side. The centre of the ceiling was a circle of clear crystal, and the sun shone down, its light flooding the room and spilling across the intricately tiled floor. Dietz saw tigers and lions, and other great cats battling beneath his feet, rending men and horses and each other.

That was not what had stopped him. Nor was it the carved columns at each corner of the room or the inset nooks holding sculptures and vases, or even the tapestries that hung between them. No, the statue facing the door had provoked his outburst. It covered the entire wall and dominated the chamber.

Dietz stepped closer, studying the carving. Much of it was the red marble of the door sculpture, though a paler, brighter red. The dark marbling had been artfully arranged to reproduce tiger stripes across the torso and limbs. The figure towered above him, its uppermost claws almost scraping the skylight. Other arms held a golden sword, a glittering black mace, a strange barbed fan and a black-headed spear. The bottom arms clutched a crimson scroll between them. Gold-set jewels hung from the tufted ears, decorated many of the claws and even pierced various points about the chest. A heavy belt, gold links connecting rubies and diamonds and other stones, hung on the hips. A curving golden spike capped the tail arcing up behind, but it was the face that captured his attention. Carved from a single slab of stone, golden brown with streaks of light where the sun touched it, the face spoke of cruelty and blood lust and a horrible intelligence. It's only a statue, Dietz reassured himself as he gasped for breath, but his heart did not believe that. No, this was She'ar Khawn, the eight-armed tiger-god of Ind, standing before him. And She'ar Khawn was not happy.

The sound of a second, lighter gong rippled through the temple air and shook Dietz from his panic. It was the first of several, and after the fourth there would be one final peal from the larger gong. Then the beastmen would return to their duties and the hall would be swarming with them again. He had to hurry.

Alaric had not known what to expect, so his instructions had been vague. 'Grab something small enough to carry, valuable enough to be worth our time and distinctive enough it could not come from anywhere else,' he had said. Dietz thought about this. The figures in the wall niches were handsome but perhaps not that unique. The tapestries were too large to carry easily. The jewels about the statue might be fused to the stone. He considered the scroll, but could not see its surface well enough to know whether it was real or a clever carving, and what good would a sculpture of a scroll be to him? Then his gaze returned to the tiger-god's face, and Dietz nodded. Since She'ar Khawn was already displeased, he saw no reason to be nice about it.

Pulling his knife, Dietz stepped up close to the statue, resisting a shudder as he passed within the compass of those eight arms. Raising his blade, he applied its tip to the bottom edge of the statue's golden face and exerted pressure, just enough to see how securely the face was held. Much to his surprise he heard a faint pop and a shrill keen, and it slid free. He caught it reflexively as it dropped, surprised by its lack of weight. Turning it over, Dietz realised why. It was not a solid carving so much as a mask, the interior carved away to allow space for a face behind it. Glancing up again, he saw that the statue still had a face the same red marble as the rest. The mask had been laid over it.

As he stepped back, sheathing the knife and sliding the mask into the pack at his back, Dietz noticed the keening had not stopped. In fact it had grown louder, and now it was joined by a strange hiss.

Trusting his instincts, Dietz hurled himself backwards. A sharp breeze tugged at his hair and beard as the hiss intensified, and he felt as much as saw a sheet of silver plummeting from the ceiling. He struck the ground hard, landing on his rear and rolling to his feet as the massive blade dropped from the ceiling and sank into a groove carved along the floor mere inches from the statue, and right where he had been standing.

'Time to go,' he muttered to himself, and turned in time to see the door sliding shut. 'Damn!' He pushed against it, but it did not budge. Beyond it he could hear the pad of feet and the scrape of claws against stone. Glancing around, Dietz saw the second door also sliding shut and dived for it, scraping through just before the heavy stone slab thudded into the doorframe. 'What have we here?' he wondered, glancing around.

This was an even smaller room, though with more traditional squared walls and corners. It had no windows, no elaborate carvings and its floor was the same smooth red granite he had seen elsewhere in the temple. A second door barring the far side of the room was of polished wood rather than stone. Clearly, this was an antechamber of some sort, but for what purpose?

Then Dietz noticed the cages.

They were small, barely the size of his head, and made from tightly fitted wooden slats. He had missed them at first because of their size and because they were all piled in the corners. Scraping sounds, whimpers, clicks and other noises told him they were occupied, as did the smell, which finally hit him. With a shudder, Dietz remembered the scroll in She'ar Khawn's lowest hands and understood. The crimson was old blood from sacrifices. These poor creatures were the victims.

'Sorry I can't help,' he told them as he hurried past to the outer door. Hauling it open, Dietz found himself facing a narrow corridor – and several beastmen charging towards him, faces twisted into snarls, blades at the ready.

A quick glance around confirmed that the antechamber had no other exits. The corridor was empty save the approaching guards, but the antechamber itself–

'Your lucky day,' Dietz said as he grabbed the cages stacked there. 'Freedom and revenge all at once.' He picked them up and hurled them, one at a time, at the charging beastmen.

The cages burst on impact, spilling angry, desperate animals into the hall. They clung to the beastmen, hissing and spitting, biting and clawing. The organised charge collapsed into a desperate attempt to remove these tiny fiends from head and arm, torso and back. In their panic, the beastmen dropped their weapons, reverting to claws and teeth, and Dietz took advantage of the moment. He darted through the frenzied mass, using one beastman's fallen axe to club anyone in his way. Finally, he was through the small throng and back in a larger hallway. Snarls and growls were everywhere, and Dietz knew he could not return the way he had come. Choosing a direction at random, he took off at a run, hoping to avoid any more surprises.

Behind him, unnoticed, the last creature he had spilled from its cage hopped off a fallen beastman, shook itself, and darted after him.

SEVERAL MINUTES AND a few hair-raising encounters later, Dietz burst through an archway onto a small balcony. The beastman he had clubbed lay groaning behind him, and he had eluded the others, so he took the time to glance around. He was facing the jungle, which was a good sign – he had already seen an interior balcony, but had avoided it, knowing it would leave him open to the beastmen's spears. This one was on the temple's exterior, along the west wall, judging from the sun. Peering down, he saw one of the temple doorways some fifty feet beneath him. A familiar figure knelt to one side of the arch, scribbling furiously.

'Alaric!' At Dietz's shout the other man glanced up and waved. 'Time to go!' Dietz added, and then looked around behind him. The beastman had rolled over and was trying to lever itself to its feet. Past him, Dietz saw several more rounding the corner. They would soon be here. The balcony was too high to jump from and the temple's exterior had been planed smooth as glass, but handsome tapestries hung to either side of the archway. He grabbed the one to the left, kicking the beastman in the head as he passed, and hauled the heavy cloth from the wall. Running back to the balcony, Dietz used his knife to slice the tapestry down the middle, eliciting a cry of dismay from Alaric below. Ignoring it, he tied one half around the balcony railing and twisted the other end around his hand. Then he jumped.

The tapestry tore under his weight; a loud rip he knew would bring the other beastmen running. However, it slowed his fall enough so that he dropped the last few feet, landing with a loud grunt, but otherwise unharmed.

'That tapestry was priceless!' Alaric complained, giving him a hand up.

'Then it won't cost anything to replace,' he snapped back, grabbing Alaric's arm and tugging him towards the jungle. 'Come on!'

A pack of beastmen burst from the temple entrance, growling and waving spears and swords, and Alaric nodded. 'Right, I'll have to come back for the tablet.' Then he took off after Dietz, who was already among the first trees.

Behind them, the small creature from the antechamber had reached the balcony. It hopped up onto the tapestry and scrambled down it, sharp claws finding easy purchase in the thick cloth. Leaping the last few feet to the ground, it darted into the jungle after the men, disappearing in the thick undergrowth.

* * *

'TAAL'S TEETH!'

Alaric slid to a stop, slamming into Dietz's back as he came upon the taller man suddenly. Only Dietz's outflung arm, grasping tightly to a thick vine, kept them both from falling into the chasm that yawned at their feet. Dietz had almost missed it, too intent upon ducking vines and low branches, and skipping over thick roots to notice the approaching line of grey that slashed across the green around them. Now, however, the wide gap was impossible to miss – the plants ended suddenly and beyond them was empty air, and another jungle-covered cliff beyond that.

'Where did that come from?' demanded Alaric, righting himself and taking two cautious steps back from the edge. 'That wasn't there before.'

Dietz rolled his eyes. 'We didn't come this way before.'

'Oh.' Alaric looked around, and pointed. 'What's that over there?'

Following his finger, Dietz saw something dark curving across the gap. 'Come on.'

As they reached it, they saw it was a bridge, though not much of one. A thick rope was strung across the chasm, with two thinner ropes above and on either side.

'You call that a bridge?' Alaric said in disgust, staring at it. 'I've seen better from orphans living in ditches!'

'Insult it later,' Dietz warned him, shoving the younger man towards it. 'Use it now.'

They both glanced back, hearing the growls and roars growing behind them, and Alaric nodded. Setting one foot upon the thicker rope and clutching the two thinner ones, he walked quickly across – for all his complaints his steps were sure and steady, and he seemed no more inconvenienced than a man on an afternoon stroll. Dietz was right behind him, doing his best not to look down. His attention entirely focussed on the ropes at his hands and feet, and the sounds behind him, he never even noticed as a small figure darted from the jungle and leaped, its front claws latching onto the leather of his pack.

'Shall we?' Alaric asked lightly as Dietz reached the other side, and was half-turned to the jungle beyond when Dietz shook his head.

'Hang on.' Drawing his knife, Dietz turned back to the bridge and sliced at one of the hand-ropes. The sharp edge of the blade slid off, repelled somehow. Looking more closely, Dietz saw a thick, sticky coating about the ropes, most likely sap. 'Clever,' he admitted.

'Leave it,' Alaric urged him, tugging at his sleeve. 'They're right behind us.'

Dietz shook him off. 'That's why I have to cut the bridge. Otherwise they'll keep chasing us.' With a sigh, he turned and started back onto the bridge. 'Get back among the trees,' he shouted over his shoulder.

As he had hoped, the sap only protected the ropes at either end. Twenty paces back it faded away and his knife sliced easily through the first hand-rope. Unfortunately, a dozen beastmen were already on the bridge and stalking towards him.

'Hurry!' Alaric shouted from the trees and Dietz snarled. What did the fool think he was doing? But he had two ropes left. A quick look at the rapidly approaching beastmen and Dietz made a decision. He stooped, just in time to avoid several spears thrown from the far side, and sliced down with all his strength, his free hand tightly curled around the other hand-rope. With a twang the rope below parted and his feet dropped out from under him. His grip held and Dietz dangled from the third rope. Most of the beastmen had not been that lucky. Their snarls turned to yowls as they plunged into the darkness below. A series of thuds a moment later testified to the chasm's depth and the presence of a solid bottom.

Three beastmen had reacted quickly when the bridge was cut, dropping their weapons and curling their paws around the remaining rope. Now the foremost began creeping towards Dietz, hauling itself hand over hand, its face twisted into a vicious array of teeth and whiskers. Dietz was not waiting around. With his other hand he lashed out again, and the knife slid easily through the last rope just behind him. The taut cord parted with a loud snap, and the remaining beastmen plummeted to their deaths. Dietz almost joined them, his sweaty hand slipping as his weight tugged on the rope, and dropped his knife just in time to grab the rope end with his other hand. The chasm wall was solid stone and his breath whooshed out as he slammed against it, but his grip held. After catching his breath again, Dietz wrapped the rope around his right hand and began hauling himself up with his left.

That was when he heard the chanting.

Looking over his shoulder, he discovered that one of the beastmen had not attempted the bridge. Standing on the far side of the chasm, this one's fur was shot with white, especially around the muzzle. One hand held a glittering black sword and the other bore a long staff of golden stone, several long claws mounted near the top. More claws and stones decorated a chain around the beastman's throat, and others rose like a crest above its head. The beastman continued chanting, strange liquid sounds rolling from its throat, and it gestured with its staff towards Dietz.

Expecting to be struck dead, Dietz was surprised when instead he felt the rope in his hands writhe. As he stared, horrified, the rough brown cord turned a glistening greenish black, its dry surface growing wet and scaly. The end, just beyond Dietz's right hand, narrowed at the tip and split across, revealing a pair of long, dripping fangs and small diamond-shaped yellow eyes just above them. The beastman had transformed the rope into a snake – and its fangs were only inches from Dietz's face.

Dietz knew this was the end. His second knife was in his boot and too far away to reach. His right hand was too tightly wrapped to get loose, and his left was still clutching to keep him from falling. He couldn't duck the snake's attack, not this close. His only hope was to let go and pray he caught on the cliff wall somehow before he struck bottom. He could almost feel Morr hovering nearby.

Even as his left hand was losing its grip, something darted past Dietz's head from behind. A small furry form lunged down, its tiny mouth wide open, its needle-like teeth latched onto the snake just below the jaws. The newcomer's mouth shut with an audible snap and the snake thrashed in Dietz's hands as its head was torn free and tossed aside. Instantly, it reverted to rope, and Dietz hauled himself the rest of the way up, pausing only to grab a loose rock and hurl it at the beastman on the far side. It snarled and dodged the missile, but backed away and disappeared into the jungle.

Alaric stepped forward and grasped Dietz's free hand once he came into view, helping the older man haul himself onto solid ground. The small creature leaped down at once from Dietz's pack and began rubbing its head and shoulder against Dietz's chin.

'Well, that was exciting,' Alaric murmured. 'Find anything worthwhile?' Dietz handed him the mask and watched his employer's face light up. 'Ah, excellent! Most excellent!' He glanced down at Dietz again. 'Good work, and where the devil did you get that monkey?'

Dietz blinked at the small creature, which stared back at him. 'No idea, but it saved my life,' he admitted. 'It can stay if it wants.' He studied it more closely. 'Maybe the antechamber – lots of small animals there. Monkey? Are you sure?'

The creature was the length of his arm, though much of that looked to be its thick tail, and covered in short tawny fur, with bands of red along its body and darker red at its head and feet, and tail end. It had a long, narrow face with a pointed nose and small round ears. Its eyes were dark and had a look of lively intelligence.

Alaric looked offended. 'Of course I'm sure. That is an Indyan tree-monkey.'

The creature reared back as if offended, and Dietz chuckled despite himself.

'Doesn't look like any monkey I've seen, but you're the expert. We'll need a name for you, little one.' He considered.

'I'll call you Glouste.' He rubbed its head and it pushed against his fingers like a contented cat. 'Well, Glouste, we shouldn't sit here all day. Come on.' Dietz stood up and Glouste skittered up his arm and settled around his neck like a fur collar.

Alaric shook his head and shoved the stone mask into his own pack. 'Yes, well, do not expect me to help you clean up after it!' he insisted as they moved away from the chasm, heading into the jungle to begin the long, dangerous trek back to their boat and eventually to civilisation.

CHAPTER ONE

'I'LL BE SPEAKING with your superiors about this!' Alaric shouted over his shoulder as he kicked his horse forward. 'The nerve,' he muttered to Dietz as they cleared the gate and entered Middenheim proper. 'Searching my bags! As if I was a common merchant, or a pedlar! This is the twentieth year of Karl-Franz's reign. You'd think he'd have brought some culture to these people by now!'

Dietz shrugged. He'd been a bit surprised to see so many soldiers at the gate when they'd arrived, including several half-familiar faces, but he couldn't fault them for searching their belongings. These were dangerous times and they were strangers here. Well, at least Alaric was.

As they passed out of the gate's shadow, Dietz glanced around, eager to see how his former home had fared of late. The sights that greeted him, however, made him wish they had chosen a different city to visit. What had happened here? When they had left, Middenheim had been the rock of the Empire, the mighty stone city that no foe could breach. Its homes had stood high and proud, its streets smooth and clean, its people rough but lively.

All that was gone. As they rode Dietz saw rubble everywhere, homes in ruins, buildings shattered. Their horses moved slowly, carefully setting hooves between chunks of stone, rotten foods, old rags, and even bodies. Some of the figures stretched out on the paving stones groaned and twitched, but others lay still; whether in sleep or worse Dietz could not tell. Those people walking past had a hard look about them, a look of despair as if they had seen the pits of Chaos and had not escaped unscathed.

'Madness,' Dietz said softly, eyeing their surroundings. He had heard about the war, of course, and the plague – the sailors had told him during their return voyage, and both he and Alaric had counted themselves lucky to have avoided such events. Clearly they had not escaped its aftermath. He found himself wondering how many of his old friends had survived both illness and combat. He was deliberately not wondering the same about his family.

'Absolutely,' Alaric agreed, but when Dietz glanced over he saw his employer rummaging through a saddlebag, not even noticing the dreariness around them. 'That lout could have destroyed these items easily, with those ham-hands of his!' Alaric exhaled sharply as his hands closed about something wrapped in several silk scarves, and pulled it loose to feel its contours carefully. 'Well, the mask is intact, at least,' he assured Dietz. 'Now, as I was saying earlier, I don't think the symbols are writing exactly. More of a pictogrammatic style, I'd guess, illustrating some significant...'

Dietz tuned out the rest of the lecture. He enjoyed Alaric's company, and liked working for the young noble-turned-explorer, but by Sigmar the boy could talk! Since Dietz didn't care to hear all the details of centuries-old writing, and Alaric could happily talk to himself for hours, the arrangement worked perfectly – Alaric continued to babble on about runes and carvings and ancient languages, and Dietz guided their horses down street after street, leading them through the city and back to Rolf's shop. At least some parts of the city were intact, and he was surprised how happy he was to see the carved wolves' heads still atop the mounting posts and the street lamps that resembled icicles, and the bite- and claw marks traditionally carved above every door, showing that Ulric had set his seal upon it and offered his protection to its occupants. Still, it was not all pleasant. Several times along the way Dietz had to kick loose hands as people grasped their saddles and reins, begging for coins or food or death, and he was finally forced to keep his gaze on the shop signs and street posts so that he would not see yet another starved, maimed wretch hobbling after them, pleading for help.

Rolf's shop looked the same, at least, its thick stone front undamaged and the heavy wooden plaque above, supported by stout chains whose links were shaped into wolves biting their own tails, still well polished. They left their horses at a livery one street over, where the stable hand remembered them and promised them the best stalls, and tossed the saddlebags onto their shoulders. Glouste made a small sound of protest as Dietz's bags rose perilously close to her, but forgave him an instant later and lowered her head against his neck again.

She had been one of the only saving graces during their long voyage back, and Dietz had distracted himself from all that water around them by testing the limits of his new pet's intelligence. He had been pleasantly surprised – though he had never had a pet himself, Dietz had known boys with cats and dogs and even tame rats, and Glouste was smarter than he remembered any of them being. She clearly understood him, at least his tone and simple words, and obeyed commands unless she was feeling unappreciated. One of the sailors, seeing the monkey pretend not to hear Dietz, had chuckled and said 'got yerself quite the little woman there, friend. Mine demands baubles and fine food afore she'll do aught for me – bettin' yers is the same.' Nor had he been wrong – though affectionate and surprisingly protective,

Glouste had shown a strong will and a sense of humour, and often resisted Dietz's instructions or obeyed in such a way as to cross his intentions. Alaric she alternately ignored and obstructed, and Dietz couldn't help feeling that his pet still disapproved of the 'monkey' label his employer had given her.

'Hello? Rolf?' Alaric strode through into the shop, side-stepping a variety of carvings and sculptures. No one responded to his hail and so he continued on to the back of the shop. Dietz followed him, Glouste emitting tiny sneezes from her perch around his neck. In the rear wall was a wide doorway that led to Rolf's outdoor workshop, and Alaric pushed his way though the thick leather curtain there. He immediately backed out again, coughing. 'Damned dust!' Pulling a silk handkerchief from one sleeve, he covered his mouth and nose, and stuck his head past the curtain again, blinking furiously to keep his eyes clear of the stone dust that swirled in the cold breeze. 'Rolf, are you out here?'

'Aye, and who's calling now?' a voice replied, and Alaric stepped outside, Dietz right behind him.

The area behind the shop had been fenced off and was littered with blocks of stone in various shapes, sizes, and states of carving. Near the far wall stood a heavy table and a large man leaned over it, chipping flecks of stone from a small block set before him. Rolf was as broad as a dwarf, though he swore no such blood tainted his line, and as tall as Dietz, with massive arms and hands, and thinning red hair tied back in a long braid. That hair looked greyer than Alaric remembered, as did the full beard, but perhaps that was simply the dust. Rolf's eyes, grey as granite and twice as hard, seemed as sharp as ever, and they widened slightly when they finally spied him.

'Alaric!' The husky stonemason laid aside his hammer and chisel and turned, wiping both hands on the heavy leather smock covering his torso. 'And Dietz as well – still with this young rascal, then?'

Dietz smiled and nodded. He had known Rolf for many years, from back when his own father had traded goods with the man, and it had been his recommendation that had first brought Alaric here. 'Can't get rid of him,' he admitted wryly, earning a glance of mock-reproach from his employer.

'Aye, and you've missed the worst of it, to be sure,' Rolf assured them as he clasped their hands in turn. 'First the siege and the war, and then the plague' – he gestured past the fence, where the roofs of the neighbouring buildings could just be seen peeking up. 'It's a wonder there's a city left!'

'We saw,' Dietz admitted, though he knew Alaric had barely noticed. He started to ask another question, but couldn't bring himself to. The stonemason understood.

'Your father's still alive,' he said softly, 'though his sight's utterly gone now. Dagmar still tends to him, poor lass. And Dracht – he lost a leg in the war and a son to the plague, but he's back in the shop now, hopping about with the aid of a stick.'

Dietz nodded, grateful for the news. Both Dagmar and Dracht still alive – that was more than he'd dared hope. Deisen had been lost long ago, as had Dehanna, and Darulf had been killed by a panicking horse only the year before – their father had always claimed he chose their names because he felt 'D' was good luck, but Dietz suspected the man had simply never learnt the alphabet beyond that point. Rolf had not mentioned Darhun, which could only mean he had died as well, though whether from a blade or sickness Dietz did not know. He promised himself he'd visit his two surviving siblings while they were here, and perhaps even look in on their father if he had the time and the stomach for it.

'Now, what have you brought me?' Rolf asked finally, leading them back into the shop and over to his scarred desk, casting an amused glance to where Alaric was hopping excitedly from foot to foot. 'It must be a rare treat for you to dance so.'

'It is, it is,' Alaric assured the larger man, setting the scarf-wrapped bundle down on the desk, safely away from a small carved wolf with impressively sharp claws. 'From Ind itself, my good man, an exquisite find indeed. I believe the markings on it…'

Dietz took the opportunity to wander away – he'd heard enough from Alaric about the mask, so much so that at times he'd regretted finding it. Now he left the two other men to discuss the matter, knowing Rolf would never cheat them beyond the normal craftsman's need for a small profit, and distracted himself by roaming the shop. Rolf was an expert carver, and though he trafficked in building blocks, most of his business was sculpture and fine carving. His work filled the large store, lintels and benches and sculptures leaning against the walls or lined up to create narrow aisles, and Dietz strolled among them, admiring several new additions. He could still hear snippets of the conversation towards the back, enough that he would hear Alaric if the younger man needed his aid or his input.

'Fine work indeed,' Rolf was saying, turning the mask over and stroking one chiselled cheek with a surprisingly delicate touch. 'I've not seen the like of it, to be honest, but the carver was a true master to shape it so thin without shattering the material.' He frowned and held it up so the light from the door shone upon it. 'Not seen this stone before, either.'

'Nor have I,' Alaric admitted. 'Much of the temple was marble, but this – I'd say some form of chalcedony, perhaps, but those bands that catch the light–'

'Aye, they're stunning,' Rolf agreed, tilting the mask again, 'and capture the sense of a cat's stripes beautifully. The problem is, since I canna identify the stone, I canna say its quality. Oh, I can vouch for the craftsmanship, certainly, but not whether this is a valuable stone or some common rock to them, or even stone that's been treated somehow.' He held up a hand to stop Alaric's protests. 'I'm not saying it's worthless – the carving alone makes it a prize for some, but without knowing the stone I canna tell you a fair price for it.'

'Of course, of course,' Alaric murmured, trying to hide his disappointment. He did not do a good job of it – as usual his handsome features reflected his mood all too clearly.

'Not to worry,' Rolf assured him, setting the mask back on the desk. 'I know a few who might be interested. I'll ask around, get a feel for it, and find out what they're willing to pay. Then you tell me if that's enough. If so I'll set up the deal as usual. If not you'll have your mask back and can take it elsewhere. Perhaps someone in one of the coastal towns knows this stone and can find a better buyer.'

Alaric hesitated a moment. He knew Rolf would try his best, but was loath to relinquish the mask at all. Still, they had brought it here from Ind to sell it, and he had already sketched it and its runes for future study.

'Done,' he said finally, and they clasped hands upon it.

'Now that's settled,' Rolf said, folding the scarves back over the mask, 'I've got a few new pieces you might want to see yourself. Came to me from a wandering tinker, a week or two back, and they're not the sorts of thing I normally buy, but I knew they'd draw your interest. Got them back here for safekeeping, not the sort of thing I'd leave lying about.'

Dietz, still half-listening, had just turned down another aisle when Glouste distracted him. She had been glancing at the objects around them, her whiskers quivering with curiosity, and more than once a small squeak had indicated interest in a particular piece. This time, however, the sound was higher, more drawn-out and strangely trilling, and Dietz knew at once it was not pleasure but fear. His pet confirmed this by leaping from his shoulders and darting back down the aisle and out of sight.

'Glouste!' Swearing under his breath, Dietz took off after her, following the brief flashes of red fur he saw far ahead. Fortunately, the doors were all closed and the windows covered in heavy metal grilles, so Glouste could not escape. Even so, it took several minutes before Dietz caught up to her, and then only because she had stopped her mad flight and was cowering within a small stone cabinet.

'There there, little one,' Dietz whispered, scooping her from her hiding place and tucking her into the front of his leather jacket. 'You're safe now.' He stroked her head gently with one finger until her fur stopped puffing and the trilling faded back to her normal purr.

'Now, what had you so frightened?' he wondered out loud, retracing his steps and still petting her. The aisle they'd entered was near the back of the shop, and the piece he had almost reached before Glouste's retreat was actually covered by a large sheet. Whatever it was stood taller than he did, and he could tell from the shape that it was more likely to be a sculpture than a building ornament, with a wide round base and projections above. His own curiosity aroused, Dietz tugged the sheet free. As its folds fell to the ground his face turned as white as the fabric, and it was a second before he could find his voice.

'Alaric!'

'What?' Hearing the panic in his companion's voice, Alaric all but dropped the scroll Rolf had been handing him and ran towards the sound. When he turned the corner and skidded to a halt, he found Dietz standing stock-still, pale as chalk, one hand still clutching the sheet. The other was inside his vest, where Alaric could just hear the frightened squeaks of that infernal tree-monkey. He quickly forgot about Dietz's unruly pet as his eyes registered the object before them, and Alaric took a step back himself.

The sculpture was large, easily seven feet tall, and roughly carved. Indeed, at first glance it looked uncarved, simply a rough block of stone. On second glance the depressions and protrusions began to assume a pattern, to show some semblance of design, and then individual features began to appear. At least, flashes of them did – Dietz felt as if he'd been watching a fast-moving deer through a thick wood, catching brief glimpses of an eye here, a leg there, an antler over there, never seeing the creature clearly, but getting an image from the scattered impressions. The image here was far less wholesome than any deer, and his head ached from the memory of it. He had a clear impression of limbs, too many limbs, some of them coiled and others bent in too many places.

Flatter spaces along the back, near the top, suggested wings flared in the act of taking flight, and both men cowered back slightly, afraid the stone monstrosity might indeed take to the air. Something about the way the statue narrowed just above its base spoke of clawed feet gouging the rock below them, as if impatient to leap free. But its face was the worst – hints of something long and vaguely bird-like, a massive hooked beak, yet Dietz was sure he had glimpsed row upon row of teeth as well. And the eyes; those he could not deny seeing. Small and faceted, several sets of them above where the beak would be, glared out at him. Most of the other features vanished again when he blinked, so that he could not find them a second time, but the eyes remained, their stare clearly intelligent, and just as clearly malevolent.

Though carved from stone, the surface glistened slightly in the dim light, as if covered in an oily sheen – as if damp with sweat or blood. Everything about the sculpture spoke of power and violence, and madness – a madness that beat at the back of your brain and threatened to burst free, overrunning your senses and your sanity if you gave it a moment's opportunity.

'It's a thing of Chaos,' Alaric whispered, backing away farther and dragging Dietz back with him. Neither of them could take their eyes from the foul carving. 'I've – I've seen drawings like this, once before, back at the university. The master kept them locked away. A traveller had made them, sketches of sculptures he'd seen on his travels – through the Chaos Wastes!'

CHAPTER TWO

A MASSIVE HAND clamped down on Alaric's shoulder, making him quake. Then a deep voice rumbled above and behind him:

'What's wrong?'

Rolf stood behind them, his hand still on Alaric to prevent his backing into the other sculptures crowded along the aisle. The big stonemason saw the direction of their glance and nodded, absently releasing his grip.

'Aye, hideous, isn't it? And would you believe that's the fourth of its kind?' He laughed and shrugged. 'Well, I'm not one to demand good taste in my clients, just coin.'

'Four of them?' Alaric risked one last glance at the statue, shuddered, and focussed his attention upon the craftsman. 'Who would want such things?'

'You know I can't say,' Rolf admonished, frowning down at him. 'Where'd I be if I started giving out names?' Then he seemed to realise how intently they were staring at him, and how pale they both were. 'Why? What's wrong?'

'What's wrong?' Dietz managed a shaky laugh. 'That's what's wrong!' He gestured back towards the statue without looking at it.

The stonemason merely shrugged again. 'So it's ugly. So what? I've seen hideous creatures perched on the sides of castles and manor houses. So've you. Wanted these to frighten away thieves, he said.' He grinned. 'I guarantee anyone coming across this fella in the night will run the other way in a hurry. "Sides, it was a challenge.'

'Rolf, don't you realise what you've done?' Alaric glared up at him. 'These aren't decorations or conversation pieces, they're daemonic icons! You've crafted sculptures of Chaos beasts! It's sacrilege!'

'What?' Now it was Rolf's turn to go pale as he stared at the statue as if for the first time. 'No! Taal's teeth, I didn't – I never–' he glanced down at Alaric and over at Dietz. 'You've got to believe me – I had no idea! Said he wanted them to spook people and paid in cash.' He shook his head. 'Told me the key was making it frightful but subtle, letting people see things in it 'stead of spelling them out. Had me start on one and make it ugly, but not too detailed. Then said it wasn't enough and told me to add bits here 'n there. Had a clear idea what he wanted, even drew me sketches to work from. Last bits were those spots at the back – that did it, and he wanted three more just like it.'

'Clever,' Alaric admitted, feeling calmer now that he was no longer facing the abomination. 'If he'd given you the complete sketches you might have suspected their origins. Instead he added one section after another until he had the appearance he wanted, but pretended it was a happy accident.' He glanced towards the statue again and barely had enough control to tear his gaze free. 'What about the face?'

'That was real particular,' Rolf admitted. 'He had a sketch all roughed out and everything. Said I couldn't shift from it at all or he'd take none of them.'

Dietz had been watching the exchange and eyeing the statue warily in between. 'What was his name, Rolf?'

The stonemason started to shake his head, and then stopped and shrugged. 'Aye, it's clear he used me ill, so I'll not be bound by scruples in return. Wilfen von Glaucht, he said it was. Member of the baron's court, recently titled and come into an estate. That's why he wanted these, to ward off trespassers. Said he didn't want anyone knowing of them aforehand – thought it would ruin the effect. Even had a warehouse where they could be delivered, so as not to wheel them right up his front walk.'

Alaric glanced at Dietz. 'Von Glaucht? I knew of a von Glaucht here in Middenland once, a minor baroness. Wilhemina, I think her name was. Nasty old harridan with yellowed teeth and a wig to cover her liver-spotted pate.' He shuddered. 'She chased me more than once, I don't mind saying – ran fast, too, for such an old biddy.'

'Her husband, maybe?' Dietz offered.

Alaric frowned. 'No, she was a widow,' he explained. 'Husband died years before – under mysterious circumstances, or so some claimed. He left her everything and no one to restrain her lusts.' He shuddered again, clearly reliving the memory.

'A son or nephew?'

Alaric shook his head again. 'She had no children, and no heirs. She was the last of the von Glaucht line.' He gave them a weak, slightly disgusted smile. 'She claimed she'd make me her baron and shower me with wealth. Ugh.'

'This Wilfen must have known about her,' Dietz pointed out, 'and chose a name close enough to confuse any who'd heard of her.' He didn't have to say the rest, that whoever this man was, he was definitely no von Glaucht. He had borrowed the old woman's family name, guessing that a title and some ready gold would keep Rolf from searching further. He had been right.

'What shall I do?' Rolf was demanding, tugging his beard absently with one hand. 'I didn't know!'

'I know,' Alaric assured him, 'and I will gladly lend my word on your behalf, but we have to tell the authorities.' He raised a hand as Rolf began arguing, and the bigger man fell silent. 'We have to tell them,' Alaric repeated. 'If we don't they'll find out somehow, and you'll have been concealing information. We'll simply tell them that you were tricked, and that you came forward as soon as you understood what you had done. That way no one can accuse you of anything worse than accepting a false commission.'

'It's a bad idea,' Dietz argued. 'They'll not believe you any more than him, and why should they? All you'll do is hasten our fate.'

'Aye, best to leave it alone,' Rolf added, nodding desperately. 'The guard have enough on their minds as it stands. Why add to their troubles?'

'Because someone will see one of these things eventually,' Alaric insisted, 'and then the guards will know. They'll trace it back here, to your shop and the fact that you didn't speak up earlier will only make you look more guilty.'

'We could move it,' Dietz suggested quietly.

Both men turned to stare at him, neither of them evidently understanding. 'Drag it out into the street,' he explained, 'plenty of rubble out there already, who would notice a little more?'

'I'll smash it,' Rolf offered helpfully, grabbing a hammer from a nearby stool. 'Then it really will only be rubble then.'

'And what of the other three?' Alaric reminded him gently. 'Those are already loosed and you cannot go after them with your hammer as easily. Nor would dragging this outside fool anyone,' he added with a hard look at Dietz. 'They'd follow the tracks back here, especially since this stone is heavy. You'd not get very far. No,' he said again. 'It's far better to own up to what happened. They're more likely to be lenient if you come forward.'

Dietz snorted behind him, reminded yet again of how young and naïve his companion was. Lenient? Not likely.

They would demand to know why he hadn't come forward earlier... and the notion that no one could accuse Rolf? Of course they could – he had seen many good men wrongly accused and unjustly sentenced in his time. The authorities saw what they wanted to see, including guilt. However, Alaric was right about one thing – lying about the statue and covering it up would only make matters worse.

'Wait here,' Alaric told them both, and strode from the store. Rolf paced back to his worktable, shoulders slumped, and Dietz followed, more to get away from the statue than anything else.

'You believe me, don't you, Dietz?' Rolf asked when they were by the desk, and Dietz started to shrug, then nodded instead.

'I believe you.' He had known Rolf his entire life, and could not picture him tapping dark magicks deliberately. Rolf didn't even trust folk magic, preferring the cold touch of stone and the bite of metal to all those 'silly ways for old folk to awe the younglings'.

'What'll they do, d'ya reckon?'

He had never seen the big man so scared, and tried to keep his own voice and face calm. 'Ask questions, nose around, fine you for being involved.'

Rolf was already shaking his head. 'You've not been here, Dietz, not since afore the troubles. That was then. They're jumping at shadows now – and with good reason. There's too many beasties wandering in the dark, too many starved refugees and veterans so desperate they'll do any-thing for stale bread, and too many ready to take advantage of it all. Afore the war no one really thought that Chaos could touch us here. We were protected, but now – now we know it can enter freely, and no one trusts anyone.'

'Alaric and I will vouch for you,' Dietz pointed out, though he realised that might not mean much. He was a son of Middenheim, it was true, and still a member of his guild, but he had been absent for months and not a true resident for far longer. Alaric, for all his airs and his noble blood, was from another region entirely. Plus the young man had a startling ability to rub people the wrong way, particularly older men in power. They would do their best, however. Rolf deserved no less.

Both men were quiet after that, Rolf idly chipping at his current work, and Dietz glancing around everywhere but at that dreaded far corner. Finally, the door swung open again, and Alaric returned, a pair of guards at his heels. One of them, Dietz saw with a sinking feeling, was the same man his employer had berated for rifling through their bags at the front gate.

'Right then,' Alaric announced, rubbing his hands together briskly, an expression of satisfaction on his face. 'They've sent for their superior. We're to wait here until he arrives and we can tell him the full story. He'll sort it out.'

It was only a few minutes before the officer arrived, several more soldiers behind him. Dietz had seen the man before, though he did not know his name – he was lean, with greying hair, but a jet-black beard, and dark, wary eyes. His armour and helmet were highly polished, but still had several dents, and Dietz knew at once that this was no ornament, but a true warrior who had fought for his city all too recently.

'Names!' the officer barked as he approached. Rolf answered first, Dietz and Alaric right behind. The officer nodded at the first two and frowned at the third, no doubt surprised to find a noble in this part of the city. 'Where is it?' was his next question, and Alaric led him over to the statue. The guards followed, and their exclamations were all too audible as they saw the hideous carving.

'What horror is at work here?' the officer demanded, his face pale and adorned with sweat. Dietz noticed a thin trickle of blood from the man's nostrils and thought he saw similar droplets at the officers' ears. The other guards seemed equally afflicted and he counted himself lucky to have received only a headache from his own encounter. He avoided glancing at the statue again to prevent a relapse.

'I believe it is daemonic,' Alaric explained, and hastened to add: 'I was trained at the University of Altdorf, and saw similar carvings during my studies.'

The officer said nothing for a moment, and then nodded. 'Very well.' He turned his back to the sculpture, and a guard hastened to toss the sheet over it again. 'You are under arrest for sacrilege and suspected treason,' the officer informed Rolf, who stood frozen as if he'd expected the charges, but had hoped to avoid them. 'Take him,' the officer added, gesturing to two guards, and they escorted Rolf from the shop.

'I will personally vouch for Rolf,' Alaric informed the officer as the stonemason disappeared through the door. 'We have known him for several years and have always found him to be a loyal citizen.' But the officer was glaring at Alaric, and Dietz did not like the look in the man's eyes.

'You two,' his glance swept to include Dietz, 'are under arrest for suspected conspiracy to commit treason.' Guards stepped up beside each of them and removed their weapons. Dietz held his arms out to allow the disarmament, but his employer stepped back, shock plain across his face.

'What? We brought you here! This makes no sense!'

'Perhaps,' the officer conceded with a tight nod, 'but what's to say you didn't summon me to conceal your own guilt?' He studied Alaric closely. 'You are not from here,' he pointed out, 'and Carrul informs me you objected strongly to a routine baggage search.' The guard from the gate grinned and tightened his grip on Alaric's arm. 'Perhaps it was you who commissioned these sculptures and the mason threatened to expose your secret. I cannot take that chance. The witch hunters will sort you out and if you're innocent you'll be released.' His tone of voice, and the way Carrul's grin widened, indicated the likelihood of that happening. The officer turned to go, but Alaric's next words stopped him.

'What about that?' He was pointing towards the sheet-covered sculpture. Carrul and the other guard beside Alaric actually cowered back, as if worried it might suddenly leap to their captive's defence.

'It will be confiscated and destroyed,' the officer assured him.

'And the other three?'

That caught the older man's attention, and he turned back to face them, his eyes locked on Alaric's face. 'What other three?' The officer's voice was dangerously soft, and Dietz prayed his employer knew what he was doing.

'Rolf was hired to carve four such statues,' Alaric announced, and then sniffed dramatically. 'A fact you would have possessed if you had bothered to question him more thoroughly, instead of hauling him away and turning upon us. Since the other three are not here in the shop, I can only assume this von Glaucht has already claimed them.' This time it was Alaric who glared. 'I suggest you retrieve them at once.'

The officer stiffened, then turned to the guard by his shoulder. 'Find out where those statues went. At once!'

'There's a warehouse,' Dietz mentioned, drawing the officer's attention to himself. He shrugged. 'Rolf mentioned it before you arrived.'

The officer nodded curtly and glanced towards the work-table. Two strides took him to the chip-strewn surface and he brushed rock dust aside, examining the table's contents. After a moment he pulled a scrap of parchment from beneath a handsome horse head sculpture.

'12 Chambers Street,' he read aloud, then tucked the scrap into his belt pouch. 'Carrul, Nodren, Filbar, escort them to the jails. The rest of you, come with me.'

'I want to see that warehouse!' Alaric insisted, but the officer ignored him. Dietz, seeing the frustration on his employer's face, knew he had to intervene.

'You should bring us along,' he mentioned quietly, and the officer paused to listen. 'Keep your guards together, keep us under control, and we're two more sets of eyes.' He shrugged. 'Not exactly out of your way.' Which was true – Chambers Street was between them and the jails.

The officer hadn't moved, and for an instant Dietz worried that the man was one of those who refused to take advice, even if it was good. But then he nodded. 'We will all go together.' He held out his hand, and Carrul laid Alaric's rapier in it. The officer nodded, slid the scabbard through his belt, and then turned and gestured towards the door.

'After you.'

'WELL,' ALARIC'S VOICE broke the silence. 'Either we're too early or we're too late.' The words travelled easily across the wide floor of the warehouse, echoing slightly in the vast, empty chamber. They had found the place without difficulty and the door had been closed but not locked. Apparently the workers had not had time to secure it properly – crates and bales and barrels lay around the wide space inside, tools for sealing them and marking them nearby. It all had the signs of a hasty departure, and perhaps an involuntary one, judging from the overturned boxes against one wall and the ball of twine unspooled and tangled upon the floor beside a half-wrapped vase.

'Find the book,' Dietz suggested, earning him a nod from the officer and a blank look from Alaric. Of course his employer had never worked in a warehouse or unloaded freight, so he hadn't known that every warehouse kept an inventory book. Everything entering or leaving the warehouse would have been recorded, along with a date, time, and destination or origin.

A moment later, one of the other guards – Nodren, possibly – came back with a large leather-bound book. The officer – whose name, they'd learned, was Herrer – set it down on an empty crate, opened the book, and began quickly flipping through it. When he growled in frustration both Dietz and Alaric crowded closer.

'This entry is from two weeks ago,' Herrer explained, pointing at the left-hand page before him. 'This entry,' his hand jabbed at the right-hang page, 'is from two days ago.'

Alaric looked at the seam of the book and immediately saw loose threads and shreds of paper. 'The pages have been torn out,' he observed. 'But why?'

'To keep anyone from reading them,' Herrer guessed. 'This way we cannot be sure when the statues arrived or where they went. We cannot pursue them further.'

Dietz had been only half-watching the exchange. A faint noise had distracted him, and now he tilted his head trying to hear it more closely. It was almost like–

'Someone's in here,' he announced, and the guards flanking him immediately dropped his arms and stepped away, hands on their blades, eyes searching the rafters and corners for an ambush.

'Who's there?' Herrer demanded, his own blade half-drawn. 'Show yourself!'

After a moment Dietz heard the sound again, slightly louder. It swelled further, and then a small, stooped figure appeared from the far end of the warehouse.

'Who's there?' a voice called out – that and the way it moved told Dietz it was an older man approaching them. 'Damn fools, making too much noise,' he added under his breath, obviously not realising they could hear him. 'You'll scare them all away.' Those mutterings had been in the trade tongue, and Dietz saw at a glance that the others did not recognise it, which was no surprise – they'd have no need for it. He had spent his youth carrying messages for the guild, however, and still remembered the tongue.

'He's talking in trade-speak,' he explained to Herrer quietly. 'I can speak it. Let me talk to him.'

Herrer nodded curtly, not needing to point out how closely they'd be watching him, and the guards stepped back to give him more space. Alaric was watching eagerly, clearly delighted at the chance to hear more of an unfamiliar language, even if it was still in use.

'We don't mean any harm,' Dietz called out in trade-speak, stepping forward to escape the guards' shadows. 'We were looking for something that was delivered here.'

'Eh?' Now the man was close enough, they saw he was old indeed, with pale yellowing skin hanging loose on his frame and a few wisps of thin grey hair bushed back over large red ears. His clothes were loose and ragged, though still serviceable, and he carried a wicked-looking knife at his belt and a small, tight-knit net in one hand. His eyes were crafty but unfocussed, and Dietz knew at once the sort of man he was. He had met enough of them over the years, men who had once been sharp, but had since grown so addled they could handle only simple tasks. Still, the man was here and might prove useful.

'My name is Dietz,' he called out, taking another step forward and holding both hands up slightly to show he was unarmed, 'and yours?'

'Franz,' the older man grunted, stopping a few paces away. 'Ye'll upset the rats, you will, stomping about like that.'

'Sorry.' Now he understood the net. 'Have you caught many tonight?'

'Aye, three big 'uns,' Franz announced proudly, patting a bulging, squirming bag at his side – its underside was wet, and sticky drops fell to floor. 'Haven't found the nest yet, but I will.'

'I'm sure you will,' Dietz agreed. 'We're looking for some packages. Three of them, large and heavy, well wrapped. They'd have come in some time these past two weeks. Have you seen them?'

'Packages?' Franz peered at him, and at the men behind him. 'Heh, what're guards wanting with packages, then? Is he in trouble?' A bony finger jabbed in Alaric's direction, where his finery stood out among the guards' armour.

'Could be,' Dietz admitted, 'if we can't find the packages. Do you remember any?'

'Don't notice much,' the old man told him. 'Too busy with the rats. Cleanest warehouse in the district,' he added proudly, 'on account o' me traps and nets.' Then he scowled. 'If'n I could just find that nest!'

Dietz started to turn away, sure he'd not gain anything more from the man, when an idea hit him. 'These packages were large,' he mentioned again, 'and the man delivering them as well. Heavy footsteps and heavy objects – the rats would've scurried away like mad.' When he saw the gleam in the ratcatcher's eyes he almost shouted, but contained himself: best not to show how important this was.

'Oh, that 'un,' Franz muttered darkly. 'Great bear of a man, he was, red and grey, stomping about and talking so loud I couldn't catch a one of 'em!' He glared at Dietz as if he had caused those intrusions personally.

'That's the one,' Dietz agreed, grinning. 'Wouldn't know stealth if it bit him,' which was true enough, and won a chuckle from Franz. He could hear Alaric behind him, repeating the words quietly, trying to commit them to memory. 'When was he here?'

'Three days ago, last,' Franz replied after a moment, idly scratching his stubbled chin. 'An' another three or four before that, and the same before that.'

'Any idea where the packages went?'

Franz snorted at that. 'Packages? You might as well call 'em boulders, that'd be closer to the truth.' He scratched again. 'Aye, the wagons creaked fit to burst with those, they did.'

Now they were getting somewhere! Dietz forced his voice to stay calm. 'What wagons?'

The old man looked at him as if he were the daft one. 'Metzer's, o' course, what else? Sent his heaviest wagon each time and still barely held 'em.'

Dietz nodded. Jurgin Metzer ran a livery a few blocks away – he vaguely remembered the place, and its owner as well.

'Thanks,' he told Franz. 'We'll try not to make too much noise when leaving.'

The ratcatcher grunted his thanks. 'Get going, and take them with ya,' he said, stroking the bag at his side. 'Nest's here somewhere and I aim to find it!'

While Franz wandered away, glaring into the shadows and stooping to study likely spots along the walls, Dietz related the conversation. Alaric, he could tell, was dying to ask translations of specific words, but Herrer was more interested in the content.

'I know Metzer,' he admitted. 'We'll ask him about these shipments.' Then he gave Dietz another grudging nod. 'You did well. I'll put that in my report.'

'Thanks.' Dietz knew all too well that, if the witch hunters wanted to find him guilty, the officer's report would mean nothing. Still, it couldn't hurt.

''COURSE I REMEMBER THEM,' Jurgin Metzer said when Herrer asked him about the packages. 'Great massive things, solid stone – had to reinforce the axles just to bear the weight.'

Metzer looked much as Dietz remembered him, a short stout man with a thick moustache on the verge of turning from brown to blond, and no hair atop his head, but a thick red-brown braid in back. He'd given Dietz a nod of recognition when they'd arrived, and if he wondered about the armed guards he didn't ask.

'Who paid for them?' Herrer demanded, and Jurgin produced an inventory book much like the one at the warehouse. This one had no missing pages, however, and he thumbed through it quickly, finally stopping on one page.

'Right,' he said, reading quickly. 'Wilfen von Glaucht. Placed the order five weeks ago. Four deliveries, same size and weight. Though I think he underestimated the weight. Damn near killed my horses, they did.'

'Where did the packages go?'

Jurgin consulted the book again. 'First one to the foot of the Howling Hills. Second one out into Reikland. Third one up into Black Fire Pass.' He looked up. 'Strange locations, but he paid well and in advance. Didn't have to meet anyone with them, either – just drop them there and head on back.' He frowned. 'Fourth one hasn't shown up at the warehouse yet – they'll let me know when it does.'

'It won't,' Herrer informed him curtly. 'It has been confiscated, and the mason taken into custody. I will need a copy of the information for the other three.'

Jurgin wrote it out without a word and handed it over.

'You may be called upon for questioning,' Herrer mentioned, and the livery master's face went pale, but he didn't protest. There was no point.

'Now you know where they were sent,' Alaric pointed out as they left the livery, 'and the orders were placed weeks ago, long before we arrived. Surely there's no reason to detain us further?'

That earned him another of Herrer's frowns – Dietz doubted the officer ever smiled. 'You could have been working with accomplices,' he pointed out, 'arriving late to establish your innocence. No, we will leave it to the witch hunters.'

Very little was said after that.

CHAPTER THREE

IT WAS A long, unpleasant night. When Dietz had been younger he had often aided his brothers Darulf and Darhun with pranks and petty thefts. Once they had been caught and had spent the night in the city jail. It was even worse now than Dietz remembered, filthy and stale and sour, each cell jammed with occupants. They had slept very little and were relieved when the guards came to escort them out early the next morning. At least until they stepped outside and the guards handed them over to several other men; men wearing the wide-brimmed hats, black breastplates and long black cloaks of the witch hunters. The men led them towards the palace itself, and with each step Dietz's concerns mounted. In his experience attracting attention from those in power was never a good thing.

Alaric, however, was not worried. 'We'll soon have this sorted out,' he assured Dietz as they followed their new guards. He had been sure their case would be shunted off to some minor functionary who would not care about their innocence, but clearly someone had recognised their importance, since they were being conveyed to the impressive building before them. As they mounted the wide stone steps, Dietz examined his clothing, doing his best to brush away the dirt from their short incarceration, and he smoothed his hair as much as possible, regretting the absence of his cloak and his rapier.

Their escort hurried them into the building, down the wide stone hall, up a broad staircase, and at last through a pair of gilded, ornately carved doors. The witch hunters paused just inside the threshold and all but hurled Alaric and Dietz before them, using enough force to send the pair crashing to the floor, where they lay stunned for a moment on the inlaid tilework.

'What have we here?' The voice carried, cutting them where they lay, and Dietz raised his head enough to look around. The sight before him made him wish he could sink through the floor. They were in a large, handsome room, its walls covered in rich brocade hangings, and its vaulted ceiling painted with scenes of Ulric and the other gods at play.

Heavy curtains were pulled back, allowing light to pour through the large windows along one wall, and against the opposite wall was a low stone platform. A heavy golden throne sat at its centre, and a second chair, handsomely carved in gilded wood, had been set beside it. Despite the splendour of the surroundings, it was less the furnishings than the occupants that made Dietz blanch. For sitting on the throne was a stout man with a square, red-cheeked face and wispy blond hair, but ice-cold blue eyes – Boris Todbringer. Elector Count Boris Todbringer, ruler of Middenland.

Beside him was a tall, narrow man with sharp features and limp black hair – Dietz did not recognise him, but the man's armour, cloak, and silver-encircled black hat showed him to be a senior witch hunter, most likely a witch hunter captain. They were in the presence of two of the most powerful men in the entire province, possibly the Empire. To make matters far worse, Alaric was already getting to his feet.

'Ah, good, an audience at last,' Alaric stated, making one last attempt to straighten his clothes. Then, giving them up as a bad job, he bowed towards the two men. 'Alaric von Jungfreud, at your service,' he gestured to his side, 'and this is my companion, Dietrich Froebel. I appreciate your seeing us so promptly, and I assure you that we will not take up much of your valuable time. Now then, I think it would be best...'

'Silence!' the man beside Todbringer snapped, his sharp tone cutting Alaric off neatly and leaving him staring, clearly offended and more than a little startled. 'This is not an audience. It is a trial! You and your companion have been accused of treachery, of conspiracy, and of consorting with Chaos! How do you plead?'

'What?' Alaric glanced around and noticed for the first time that, rather than courtiers, the room was filled with more of those same sinister men who had accompanied them here. Right, he decided, time to set aside the niceties. 'This is preposterous!' he replied coldly. 'We are innocent, of course. It was only through our actions that your men learned of the danger at all! Yes yes, I know,' he said loudly, cutting off the thin man before he could speak. 'We could have arranged that to conceal our own involvement. The guard captain suggested as much, but surely we would have known that you would see through such an obvious lie? Surely we would realise that you could not be fooled by so transparent a ploy?' As he'd hoped, the man sat back, a proud smile flashing across his lips as he accepted the compliments. This, Alaric thought to himself, would be far easier than debating the merits of the ancient trade routes with Professor Untegaar.

Dietz had finally stood up, but kept back a pace, watching Alaric work. He had to admit, he was impressed again – his employer often seemed a flighty young noble, but he could become intensely focussed when necessary, and he was still the most intelligent man Dietz had ever met. Right now, he was relating the incident to the men on the platform, which gave Dietz himself a chance to glance around a little. The one thing that struck him most force-fully was a clear absence.

There were no priests of Ulric present.

For that matter, since they had been accused of heresy, their trial should have taken place in the Great Temple and been overseen by a priest, if not the Ar-Ulric himself. The fact that they were here in the palace, being accused by a witch hunter captain and the elector count, made no sense.

'…and that is the extent of our involvement,' Alaric concluded with a second bow. 'Of course your men apprehended us, a perfectly understandable precaution, but I think I have explained our presence adequately, and a simple check can verify when we entered the city and that we have been absent many months. I can also provide several character references, both here and in Altdorf, to verify that we are men of our word and loyal citizens of the Empire.'

'An impressive recitation,' the thin man acknowledged coldly after a moment, 'but it does nothing to disprove your guilt. The servants of Chaos are cunning, and often conceal their true natures for years before daring to strike. You set these plans in motion during a previous visit to our city, or through intermediaries, and expected them to be finished by the time you returned.'

'Yes, but why weren't they, then?' Alaric responded. 'If I had planned this all so carefully, why was the last statue still sitting there when I arrived? Why not have it delivered to the warehouse like the other three and carted off by a wagon as they were? Why run the risk of being associated with it at all? You have a very low opinion of my so-called cunning if you believe I would be so careless.'

Todbringer leaned over and muttered something to the thin man, who whispered a reply. Alaric was too far away to hear what they said, but Dietz, who was a few steps behind him, could hear clearly – not the two of them, but the witch hunters guarding the door behind him.

'He's not going to send us after them, is he?' one of them said.

'Not a chance,' another replied. 'He can't risk Valgeir's gaining the upper hand again. If his knights rally, Halmeinger'll need every one of us here to hold them back.'

'Can't just leave those things out there, though,' a third commented, 'could wind up causing all manner of havoc, and it'd reflect badly on us if anyone knew we'd known about them and done nothing.'

The snippet of conversation explained a great deal, and Dietz sidled forward until he was right next to Alaric. 'Tell them we'll do it,' he whispered, and his employer glanced over at him curiously.

'Do what? Speak up. I can barely hear you.'

'Tell them we'll get rid of the other three,' Dietz explained, still whispering and watching the two men on the platform. They seemed to be finishing their own consultation, which meant they only had a moment.

Fortunately, Alaric understood immediately, and stepped forward, giving a discreet cough to recall the two men's attention.

'My lords, I have a proposal,' he stated. 'One which will both prove our innocence and eliminate any further danger these items might pose. Three of those sculptures have already been delivered to various points throughout the Empire, clearly intended for some nefarious – one might safely say daemonic – purpose. You,' he bowed to Todbringer, who nodded back, 'are of course busy maintaining this city and this province and defending it from attack. You,' here he bowed to the thin man, whose only response was a slightly raised eyebrow, 'must maintain constant vigilance against the foes of the Empire. These sculptures must be found and destroyed, yet surely this matter is beneath men such as you.' He smiled. 'My companion and I, however, are lesser men and thus well suited to the task. I am also a scholar of Altdorf, and well-versed in ancient languages. We would happily undertake this mission on your behalf. Allow us to destroy these sculptures, bringing back proof of their destruction. Thus we can demonstrate our loyalty and remove the threat, all without requiring you to divert your own forces from their necessary duties.'

The two men seemed to consider the proposal, whispering back and forth. It was clear that Todbringer found merit in the idea, but Halmeinger did not approve. Finally they reached an agreement, and the elector count turned towards them. Just as he opened his mouth to speak, however, a loud thud echoed through the room.

It sounded again, and all eyes turned towards the double doors, still reverberating from the force of the blow. Once more it sounded, and then at a gesture from Todbringer the doors were pulled open to reveal a pair of men in the hall beyond. They wore fur pelts across their shoulders, but were unarmoured, and each carried a massive two-handed warhammer; even without the wolf's-head clasps at their necks, everyone would have recognised them immediately.

They were the Knights of the White Wolf – Templars of the Cult of Ulric.

The two knights entered and stopped just inside the door, forcing the witch hunters there to retreat a few paces. Two more knights followed behind them, though these advanced to the centre of the room – Alaric and Dietz took the opportunity to move to one side. Behind the second set of knights strode a tall, powerfully built man in full armour, his breastplate adorned with the wolf's head of Ulric and a thin silver circlet upon his thick white hair. A handsomely carved silver hammer hung from his belt, and his eyes were black as obsidian.

Though he had only seen the man a few times in his youth, Dietz knew immediately that this could only be Emil Valgeir, the Ar-Ulric.

'Greetings, my count,' announced Valgeir, inclining his head as one equal to another. He spared a single, hard glance at the man beside Todbringer. 'Witch hunter captain,' he said in clipped tones. Then he forced a smile to his face. 'I had hoped to discuss certain defensive repairs with you, count, but if you are otherwise involved I would be happy to wait.' His glance swept across Alaric and Dietz before returning to the throne, and the two of them admired the man's move. Even Todbringer would not dare send the Ar-Ulric away, which meant either including him, or ending whatever they were doing in favour of discussing his own goals. He had probably heard of their arrest and had staged his entrance perfectly to interrupt the trial, which by rights was his to conduct.

'Not at all, my dear Ar-Ulric,' Todbringer replied, smiling with only a little awkwardness. 'It is always the pleasure of the court to hear the wisdom of the Cult of Ulric, and the recovery of our city is of paramount importance.' He turned his attention to Alaric and Dietz, and then visibly dismissed them. 'We were merely discussing a small journey these gentlemen proposed, and had just given them our permission to embark.' He gestured and a heavy-set man with a grey-flecked beard and a fine velvet cloak stepped to the edge of the platform. 'Take care of the arrangements, Struber,' Todbringer instructed him, and the man nodded and stepped away, bowing to him and to the Ar-Ulric and the witch hunter captain before beckoning for Alaric and Dietz to follow him out. They did so quickly, with several bows to the three powerful men, each of whom pretended not to watch them depart.

'We will need our weapons back,' Alaric pointed out after they had descended to the main level, and Struber nodded impatiently.

'Yes yes,' he said quickly. 'The guard have them. We can retrieve them now.' He stopped and turned to face them both. 'You understand that if the Cult of Ulric takes an interest in your activities…'

Alaric spread his hands. 'We are merely travelling the Empire in search of old ruins, a favourite occupation, but one that sadly yields little of value or significance. We had hoped to study several promising sites along the edges of Middenland, hence our asking the count's permission.'

Struber nodded. 'Just so.' He led them back to the jail, and they stepped inside just long enough for Alaric to retrieve his rapier and Dietz his club and knives. Just before they left, Dietz glanced up at the rafters and whistled.

'Glouste!' A dark form scuttled along a nearby beam and dropped to his shoulders, happily nuzzling his cheek as he stepped out and shut the door solidly behind him.

'Well,' Alaric commented. 'Let's get our horses and be off, then.'

Struber shook his head. 'You will leave in the morning,' he informed them, leading them down another street to a small inn named the Dancing Frog. 'You will spend the night here.'

'I'd really rather get started right–' Alaric began, but Struber shook his head again and pulled open the inn's front door.

'The elector count insists,' he explained quietly, but clearly, putting an emphasis on the word 'insists.' 'You must be well rested before your journey.' He glared at them, as if daring them to object again, and glanced meaningfully behind him, where Alaric and Dietz suddenly noticed a pair of the same black-clad soldiers waiting a short distance away. Evidently their stay here was not a request.

'Yes, well, I suppose I could do with a good night's sleep,' Alaric admitted gracefully, waving cheerfully at the soldiers and allowing the courtier to usher him into the inn. Dietz followed along, happy enough to be anywhere but jail, but unable to shake the feeling that he had merely traded up for a larger cell.

THE DANCING FROG was a fine place, it turned out, not fancy, but clean and well tended. The food was hearty, the beds were solid, and there were real mattresses, one for each of them. The room even had a pitcher of water and a basin for washing in. They had certainly stayed in worse places.

Struber's reasons for insisting on their stay became clear when a man approached them during dinner. Though of average height, the stranger's broad shoulders made him seem to tower over their table, and his angular face peered down at them from beneath his broad-brimmed hat.

'Alaric von Jungfreud and Dietrich Froebel?' he inquired with the bored tone of a man who already knew the answer. 'I am Oswald Kleiber, witch hunter. I will be accompanying you.'

'Thanks all the same,' Alaric said, glancing up from his roast, 'but we don't need any assistance.'

Kleiber's thin lips narrowed further. 'It is not a request. Witch Hunter Captain Halmeinger has detailed me to escort you.' His gaze flickered across them. 'Should you prove to be Chaos worshippers I will dispatch you and return with your heads.'

'We'll do our best to pray quietly then,' Alaric muttered, and then winced as Dietz's elbow struck him hard in the ribs. 'We welcome the knowledge and spiritual guidance of a witch hunter,' he amended more loudly, but Kleiber bowed as if he thought the statement sincere.

'I will be waiting at first light,' he informed them, before turning and striding out of the inn.

'Charming,' Alaric commented, watching the man's exit, 'and just what we needed, our very own fanatic.'

'Better than our very own beheading,' Dietz pointed out, returning to his own food. He had barely managed two bites before another shadow fell across his plate.

'Kristoff Magnusson, at your service,' the gentleman announced, pulling out a chair and dropping into it. 'May I?' Since he was already sitting down they couldn't very well refuse, but his grin said he knew that. 'The trading guild sent me,' he said, helping himself to a glass of wine. 'I understand you're off on a mission of some importance and delicacy. They thought an experienced trader might prove useful.'

More likely they want to know what Todbringer and Halmeinger are up to, and to get their hands on anything valuable we find, Dietz thought to himself, but he said nothing. He knew better than to voice such opinions, and besides he found himself liking the short man with the unruly brown hair and the needle-thin nose.

Kristoff proved an entertaining fellow, and was regaling them with a story about a seasick merchant and a lusty sailor when a tall, portly gentleman of middling years stepped up to their table. 'I believe you are the gentlemen embarking for the Howling Hills?' he asked, hands resting on the back of an empty chair, and Alaric and Dietz exchanged glances. They had, in fact, chosen the Hills for their first stop, if only because it was the closest of the three locations. When they nodded the gentleman cleared his throat and, after Alaric nodded him to the chair, smiled graciously. 'Fastred Albers is my name–' he began, but was cut off before he could finish.

'Albers?' Alaric leaned forward, his pose of nonchalance vanishing, 'from the Guild of Explorers?' At Albers's nod, he grinned and reached out to shake the man's hand. 'You lectured to us once in Altdorf, a few years ago, about establishing trade routes and their cultural significance, particularly to nomadic tribes.'

'Ah, yes,' Albers beamed, a wide smile above his neatly trimmed white beard. 'My friend Waldemar asked me to speak – I'd just returned from Bretonnia and he said his students could do with a bit of practical knowledge.'

'Has the guild sent you to join us, then?' Alaric asked, and at Albers's nod his own grin widened. 'Excellent! Oh, I have many questions for you, and I would dearly like to tell you of my own travels – perhaps you'll be able to help me make sense of them all.' He poured Albers a glass of wine, and soon they and Kristoff were happily engaged in swapping stories and comparing notes. Dietz took advantage of the time to finish his food – he was used to letting Alaric talk unheeded, and now he discovered he could manage that trick as easily with three as with one.

THE NEXT MORNING, after a solid night's sleep, Alaric and Dietz gathered their belongings and stepped out of the inn. Albers and Kristoff were waiting for them, as was Kleiber. So were several others.

'Renke Jülicher,' a small, slender man informed them, stepping forward and bowing with precision. 'Imperial Geographic Society.' His short tones, and the disapproving glance he gave Dietz, indicated his attitude clearly, and Dietz was quite pleased to let the man direct all his attention to Alaric.

The remaining strangers, however, stepped towards both of them, and so Dietz found himself dealing with them while Jülicher pulled a map from the long leather case at his back and began discussing probable routes. The newcomers were almost two dozen, most of them clearly soldiers from the count's militia, wearing the Middenland tabard over chainmail and carrying swords and shields. One had a plume atop his helmet, designating him as squad leader. The last man wore leathers instead of mail and bore a longsword at his side and a longbow across his chest.

'Adelrich Jaarl,' he introduced himself, offering Dietz his hand. 'Scout for the count's army.' Adelrich was a rangy fellow with long features, weather-beaten skin and short black curls, and Dietz liked him immediately, sensing a kindred spirit. 'This lot are along as well,' Adelrich added, gesturing towards the soldiers. 'One full unit, twenty men, members of his guard, Sergeant Holst commanding. Orders are to assist in your mission and protect the other travellers as necessary.'

'Glad to have you,' Dietz said, and meant it. He could see that Kristoff and Albers might be useful for their knowledge, and Kleiber for his religious authority – even Jülicher might be handy in a pinch, but soldiers would definitely increase their chance of survival, and a good military scout was worth his weight in gold.

As they packed everyone's gear and got ready to depart, Dietz found himself next to Adelrich, and they traded comments as they worked.

'He carries a fine blade,' Adelrich commented at one point, gesturing to where Alaric stood by his horse, his rapier visible at his side.

'Aye,' Dietz replied, trying to control his disgust, 'and he makes a fine show with it, if you stand still long enough.' They both laughed, and Dietz admitted to himself that he felt better about this trip than he had since they'd agreed to it.

'I still don't like taking orders, particularly from witch hunters,' he mentioned to Alaric as they led the others through the gate and out of Middenheim. 'They should be doing their own dirty work.'

'Never mind that,' Alaric replied, his eyes already alight with a look Dietz knew all too well. 'Think about what we're doing, where we're going! We're in pursuit of real Chaos icons! And we're going into the Howling Hills! I can't wait to see what we find!'

'Oh, I can,' Dietz muttered softly. 'I can definitely wait.'

CHAPTER FOUR

ALARIC AND DIETZ had worked together for more than a year, and had travelled to many interesting places. They had sailed on ships, ridden with caravans, hiked over mountains, and frequently walked or ridden alone, but this journey was a new experience for both of them. They had travelled with large groups before, but it had always been a matter of convenience – settlers or traders, or miners who were already heading in the same direction and welcomed an extra pair of hands and swords (well, one rarely-used sword and one oft-used club). This time everyone was going to the same destination. It was a single expedition, with a single purpose, and a single leader: Alaric.

They had discovered this the first night, when the beefy army sergeant, Holst, had approached Alaric close to sunset.

'It's getting dark, sir,' the scarred veteran had mentioned quietly. He seemed slightly embarrassed.

'Hm?' Alaric had been having a fascinating conversation with Fastred and Kristoff, and it took him a moment to realise the sergeant was addressing him. 'Is it? Yes, I suppose so.'

'Might be best to stop soon,' Holst added after a moment, just as Alaric had turned back to his two companions.

'Do you think so?' Alaric had glanced about again, frowning slightly. 'I'd hoped to get a bit farther before turning in.'

'As you say, sir.' Holst had faded back to his men, leaving Alaric a bit confused and Fastred and Kristoff chuckling.

'I think he was hoping for a more decisive answer,' Kristoff explained with a grin.

'What? Answer from whom?' Alaric glanced over his shoulder, and back at his two new friends. 'What, from me? I'm not in the militia!'

'No, but you are the leader of this expedition,' Fastred pointed out. 'He's taking his orders from you.'

'Orders?' Alaric thought about that one. Growing up, servants had sometimes taken orders from him, though more often his father had already given them instructions and nothing he said could change them. Dietz worked for him, and that meant he was supposed to take orders, but somehow it never worked out that way – they discussed things and often Dietz convinced him to do something a different way or to give it up altogether. Now this sergeant was expecting orders? That would make him the first person to be actively soliciting such command decisions, and Alaric discovered the idea made him a bit nervous.

For the next two days he second-guessed himself constantly and asked others' opinions on everything. Finally Dietz lost patience.

'What is wrong with you?' he demanded after Alaric had questioned whether they should in fact refill their waterskins. 'You're acting like an idiot!'

'What?' Alaric drew himself up to his full height, which never helped since Dietz loomed over him anyway. 'It's not easy being in command, you know.'

'Ah. Is that what's wrong?' Sometimes Alaric swore his companion was reading his mind. 'Relax. Just do what you'd normally do. I'll let you know if it's wrong, and don't let them see you worried.'

Alaric considered the advice. Act as usual. Well, they had travelled extensively and had always managed fine, so obviously he did know when to stop for the night and where to get water, and how to hobble the horses – though Dietz usually handled the actual chores. Trust Dietz to stop him from blundering – that much he was used to. Never show concern or hesitation. At last his father's discipline would be useful for something!

After that the trip became much easier. He grew more comfortable giving orders, and Holst visibly relaxed once Alaric took charge, which made it even easier. Their companions were all seasoned travellers in their own right, which certainly helped – they didn't really need instruction on how to water a horse or set up a fire, and so he could say something as simple as 'Let's set up camp' and it would be done.

Dietz also found himself relaxing as they travelled. Despite the size of the group everyone worked together fairly well, and within a few days they had all become much better acquainted. Magnusson and Albers had become Kristoff and Fastred almost immediately, and proved to be excellent travelling companions, full of stories and local knowledge and practical experience.

Adelrich could have been Dietz's cousin they had so much in common, including their attitudes and their quiet, no-nonsense speech, and they quickly became fast friends. Kleiber was still stiff and arrogant, and kept to himself, but he was an expert horseman and had sharp eyes – he was the first to notice approaching riders or birds of prey and alerted the others at once. Even Jülicher, stiff, officious little man that he was, became Renke and showed that he snored loudly, but was a surprisingly good road chef. The soldiers kept to themselves, camping around the others at night and riding behind them by day, but they seemed decent enough, and Adelrich knew them all and vouched for them. Their sergeant, Holst, was a career soldier of the better variety and Dietz quickly saw that he was hard but fair, and well respected by his men.

The Howling Hills lay almost directly south of Middenheim, and if they'd been alone Alaric and Dietz would have cut straight through the Drakwald to save time. However, a group this big would take forever weaving between the trees and could never hope to outrun an ambush, so they were forced to follow the road. It cut down through Leichlinberg, past Malstedt and Gerdav and Sotturm, before finally branching at Mittelweg. They took the western path, towards Hochland, and the ground grew steeper, the trees thinning and becoming shorter, interspersed with scrub brush. As the terrain rose the temperature dropped slightly and the wind picked up, until they halted just beyond Eldagsen and listened to it whistle and rumble, and howl ahead of them.

'Welcome to the Howling Hills,' Fastred announced, bowing and sweeping one arm before him as if he were a host welcoming guests into a favourite room. 'Home of bandits, brigands, and beastmen.' The scenery behind him seemed well suited to such denizens. It was bleak, scraggly bushes clinging stubbornly to rocky hills, their leaves and limbs as cracked and harsh as the soil from which they sprang. The wind had carved narrow, twisting canyons between the hills and leaped through those passages, scouring them clean of dirt and plants, and pelting the travellers with the debris from its passage, forcing them to raise their hands to stop the fast-moving pebbles and twigs from striking their faces.

'A desolate place,' Renke sniffed, glancing about, 'and very little of significance. Our maps have only vague markings for this area.'

'Where was the statue delivered?' Dietz asked Alaric. On their third night they had told the others the purpose of their mission, reasoning that it made little sense to hide the details. Besides, the others would not be much help if they didn't know what to look for.

'Between Eldagsen and Zilly,' Alaric replied, reading the information from the ledger copy Struber had provided them. 'Halfway, it says.'

'Zilly is a day's ride farther on the trail,' Kristoff pointed out, running a hand through his hair. 'If we ride another three hours that should place us roughly midway.'

Alaric nodded. 'Let's be off, then,' he told them, kicking his mount into a slow walk. 'We'd best keep our eyes open, though. They may not have followed their own directions so precisely.'

There was another reason to stay alert, Dietz thought as he followed his employer closely. He had no desire to meet any of the locals Fastred had mentioned and he doubted their welcome would be one he'd enjoy. The others no doubt felt the same, and it was a quiet, wary group that rode along the path, weapons loose in their scabbards and eyes scanning both ground and horizon.

Not surprisingly, it was Kleiber who reined in almost four hours later. The ride had been uneventful, the landscape as boring and stripped bare here as it had been hours before. Yet the witch hunter's sharp eyes spied something amid the rock and dirt and bushes.

'There,' he announced, pointing off to one side. 'Something heavy was moved off the road.' Dietz dismounted and examined the spot the witch hunter had indicated, Adelrich right beside him.

'I hate to say it, but he's right,' Adelrich admitted quietly as they studied the area. Up close they could see where the grass had been matted down and the brush crushed by something very heavy. The destruction led south and east, into the hills proper, and they left the road behind as they followed this new path, Adelrich on foot to scout ahead. Dietz followed behind him, Adelrich's reins looped around the top of his saddle, and the others followed after, with the soldiers bringing up the rear.

They considered themselves quite lucky that it took a full day before they were attacked.

ADELRICH HAD JUST returned to report signs of beastmen in the vicinity when a crude spear flew from behind a nearby tree, just missing both him and Alaric. Several more spears appeared, and then a coarse bellow announced several beastmen an instant before they burst from cover.

These were the beastmen Dietz had expected in Ind, crude figures with rough armour and poorly maintained weapons, dirty and savage and little more than beasts with human hands. They had always struck him as being closest to goats, with long faces, short tufts of fur below long, narrow jaws, and short horns curving up from their brows. Their hides were thick and coated with shaggy fur and their legs bent backward, ending in strong hooves. Many had tails, though fortunately they were useless – he didn't relish the idea of facing a creature that could wield a weapon from there as well. Still, this was not the time or the place to study the locals. He dispatched one with a quick knife throw and battered aside another's club before using his second blade to spill its guts.

Glouste, recognising that her sharp teeth might not even pierce the beastmen's thick hide, took refuge inside Dietz's leather jacket and avoided the fight altogether. Adelrich, realising they were too close for a bow, had drawn his longsword and was slashing his way through their attackers, ducking beneath their clumsy attacks and weaving his way behind them.

Kristoff had drawn a wicked-looking blade and was wielding it with surprising enthusiasm and skill, while Fastred fired a handsome crossbow without apparently needing to reload. Kleiber held a longsword in one hand and a pistol in the other, which he traded for a long dagger after firing it. He handled both blades with such skill and ferocity that the beastmen began avoiding him. Renke had drawn a short sword and was proving to be no slouch at combat, while Holst and his men were attacking with their spears and swords, and circling around to keep the beastmen from escaping. Alaric, meanwhile, sat on his horse at the centre of the mêlée, sword in hand, but rarely using it to do more than slash casually at any beastman who ventured too close.

The battle was over quickly. The beastmen had been badly outnumbered, not to mention outmatched and out-equipped, and the party had been ready for an attack, responding quickly and easily. The victory, and the exertion, only served to tighten the bonds within the group, and everyone was in good spirits as they rode away, leaving the beastmen's corpses behind among the trees and the tall grass.

BEASTMEN ATTACKED SEVERAL more times over the next few days. Each time the group fended them off with no casualties and no serious injuries, though several members suffered minor cuts and bruises, and one soldier's arm was broken by a poorly blocked club strike. Adelrich proved his worth as a scout – he detected each beastman band in turn, and provided ample warning so the party was never taken by surprise. Twice, he also warned them of a much larger band nearby, one that would significantly outnumber them and that possessed several of the larger, tougher beastmen who seemed to be commanders rather than mere soldiers. Each time, Alaric chose to evade rather than fight.

'Yes, I know we might win,' he replied when Holst objected the first time, 'but we might lose as well, and if we did, that statue would still be out here, doing who knows what, and it would be our fault. I am not prepared to allow that, thanks very much, so we'll step aside and let this band pass, shall we?' Holst had not been happy, but Alaric had finally got the hang of giving orders and did not give the sergeant a chance to counter his instructions.

'Quite a few around here,' Dietz mentioned that night, and it was Kristoff who replied.

'It was not this bad the last time I was here,' the trader admitted, idly flicking bits of bark into the fire. 'Beastmen hid here, of course, but only a few and never this aggressive. The war changed everything.'

'We drove the evil from our lands,' Kleiber objected, and Kristoff smiled indulgently at the indignant witch hunter.

'No, actually,' he replied. 'We defeated their army, yes, and held the city, but when their attack faltered many of the lesser soldiers fled. Most of those are still within the Empire somewhere, and many are here in Middenland – they cannot escape to another province without drawing attention, so they hide within the forest or here in the hills and survive by ambushing travellers, stealing from locals, and killing one another.' He shrugged. 'I'd heard many beastmen fled here, seeking refuge within the Howling Hills. It seems those tales were true.'

'We must cleanse this land of their filth,' Kleiber insisted, but Alaric shook his head.

'That's not our goal,' he pointed out, ignoring the witch hunter's glare. 'We're after the statue. I've no problem killing any beastmen who get in our way, but we aren't going after them. We will find the statue, destroy it, and leave.' He grinned at Kleiber. 'You're welcome to stay and eliminate the other beastmen when we go, of course.'

Kleiber refused to acknowledge the taunt. 'My first task, as always, is to hunt the agents of Chaos,' he announced. 'These creatures are little more than pawns, though still their foulness offends me.' He sniffed. 'I will send word to the witch hunter captain,' he decided finally, 'and others will rid these hills of their filth.'

IT WAS NEAR noon the next day when Adelrich reappeared from the trees, tapping Dietz's foot in passing before Dietz had even registered his presence. Adelrich nodded, but didn't stop, stalking back to Alaric, and Dietz turned in his saddle to hear the scout's report.

'One beastman, alone, back two hundred paces that direction,' he reported, jerking a thumb back over his shoulder. 'Nothing else around.'

'Did you kill him?' Kleiber demanded, and snarled when the scout shook his head.

'He didn't see me,' he explained, 'and I couldn't take the chance.'

'What, that he might overpower you?' Kleiber sneered, and seemed delighted when Adelrich's hand reached for his sword, but the scout caught himself and settled for resting his hand on his belt instead.

'I couldn't risk his being a scout,' Adelrich replied slowly, as if Kleiber were an idiot. The witch hunter's eyes bulged and his face turned red, but Adelrich ignored him, turning to face Alaric again. 'Beastmen don't normally travel alone,' he explained. 'Pairs and threes are more common, or small packs like the ones that have attacked us already. If he's alone, he might be a scout for a larger group – much larger. Killing him could have drawn their attention.'

Alaric nodded, as did Kristoff and Fastred. 'So we circle around him,' Alaric decided, 'and you make sure he doesn't see us. If he does, kill him. If not we can move on and leave him none the wiser.'

It was a good plan, simple and effective, which surprised no one more than Alaric himself. Apparently he had been paying attention during some of those strategy lessons long ago – who knew?

It was a shame, and no real fault of his own, that the plan didn't work.

LATER, ADELRICH GUESSED that the warband had more than one scout – he had noticed one, but another had seen him first and deliberately ducked out of sight. That scout had tailed him back to the group, and then returned to report their presence and their location.

All this was later, however. That day they had continued riding, secure in the knowledge that they were avoiding another fight. It was not until a spear had pierced one of the soldiers through the neck, knocking him from his horse and leaving him dead upon the ground, that they realised their error.

By then it was already too late.

Beastmen poured from the trees. This was easily the largest band they had seen in the hills, larger than the two they had avoided. Within seconds, the hills echoed with the clang of metal against metal, the rasp of steel entering flesh, the growls and snarls of the beastmen, the shouts of the defenders, and the gasps of pain when a weapon found its target.

Not only were these beastmen more numerous than in any previous encounter, they were better organised. The weapons were the same, crude spears and axes and clubs, and the occasional plundered sword or mace wielded by larger ones, but the beastmen showed more cunning in their attack. First had come a wave of spears from every side, and then the bestial warriors had launched themselves, closing the distance too rapidly for the soldiers to return fire. The larger beastmen, the ones clearly in charge, wove in among the horses, using their speed to strike and duck before their target could attack in return. Several of them stabbed horses instead of men, letting the wounded steeds topple and pin their riders. Others menaced horses with their spears, causing the mounts to rear and throw their riders to the ground, where they were quickly dispatched.

'We can't win!' Dietz shouted to Alaric, burying his knife in a beastman's eye and barely retrieving it in time to block another attacker's axe. 'We need to pull back!'

'Back to where?' Alaric shouted, slashing a beastman across the throat and kicking another that tried pulling him from his saddle. 'They've got us boxed in!'

'Pick a direction!' Dietz replied, concentrating on the two beastmen now menacing him. Adelrich stepped in and carved one open from behind, but that left him open to attack, and Dietz cursed as his friend fell to a heavy mace across the head.

'Stay together!' he heard Kleiber bellow, and glanced up in time to see the witch hunter remove a beastman's head with one blow and then slash another's throat on the return stroke. A movement just beyond that caught his eye, and he focussed upon it to see Renke fall before a burly beastman with a massive gnarled club.

'Renke is down!' Dietz shouted to the others. 'So is Adelrich!'

'Grab Adelrich and let's go!' Fastred replied. The portly explorer turned his own mount towards Renke, charging the pair of beastmen gathering around the little man's body. The first fell with a crossbow bolt blossoming from his chest, but the second danced back and lashed out, his clawed hand carving bloody tracks across the face of Fastred's horse. The panicked steed reared, toppling him from his saddle, and disappeared into the trees as Fastred hit the ground. His head struck a rock with an audible thunk and the large man groaned, and collapsed.

'Go, go, go!' Kristoff was urging Dietz on and fending off three beastmen at once. Alaric had already wheeled his horse about, using the gelding's iron-shod hooves to keep more beastmen at bay, and on his other side, Kleiber was menacing them with his flashing blades. Dietz turned back to Adelrich's body and cursed anew as he saw more beastmen dragging the scout away. He wanted to chase after him, but knew he would fall victim himself if he did. Finally, with one last curse, he turned his horse and rode closer to the others, kicking a beastman out of his way.

Holst and his soldiers had not been idle all this time and now they regrouped around the others, using their spears to keep the beastmen back. With this new formation the beastmen could not get close, and after several more minutes one of the larger ones threw back his head and howled. The sound echoed through the clearing, and the other beastmen responded by fading back into the trees, only their dead and several distant howls and barks lingering behind.

'Is anyone hurt?' Alaric demanded after a moment, when he was sure they were not about to suffer a second attack. Kristoff was wrapping a scarf around a nasty cut across his upper arm and Kleiber was checking his sword arm where a mace had battered it, but both shook their heads. Dietz had a few cuts and scrapes, but nothing severe. Alaric himself was untouched.

The soldiers had not fared so well. 'I lost four men,' Holst reported grimly, 'and two more are too injured to fight. Three others were taken.'

'So were Adelrich, Renke, and Fastred,' Dietz added. He waited, as did the others, while Alaric considered this information. It didn't take long, and for once Dietz was glad of his employer's romantic notions.

'Well,' Alaric said, letting out a sigh. 'I suppose we shall have to go after them.'

CHAPTER FIVE

'THEY'RE GOOD AS dead already,' Kristoff protested, raising his hands apologetically when the others turned on him. 'Look, I liked them as much as you did, and I'm sorry they're gone, but I know beastmen – I've had run-ins with them before.' He had regaled them with a few of those tales on previous nights, when they had sounded like charming little scrapes. 'They're vicious bastards, the lot of them.'

'So we have seen,' Kleiber affirmed, flexing his sword arm and wincing.

Kristoff shook his head. 'That's not what I meant. Yes, they're nasty in battle – this band was bigger and smarter than most, but they're all bloodthirsty brutes. It's after the battles I'm talking about.' He shuddered slightly, and then leaned forward, his narrow face intense. 'They don't take prisoners. No use for them.'

'They took Adelrich, Renke, and Fastred,' Dietz corrected him, 'and three of Holst's soldiers.'

'Yes, I know, but not as prisoners.' Kristoff shuddered again. 'As sacrifices and as food.'

'What?' Alaric had been sitting quietly, listening, but now he leapt to his feet. 'You're saying they'll eat them?'

Kristoff nodded. He looked miserable. 'If they haven't already.'

Alaric wheeled his horse about. 'We've got some time though, yes? Until they reach their camp, light their fires, pray to their gods, and thus forth?'

Kristoff shook his head again. 'No, no fires,' he explained softly. 'Beastmen like their meat raw.'

'We must save them!' Surprisingly, it was Kleiber who shouted out. He had both blades unsheathed, and a manic gleam in his eye. 'We must not allow them to sully our companions or taint their souls with such foul appetites!' For the first time since they'd left Middenheim, Dietz found himself actually liking the witch hunter. Well, perhaps 'like' was too strong a word, but he certainly appreciated Kleiber's sudden show of loyalty.

Alaric seemed to agree, for he nodded enthusiastically. 'You're right. They aren't long gone, and we've horses while they're afoot. We can catch them, cut them down from behind, and rescue the others, but we have to go now!' Without waiting to see if the others were following, he charged off in the direction the beastmen had disappeared. Kleiber was right behind him, as was Dietz. Kristoff, Holst and the soldiers followed a moment after.

They made no attempt at subtlety. That time was past. Now what they needed was speed, and Alaric spurred his horse on recklessly, weaving among the trees and frequently ducking low branches or leaping upthrust roots and small bushes.

Dietz, not far behind him, worried that they might be riding into yet another ambush, and he patted the comforting bulk of the crossbow he'd retrieved from where Fastred fell. He was not an expert shot by any stretch, but it was far better than a thrown knife, particularly if he needed to fire in a hurry.

They had ridden almost an hour before Alaric slowed his horse to let the animal breathe. The others reined in around him.

'Are we sure we're going the right way?' Kristoff asked, glancing about. 'I'd have thought we'd be upon them by now.'

'As would I,' Kleiber agreed, gripping his sword hilt tightly. 'Perhaps they doubled back?'

'Perhaps,' Alaric started to say, but Dietz stopped him, raising one hand for quiet.

'Listen,' he whispered, and the others strained their ears. After a second they heard what he had already noticed – the sound of snarls, barks and whines, accompanied by an unmistakable noise that chilled them all to the marrow: the sound of bone cracking between teeth.

'Close, very close,' Dietz murmured, dismounting and edging first to one side and then the other. 'This way,' he said finally when the sounds grew slightly louder. The others dismounted as well, ground-tying their horses in the tall grass, and Kleiber inched forward behind him, his steps almost silent on the dew-damp grass.

'Yes,' the witch hunter said softly a moment later. 'I see them. A small clearing, not forty paces ahead and to the left. There are perhaps twenty in all. They are gathered around' – he paused for an instant, and then hurried on – 'around a pile of bodies.'

'We can take them by surprise,' Holst hissed, signalling his remaining men. One stayed with the two injured soldiers, but the rest readied their spears. The travellers remounted, moving carefully to keep the jangle of reins, spurs and saddlebags to a minimum. It was only at the last minute that Holst remembered to look to Alaric for permission to attack.

'Kill them,' the young noble snarled, giving a tight nod. He spurred his horse on at the same time, and together the group burst into the clearing, shouting and cursing and waving weapons aloft.

It was over quickly. The beastmen had not been expecting an attack. Flushed from their apparent victory, they had left the battle far behind and stopped to enjoy their spoils. When the soldiers and the other riders fell upon them, most of the beastmen were unarmed, their weapons leaning against tree trunks or resting on the ground beside them. Those died before they could reclaim their weapons, most of them trampled by the horses. The soldiers' spears pinned several to the ground or to trees, and Alaric, Kleiber and Kristoff's swords cut down many others. Dietz shot one through the eye with Fastred's crossbow, and almost dropped the weapon when he felt another bolt slide into place from a compartment by the trigger. He recovered in time to shoot a lunging beastman through the chest, however, and then took another through the throat with a lucky shot.

Within minutes the battle was over. Holst and Kleiber dismounted and dispatched those beastmen still living, while Kristoff searched the clearing. It was Alaric, however, whose shout caught them all by surprise.

'Over here!' He was already dismounting and raced across the small clearing to the pile of mail, shields, and weapons. It was only when he shoved a shield aside that the others saw what he had noticed from his higher vantage – a hand thrust up from the mound. In an instant Holst and Kristoff were beside him, tossing the equipment aside. Beneath what had obviously been the soldiers' gear was Fastred, still unconscious. Beneath him and all but smothered by his bulk were Adelrich and Renke.

'Stand back!' Kristoff demanded as they all gathered round their comrades. 'Give them some air!' They obeyed silently, watching as he laid each of the three out on the ground and bent to rest his head against their chests in turn. Finally he straightened and grinned. 'They're alive,' he pronounced. Alaric felt like cheering, but one glance at the discarded armour and weaponry sobered him again and he turned to Holst.

'I'm sorry about your men,' he told the sergeant, who nodded.

'It could have easily been them we saved,' the warrior pointed out quietly.

'We would have been just as relieved,' Alaric replied, which earned him a grateful look and a sharp salute. Then Holst set his remaining soldiers to guarding the clearing's perimeter, and he and two others began building a small fire and collecting the remains of their comrades. Alaric knew the fire might draw attention from other beastmen, but couldn't bring himself to forbid it. The ground here was rocky and hard, digging near impossible, and those men deserved a decent funeral. A pyre was the best they could offer, and even if it brought all the savages in the Howling Hills upon them, they would honour those soldiers properly.

Thinking about that, and about how this was one more scrape they had survived together, Alaric glanced around and had a horrible realisation, followed immediately by a panicked shout. 'Where is Dietz?'

AFTER SHOOTING THE beastman through the throat, Dietz had glanced around for another target. Most of the other beastmen were already dead, or engaged by one of his companions, and Dietz knew himself well enough not to risk shooting that close to an ally.

Then he saw a bestial figure off by itself, and slipping out of the clearing.

'Oh no you don't,' Dietz muttered, spurring his horse after the figure. He remembered what Adelrich had said earlier about this band's scout, and knew that if this one escaped he could potentially bring more after them. He was not about to let that happen.

The beastman moved quickly, racing on all fours and darting between trees Dietz's horse could not clear. He considered dismounting, but knew he could not match the savage's speed on foot. The delays caused by backing and turning were balanced by his steed's speed through sparser terrain, and he managed to at least keep the beastman in sight, though never well enough or for long enough to loose a shot.

Finally, after an hour or more, the beastman faced a low hill. He charged up it without pause, and Dietz, a short way behind, reined in for a moment. The creature was framed perfectly against the rocks, and Dietz raised the crossbow and sighted down it carefully.

Twang!

The bolt slammed the beastman into the hillside, its arms and legs collapsing under it, and it half-slid half-rolled back down. It was dead by the time its head slammed into a rock near the bottom.

Dietz rode up to be sure and it was then he heard the noises: barks and growls, all too familiar – and coming from the other side of that hill.

IT WAS A sombre group that dined together that night. Adelrich and Renke had recovered quickly and seemed fine other than bruises and tender skulls. Fastred had taken a harder blow and was having trouble focussing his eyes, but Kristoff assured him it would pass with a few nights' sleep. Their good fortune was offset by the loss of the soldiers and by Dietz's mysterious disappearance.

No one, not even Kleiber, suggested that Dietz had fled. They had all seen him fighting the beastmen, and more than one had noticed his reluctance to leave the earlier battle when Adelrich had fallen. Nor could they find his body – or that of his horse. It was the last that convinced them he had not simply fallen victim to the beastmen.

'He'll turn up,' Alaric had announced after he had explored every inch of the clearing and its surroundings. He repeated this several times, both out loud and to himself. Dietz would turn up.

Adelrich had examined the area as well and had found a horse's tracks off to one side, well away from where the party had entered. Beastman tracks were there as well, though he could not be sure which had come first. He had offered to follow them, but Alaric shook his head.

'No, we can't risk losing more people,' he decided, but the nods he got from both Holst and Kleiber did nothing to make him feel better. This was why he'd always avoided command before – the hard decisions. No wonder his father, brothers and cousins had always looked so miserable.

After eating they had turned in, leaving one person posted on watch at all times. It was Olgen, one of the soldiers, who was pacing by the pyre's remains, who heard something or someone approaching.

'Something's coming,' he announced to Holst after nudging the sergeant awake. Holst was on his feet in an instant, tugging his mail shirt over his head and grabbing his spear as soon as his hands were free. He woke two other soldiers and together the four of them readied themselves to face the noises. Hands tightened on spears, mail rustled as their muscles tensed, leg muscles tightened, ready to spring...

...and a horse rode into the clearing, stopping just shy of the first spear point.

'Careful,' Dietz called down, grinning. 'I've not been called a beast since I was knee-high and raising havoc in the marketplace.'

His arrival roused the others and soon they were all gathered round to hear his story as he wolfed down some food and followed it with draughts from a wineskin.

'Caught him just in time,' he finished, wiping his mouth with the back of a hand and idly tossing a piece of meat to Glouste, who had emerged from his jacket and was stretched out along his legs. 'Other side of that hill was a camp, and a big one. Big enough for three, maybe four times as many as we just fought.'

'An army,' Kleiber whispered, anger written across his face. 'These foul creatures have gathered to strike at us a second time!'

'They're not smart enough for that,' Fastred argued, still rubbing one temple with his hand and wincing from the torches they'd lit upon Dietz's return. 'It would take a powerful leader to unite beastmen into a proper militia. More likely this is a single tribe – they were called to war together and now the battle's over they're too far from home to return safely, so they wound up here.'

Kristoff agreed. 'All the ones we fought today had the same markings,' he pointed out. 'They're a single extended family, and you just found their base.'

'Hooray for me,' Dietz muttered, but Kristoff smiled.

'Yes, actually,' the trader agreed. 'Now we know where they are, we can travel around them.'

'Or straight to them,' Adelrich pointed out. 'We do need to find that statue and a strong tribe might have it.'

'I didn't see it,' Dietz admitted, 'but I wasn't looking that closely.'

'We can check in the morning,' Alaric suggested, clapping a hand on Dietz's shoulder. 'For now, get some sleep. You need it.' He had meant to say how glad he was that Dietz was all right, but something in the older man's nod told him he didn't have to.

THE NEXT MORNING, Dietz and Adelrich scouted the base. The others rode behind, far enough back not to draw attention, but near enough to ride to the two men's aid quickly.

'Definitely a village, or at least a settlement, rather than a military camp,' Adelrich confirmed quietly when he and Dietz lay on their bellies just below the crest of the hill, glancing down into the small valley below. In the daylight, Dietz could see what he meant. Last night all he'd noticed was how many beastmen were crouching or stalking, or sleeping down there. Now he could see the lack of organisation. Beastmen milled about, apparently eating and sleeping, and relieving themselves anywhere they liked. He saw one try to lie down next to another, only to be kicked by a third – the first one then got up and slouched away to a fourth and lay against that one instead. It definitely looked like an extended family.

'No sign of the statue,' he reported when he and Adelrich had crept back down the hill a short while later, 'and they've got no buildings or tents so we'd have seen it if it was there.'

'Definitely not there,' Adelrich agreed, 'and definitely one tribe. It's a big one – too big for us.'

'We go around, then,' Alaric decided, ignoring the glare from Kleiber. The others nodded and they backed away from the hill, letting Adelrich lead them a short distance back before looping around well clear of the valley.

THEY MADE GOOD time, though they had no idea where they were within the hills and nor where they were going. Several times, Adelrich spotted more beastmen, and when it was a small band Alaric let the party attack. When it was a larger band or a lone scout he held them back, though Kleiber frothed to go after the savages. Twice they encountered beastmen from the same tribe, though both times in much smaller packs.

They were just finishing a late lunch one day when Adelrich stepped out of the trees and approached Alaric.

'You'd better see this.'

Alaric nodded and followed the scout, with Dietz right behind him. The three of them walked for perhaps an hour before reaching another hill. Adelrich led the way up, motioning them to stay quiet and keep hidden, and paused just below the top. Feeling as if he had done this not long before, Dietz crept up to the scout and lowered himself to his belly so he could peer over the edge.

At first he thought they had made a large circle and returned to the beastman camp. Below him was a small valley nestled between three hills, and it was filled with beastmen. Then he noticed several differences.

The first was the weapons. These beastmen had fewer spears and clubs, and more axes and swords; the latter definitely scavenged from human soldiers.

The second difference was the grouping. This base was a little smaller than the first and organised in dense clumps scattered in a circle around the valley floor.

The third difference was the base's focus. Those clumps were centred on a small clearing – and the large, rough stone block within, its shadow suggesting a hideous beast rearing up, wings outspread, limbs waving in menace. Dietz recognised it at once, and a hiss beside him said Alaric had as well.

'Well, we've found our statue,' Alaric confirmed as they slid back down the hill. 'Now how do we get through a tribe of beastmen to destroy it?'

'WE CUT OUR way through, of course,' Kleiber announced when Alaric related the details to the others back at their camp. Everyone stared at the witch hunter, who continued, oblivious to their shock. 'Sigmar himself will bolster our arms and sharpen our blades so that none may stand against us!'

'I counted at least one hundred and fifty down there,' Adelrich pointed out. 'I'd guess it's closer to two hundred, not counting any out hunting. We've fewer than twenty. You want us to wade in? You're mad.'

Alaric stepped between them before the witch hunter could draw his blade, which he looked ready to do. 'Let's not do their work for them,' he pointed out, and both men retreated though they exchanged harsh glances across the camp. 'Adelrich's right. No matter how blessed we may be we cannot take two hundred of them. We need another way.'

'Can we destroy it from a distance?' Renke asked. Alaric looked to Dietz, who shrugged.

'It's solid stone,' he said, 'and well carved. A heavy enough blow could shatter it, but I doubt a spear could strike that hard from a distance. A crossbow bolt maybe, though I'd not want to chance it failing.'

'Shame we have no blackpowder,' Holst grumbled. 'That would do for it, but the count refuses to equip us with such things.'

They all glanced at Kleiber, the only member of their party armed with a pistol, but he shook his head.

'I have some blackpowder,' he admitted, patting a small horn at his belt. 'But I carried only enough for ten shots – four now. That would not be sufficient to demolish solid stone.'

Dietz was eyeing the horn. 'Perhaps it would, if it hit hard enough,' he mused aloud. 'For that matter, one shot from a pistol might do, if it struck the right place.'

'We'd still need to be close,' Kristoff pointed out. 'Closer than the top of that hill, at any rate, and once we're over that peak they'll swarm us under.'

'Not if they're distracted,' Fastred commented. 'Herr Kleiber could wait with that pistol of his while the rest of us charged from another hill, drawing their attention. Then he could ride down and fire at the statue.'

The others considered it, but finally Holst shook his head. 'Still not enough of us,' he stated with the confidence of a trained military man. 'We'd never survive it.'

'I will gladly give my life to protect the Empire!' Kleiber announced, and several of the soldiers nodded.

'Yes yes,' Alaric said finally. 'But what about the other statues? Let's not throw our lives away while those are still out there somewhere, hm?' That quieted Kleiber, and Alaric glanced around at the others. 'Let's mull it over tonight,' he suggested, 'and discuss our options again in the morning.' No one disputed the suggestion and so they settled in for the night.

THE NEXT MORNING Dietz awoke to the sound of clattering hooves. His first thought was of an attack, forgetting that the beastmen did not ride mounts. Regardless, the sound was too near to ignore. He rolled to his feet, one hand drawing a knife while the other brushed sleep from his eyes. He dropped into a crouch, glancing around for the source of the noise. He found it an instant later, over where they had tethered their horses for the night. One of the horses was loose, and he watched as it galloped from the clearing. It was not without its rider. Despite his rude awakening, Dietz blinked his eyes clear in time to recognize Kleiber's distinctive hat atop the rider's head, just before horse and rider crested a low hill and vanished from view.

'What is that maniac doing now?' Dietz muttered, stumbling over to Alaric. His employer was still asleep – bitter experience had taught Dietz that the younger man could sleep through anything – but beside him was an unfamiliar cloth-wrapped bundle. Using his knife tip Dietz nudged it open to reveal Kleiber's pistol, the powder horn, a small pouch Dietz knew held the ammunition, and a note. Deciding this was beyond him, he nudged Alaric none-too-gently in the side with a boot tip until the young noble awoke.

'Wha-what?'

'Kleiber's gone,' Dietz reported, getting in one last nudge. 'He took off, but left that for you.'

Alaric rolled over and sat up, rubbing at his face. 'Gone? Where?' He picked up the pistol with one hand as if he'd never seen one before, then set it back down and unfolded the note.

'"I will bring a distraction. Be ready to fire",' he read. He read it again, more slowly, and then turned the scrap of parchment over as if hoping the blank reverse might hold some explanation. Finally, he hauled himself to his feet, snatching up the pistol, horn and pouch as he did so.

'He's mad,' Alaric grumbled as he stalked over to the others, who had also been awakened by Kleiber's departure.

'That's what I said,' Dietz agreed, following him and absently petting Glouste. His pet had been forced to spend more time within the shelter of his jacket lately, and was enjoying this brief quiet by draping herself in her favourite position around his neck and across his shoulders.

'I don't know what Kleiber intends,' Alaric informed the others after he'd read them the note, 'but he clearly believes it will be enough to draw the beastmen away from their camp. If he is right we'll need to be ready.'

'And if he's wrong?' Renke asked.

'Then,' Alaric said, grinning, 'we will have to save him.' The idea of rescuing the arrogant witch hunter amused everyone, and a sense of cheer filled the camp as they gathered their gear and readied for battle.

'You'll be needing this,' Dietz told Fastred, holding out his crossbow, but the older man shook his head and handed it back.

'My sight is still cloudy,' he explained, 'and that's not something you want when firing into a crowd.' Instead, he drew a long curved sword from a scabbard hanging off his saddle. 'This will do for now.'

Next Dietz wandered over to Alaric, who was standing to one side, staring off in the direction of the village.

'Who's handling the pistol?' he asked bluntly.

'I will,' Alaric replied absently, then turned and laughed at the look on his companion's face. 'Don't worry, Dietz! I do know how to handle a pistol, you know. Decent shot, in fact – my arms instructor was quite pleased. Father was more angry than ever, though – I think he'd rather I'd been terrible at it than have the talent but not the inclination.' He didn't explain further, and Dietz knew better than to ask – over the past year he had learned enough about Alaric's youth to know it would not be a cheerful tale.

Finally they were ready. They rode towards the beast-men's camp and reined in the horses just shy of the obstructing hill. Alaric, Dietz and Adelrich climbed to the peak again while the others remained mounted below, ready to charge if necessary.

The encampment looked unchanged, and beastmen still fought and slept, and snarled and ate everywhere. Clearly Kleiber's intended diversion had not yet begun.

'Now we wait,' Alaric commented, ducking back below the rise and settling onto his haunches. He loaded Kleiber's pistol and set it beside him, within easy reach, stuffing the pouch and the horn back into his belt. Dietz had Fastred's crossbow beside him, its bolt chamber fully loaded, and Adelrich had his longbow at his side and an arrow held loosely against it.

An hour passed. Growls and barks echoed up from the valley behind them, but there was nothing unusual. Dietz found himself dozing in the warm sun that had pooled about them, and kept shaking himself awake.

Adelrich was asleep, showing a soldier's knack for
falling instantly into slumber and just as quickly emerging from it when necessary. Alaric alone did not
succumb, but sat brooding upon the hill, worrying
about what they would be doing and its possible out-
comes.

It was almost noon when the volume of snarls, whines
and howls increased. Adelrich was awake at once, nock-
ing his arrow even as he turned to glance over the
hilltop. Dietz started and then turned, raising the crossbow. Alaric shifted so that he was kneeling, the pistol
balanced on a small outcropping and aimed down into
the valley. Behind them the others readied themselves.

Adelrich spied him first, and gestured with the arrow.
'There.' Dietz and Alaric glanced where he indicated and
saw a horse charging down a hill opposite them, directly
towards the camp. Kleiber had both sword and dagger
drawn and they could hear him shouting dedications to
Sigmar as he rode.

Then the growling grew even louder as more beastmen topped the hill behind him and swarmed down
after him.

'He's pinned!' Alaric gasped, starting to stand, before
Dietz yanked him back down. 'And they're driving him
back into their camp!' Adelrich, watching the witch
hunter's approach, smiled slowly.

'Clever bastard,' he said softly, gesturing towards the
rider with his chin. 'Look. He's not fleeing – he's leading. They're chasing because he wants them to.'

Dietz studied the scene and nodded. Kleiber did not
look desperate, only driven. Several beastmen actually
tumbled past him down the hill. Instead of turning to
attack him as he approached, however, they ignored the
witch hunter now behind them and charged forward –
into the camp. Dietz suddenly understood what he was
seeing.

'It's the other tribe!' he all but shouted. 'He's brought
the other tribe!'

Adelrich nodded, grinning as he rose up, bow in hand. Alaric followed him, finally registering what Dietz had already noticed – these beastmen had different markings and different weapons from the ones below. Kleiber had apparently gone back to the settlement they had passed before and had led those savages here. Now, faced with a rival tribe, they were in full battle-frenzy.

Nor was the second tribe of beastmen sitting idly by. As the invaders charged, the beastmen below gathered their weapons and ran forward, snarling and slavering as they moved to defend their home. The first from each side collided, fur and blood flying, and soon it was a mass of bodies and weapons. Kleiber had ridden past the defenders and wheeled his horse around, cutting down any beastmen who made it through the tumult.

The others were already on their way down as well. Adelrich, Alaric and Dietz had charged down as soon as the beastmen were occupied, and were now approaching the outskirts of the camp. Renke, Kristoff, Fastred, Holst and the soldiers were right behind them, but despite their horses most of the beastmen paid them no mind. They were too intent upon killing one another.

Finally Alaric paused, not forty paces from the statue. It was as hideous and unsettling as the one they had seen in Rolf's shop, though that one had still been pristine. This statue was covered in gore, and the bones at its base indicated the sacrifices it had received. Dietz thought it seemed larger than the other and more organic, its edges softer and a bit blurred as if it was flesh rather than stone, and it was shifting slightly, as if to take a breath.

'It's magnificent,' Alaric whispered, staring at it. 'I couldn't get a good view in Rolf's shop – the lighting was too dim. Those runes around the base – I've seen similar, but none so complete or so extensive! Most likely they're–'

Dietz slapped the younger man across the cheek, almost sending him sprawling. 'Don't look at it!'

'Right, right.' Alaric recovered his balance, straightened, and raised the pistol. He paused again, the barrel shifting before him, and then pulled the trigger.

Blam! The crack echoed through the valley, causing many of the beastmen to halt their attack and glance around. The bullet struck true, impacting the statue where neck and head would have met, and sending a long crack shivering through the stone. However, it did not crumble.

'Damn and blast!' Dietz raised the crossbow, squinted, and fired. His aim was not as good, however, and the bolt skittered across what might be a wing. He fired again, shifting the stock down and to the right, and this time struck it near one shoulder. The bolt embedded itself in the statue, sending another crack through it, but still the icon held together.

Adelrich had been eyeing the beastmen, several of whom had quit their tribal warfare to deal with this desecration, but now he turned and loosed a quick shot towards the statue as well. The arrow sped true, its head driving into the gap Alaric's first shot had created and widening the crack farther. Now the gap extended from the neck to the stomach and was wide enough in places to insert a finger.

Alaric had been quickly but carefully reloading, and now he fired again. His second shot was just to the left of his first and produced a second crack that paralleled the other, intersecting it just below the chest. Dietz's next shot struck a hand, chipping what he thought of as a claw, but his fourth hit the same shoulder as before, and with a loud crack the joint shattered. That side – he shuddered as he realised it was an arm – pulled free, splintering the limb below as it fell and shattering as it struck the hard ground.

Adelrich had his back to them and was shooting approaching beastmen. Most of the savages were still occupied battling each other, but enough had broken off to require his attention. Then the soldiers arrived, Kristoff, Fastred and Renke beside them, and while they dealt with those savages nearby, the scout returned his attention to the stone target before him. An arrow slammed into the first crack a foot above the previous impact, widening it yet more, and another struck the second crack, but glanced off.

Alaric had loaded a third time and raised the pistol again. He aimed carefully and fired.

Bang!

The steel ball struck the statue just below what would be the chin, between his first and second shots, and the already weakened neck could not withstand the additional impact. With a resounding tear eerily similar to the sound of rent flesh the neck disintegrated, the head toppling backward. It tore the wings from the body as it struck them and continued its descent, exploding when it hit the ground.

The repeated blows had weakened the statue throughout, and when the wings broke free the remaining arms crumbled as well, along with large portions of the torso. The jagged chunks of stone were large enough to demolish more as they fell, and soon little remained but the base, one foot and part of a leg. A cloud of dust filled the air around them, sending the men into a coughing fit as they frantically rubbed to clear their eyes of grit.

Seeing this, the beastmen from the camp howled in rage. Many of them turned towards the trio, intent upon destroying them in turn, but the invaders took the opportunity to attack from behind and soon the savages were forced to focus upon the rival tribe again.

'Time to go,' Dietz pointed out, dragging Alaric away just as the younger man pulled a small notepad from his pouch.

'I need to–' Alaric protested, but gave up when he saw the beastmen still fighting not a hundred paces away. 'I suppose I can study the next one,' he admitted, tucking the notepad away again.

'Where are you going?' Kleiber demanded, riding up to them as they began climbing back up the hill. 'We must destroy these foul creatures!'

'No, we came to destroy the statue, which we did,' Fastred replied, wheeling his horse about to give Alaric, Dietz and Adelrich cover as they ran. 'Time to move on.'

'Besides,' Renke added from nearby, 'they're killing each other anyway. By nightfall both tribes will be too weak to pose a threat to anyone. Most of them will be dead. Does it matter who killed them?'

Kleiber stopped, surprised at the small man's pointed remark, but after a moment he nodded and sheathed his blades. 'Sigmar's work is done,' he announced, glancing back a little regretfully. 'These beasts will hunt no more.' He turned his horse and followed the others up the hill.

They did not pause once they'd reached the safety of the other side, but continued on, riding for several more hours. Finally they stopped long enough to eat and feed the horses and relieve themselves.

When they were dismounted Kleiber marched up to Alaric. The young noble assumed the witch hunter wanted his pistol back and proffered the weapon, but the fanatic took it with barely a glance. 'You fought well,' he intoned, glancing first at Alaric and Dietz and then at the others. 'Through your efforts that foul statue was destroyed.' He grimaced as if the words pained him, but set his jaw and continued. 'I… approve of your actions.' Then he walked away again.

'Great,' Dietz muttered to Alaric as he watered their horses. 'If we survive breaking two more statues and facing who knows what perils, he might even admit we're decent folk.'

'It's something to look forward to,' Alaric replied with a smile, stroking his horse's neck. He turned as Holst approached.

'Where to next, sir?' the sergeant asked, and despite his low tone Dietz knew everyone was listening.

Alaric realised it as well, and frowned. He considered the two possibilities carefully, trying to block his own bias, and finally shrugged. 'Best if we keep moving south,' he said, swinging back onto this horse. 'That way we won't leave one of these things behind us.' He kicked his steed into motion. 'We ride to the Reikland.'

Only Dietz knew his employer was from that province, and only he noticed how hesitant Alaric had been to select that destination.

CHAPTER SIX

THEY SPENT THE next week riding. Adelrich pointed out, late one night when he and Dietz were the only two on guard, that he would have cut south and west through the Howling Hills until they'd reached the Hulzrenne. Following that small river would have led them down to the River Talabec, which flowed straight to Altdorf. Most likely they'd have found a boat along the way.

Instead of this quick, painless route, Alaric had led them back to Eldagsen, then back to Mittelweg. From there they had followed the road's other fork, veering south-west towards Altdorf. At Kutenholz the road had split again, but instead of staying south towards the Reikland capital, Alaric had turned his mount west towards the Ridge Way and the Wastelands.

'Why are we taking this route?' Renke had demanded when they had camped earlier that night. As a member of the Imperial Geographic Society he had access to the Empire's best maps and he had demonstrated on their way to the Howling Hills that he had an excellent knowledge of

the area. He had agreed completely with Alaric's choices on
the way to the Howling Hills, but now the little man
seemed genuinely surprised and even slightly affronted.

'We're heading towards the Barony of Drasche,' Alaric
replied casually, though Dietz noticed his employer's hand
tightening on the water skin he held. 'This is the best route.'

'Surely taking Talabec to Altdorf–' Renke began, but
Alaric cut him off.

'We're not going through Altdorf.' His harsh tone startled
the slender geographer into quiet, but now Kristoff joined
the discussion.

'Why not?' he asked, taking a swig from another water
skin and wiping droplets from his beard with his free hand.
'It does seem the fastest way into Reikland.'

'It is,' Alaric agreed tersely, but after a second he realised
this answer would not satisfy the others. 'We need to head
west, not south. We can pick up the River Reik at Carroburg
and follow it west to the Hundleir. That is the southern
edge of Drasche and takes us right to Merxheim, though,'
he admitted quietly, 'I'm in no hurry to visit the region or
its ruler.'

'You have an impressive knowledge of Reikland,' Renke
commented after a moment. 'I admit I'd not thought of the
Hundleir.'

'It's only a small tributary,' Alaric said with a shrug, 'and
easily overlooked. For our purposes, however, it is perfect.'

'I still wonder why we do not stop in Altdorf first,' Fastred
asked, accepting the wineskin from Kristoff with a nod. 'We
could resupply there and send reports back to Middenheim.' His sly smile reminded them that each member of
the small group might wish to report, but to completely
different people. Though united on their mission, everyone
served a different master.

'Carroburg is large enough for that,' Alaric pointed out,
'and still within Middenheim, which should make both
tasks easier. It is also far quieter than Altdorf. Much as I love
that city, entering it would distract us from our task and
most likely cause us several days' delay.'

The others nodded and let the matter drop, satisfied that Alaric's reasoning was sound. Dietz knew better, however. His employer did indeed love Altdorf, almost to distraction, and rarely passed up a chance to enter its walls. They were not avoiding the city, but the area around it. From Altdorf they might have taken the Weissbrock Canal, which ran through the Reikwald Forest and could have deposited them in farmlands south of their destination. That would put them within range of Ubersreik to the south, and that was the home of the von Jungfreuds – Alaric's kin. Clearly the young noble wished to avoid his family at all costs. Since the detour was not that difficult, adding a few extra days in the saddle, but no other complications, Dietz was content to leave it alone.

'He wants to get in and out of Reikland as quickly as possible,' he told Adelrich in reply, which was certainly true. 'So we're heading straight for our destination.'

'I'd have gone by the river,' the scout repeated with a shrug, 'but then I'm a man of Middenheim and not familiar with the ways of our south-west neighbour. He seems confident in his route and I'll trust in his judgement.'

ALARIC HAD CERTAINLY been right, Dietz mused as they passed through the city gates. Carroburg was large enough. As the former capital it was the largest city in the province after Middenheim itself, and though it lacked his own home's rugged exterior, this place had enough people, wares and energy to satisfy any traveller. Not that Carroburg had escaped the war, of course, but it had not been involved in more than peripheral skirmishes. The brunt of the war's impact here had come when refugees from eastern towns had arrived seeking shelter and protection. Tents and shanties still lined the space outside the city walls and filled every alley within. The resulting crowd was thicker than Middenheim had suffered at its height, and Alaric admitted he found it hard to breathe with so many bodies jammed so close together.

They wasted little time in Carroburg, however. The party took rooms in a modest inn halfway up the riverbank, high enough to avoid water and waste, but low enough not to be extravagant, and spent the next day replenishing their supply of food, drink and feed. New bolts and arrows were bought to replace the ones used in fighting the beastmen, and Dietz saw Kleiber tying a fresh powder horn to his belt beside a new pouch of pistol balls.

The witch hunter had also penned a long report, which he had then taken to one of his peers within the city. He assured Alaric and Dietz over dinner that the report mentioned their dedication and would clear their name at once. Fastred had sent copies of his journal entries to his fellows at the guild, and Kristoff had given a written account to a cohort at Carroburg's trading guildhouse. Holst had arranged for his wounded men to stay in the city and travel back to Middenheim when they could, taking his short report and a list of their slain brethren back with them. Only Adelrich and Renke had not sent word – the scout pointed out his job was merely to help them get where they were going safely, and Renke was updating his maps as they travelled and saw no need to send them off half-finished, or to leave copies of the uncompleted versions with his counterparts there in town.

That night they all slept well and the next morning they departed. Alaric had hired a boat and, once men and horses were loaded, they set off along the river towards Marienburg.

RIVERBOAT TRAVEL WAS an easy, comfortable thing. The sailors handled the sails and steered from the rudder at the rear, leaving the travellers nothing to do but laze about in the sun and enjoy the quiet. They passed several other boats along the way, ranging from one-person skiffs to longboats twice the size of their boat, and each time the boatmen exchanged news and information about their route. Dietz admitted to Adelrich that, if he was forced to travel by water, this was the least upsetting method. Still, he could not shake his sense of dread whenever he looked out over the silver waters or realised just how far they were from each bank, or how deep the water ran below them. He slept fitfully, waking from nightmares of lying chained on the riverbed as boats glided by above him.

Glouste did her best to distract her master, nipping him awake whenever he cried out. During the day the tree-monkey delighted in racing about the ferry, scampering under and sometimes over the horses, and weaving in between baggage and people at top speed. The rest of the party had grown accustomed to her antics during their ride through Middenland and watched her with amusement, complaining half-heartedly when she nipped their feet or hands or scurried up their arms or legs. The sailors were less comfortable, and after a near miss with an oar on the first day, Dietz warned her not to bother the sailors or get in their way. Glouste seemed to take this as a challenge and spent the rest of their voyage keeping just beyond the sailors' reach and just at the edge of their sight.

THE RIVER BARGE finally reached the Hundleir. Middenland lay on the north side and Reikland on the south, Uder and Merxheim representing them respectively. Alaric paid the ferrymen and the party disembarked on the Reikland side, leading their horses onto the dock and down into Merxheim proper. It was not until the ferry had swung back into the current and floated on down the river that the travellers examined their location.

Merxheim was not a large town, perhaps a hundred buildings in all, and many were in sad repair. Deitz had grown up among the stone of Middenheim and still found it strange to see wooden houses and dirt roads, but he had learned to appreciate the warmth of a well-built wooden structure. The buildings he saw beyond the docks did not match that ideal – their planks were worn and grey, the roofs sagged, the walls drooped, and the buildings themselves leaned, often in more than one direction.

Doors hung crooked and shutters flapped in the breeze, revealing darkened interiors. No one moved around them.

'Where is everyone?' Alaric wondered out loud, glancing about. 'I've always thought Merxheim a dirty little hovel, but last I was here it had mud-spattered children and dogs playing in the road, old women trying to sell fish and soap, and brutish men offering to hire as guides and body-guards.' He looked around again, as did the others, but still nothing moved but them, the doors and shutters. The town seemed deserted.

'Perhaps it was the war,' Renke suggested, though he did not sound convinced. As far as they knew the forces of Chaos had not crossed the Reik.

'Plague,' Fastred offered with a shudder, an explanation that was both more plausible and more chilling. Normally plague houses were fired with the victims inside, but the buildings here, though dilapidated, were unburned. Adel-rich and Dietz jogged quickly among the buildings but saw no people nor any traces of them. Finally they returned, no less confused than before.

'Well, whatever happened here is not our concern,' Alaric decided, swinging up into his saddle. He frowned, 'Although this was the drop-off point for the second statue. I hope its presence was not the cause of the town's empti-ness.' He raised his head and grabbed his reins. 'Still, it's clearly not here so we'd best get moving.'

'But where should we go?' Kristoff asked, still looking around warily. 'Do we have any idea who might have taken the statue, or where it might be?'

'None,' Alaric admitted. He grinned. 'But Drasche is not that big, no matter what its baron might think. If we head south along the river we'll be out of the trees in a week. Another two will see us to the foot of the Grey Mountains and I very much doubt that anyone carried it up there. If we have not found it by then,' he shrugged, 'we head north along the mountains' base until we hit the Fleudermeiser, which forms Drasche's – and Reikland's – northern border.

That will lead us back to the Reik. If we reach the Reik again without seeing signs of this statue it is not in the barony, I guarantee you.'

The others looked less certain, but none of them knew the terrain as well as Alaric did, and he had already demonstrated his leadership to be competent, so they nodded, mounted, and followed him from the empty town. Dietz kept glancing back as they rode away, worried that something might be lurking there to leap at them from behind. He was not the only one.

TWO DAYS LATER they reached another village, this one so small it did not appear on Renke's maps. Nor was it likely to do so now, Alaric thought as he studied the blackened remains of buildings, posts – and people. Merxheim at least had been intact. This nameless place had been burned to the ground and its inhabitants had perished with it.

'It could have been plague,' Fastred confirmed, tossing aside several charred planks to examine a body beneath them. 'I see no evidence of sickness, but the fire would have burned it away.'

'Sigmar's holy flame cleanses the world,' Kleiber agreed, though Alaric noticed the witch hunter kept his mount well back from the destruction. Perhaps, he thought, the fanatic was not so confident in his god's favour, or in Sigmar's power to protect him, as he often claimed.

'Whoever did this was efficient,' Holst commented, his eyes skimming across the wreckage. 'More bodies at the centre, and more ash – they started there and worked outward, burning as they went.' He shook his head. 'Militia, I'd wager my sword on it.'

'Reikland's soldiers do have a reputation,' Kristoff pointed out lightly, and Alaric was glad he was standing slightly ahead of the others when the trader said it. That way he knew his expression wouldn't betray him.

'Oh yes,' he replied, forcing his tone to stay casual. 'We have some of the finest soldiers in the Empire. No offence,' he added, nodding to Holst, who nodded back.

'None taken, sir,' the warrior replied. 'I've fought along-side several from Reikland and always been impressed with their skill.' The burly sergeant frowned. 'I'm not sure why soldiers would burn a village, though, unless it was plague.'

'Or bandits,' Adelrich added, returning from a quick survey of the area. 'I've heard stories of small towns that preyed upon travellers, and they're well-situated for it here.' It was true – the nameless village had stood along the bank of the Hundleir, still well within the north-west edge of the Reikwald Forest. It would be easy to ambush anyone coming down the river or through the woods.

'No signs of the statue,' the scout added, falling in beside Dietz and Alaric. 'Nor can I see traces in the forest of a wagon or cart carrying such a weight.'

'It did not travel by land,' Alaric agreed, turning away from the burnt village and leading them farther along the river. 'Whoever has it must have received it at Merxheim and taken it south by boat.'

The others nodded. That made sense – the Hundleir was right here and Merxheim stood at the junction between it and the Reik. The forest was dense enough to make even riding on horse back difficult – no one could have brought a massive stone sculpture through the trees intact, but the river provided an easy alternative. By riding alongside the river they were tracing the same route as the statue, but could stop to study clues at any time. Alaric could not help but notice the nod Adelrich gave him – it was the gesture of a man who agrees with your decision and respects it – and that buoyed his spirits, which had been low since they had boarded the river boat and crossed into his home province. He was not accustomed to making decisions and even less familiar with having them turn out correct. For an instant he wished his father could see him now, but he quickly quashed that notion.

ADELRICH SPOTTED ANOTHER small settlement a few days later, this one deeper within the forest and well away from the riverbank. It too had been destroyed, but not burned – the buildings had been shattered and torn down. They detoured to examine it and Holst confirmed the others' first impressions.

'Axes did this,' he stated, running one finger along a broken board, 'and longswords. More soldiers.' He squinted up at the surrounding trees. 'They didn't dare risk a fire spreading so they tore the place apart instead.'

'No sign of the people,' Fastred was saying, but Kleiber interrupted him.

'Over here.' The witch hunter gestured and the others followed his finger to a low mound just beyond the furthest building. The ground was still damp and loose. 'Fully forty people could be buried there,' he declared, his voice unusually soft, 'possibly the village's full occupancy.'

'Plague again?' Fastred wondered aloud, but corrected himself. 'No, they'd have burned the bodies, at least. Bandits, then? It is an ill-omened place,' he said, looking at the trees looming over the wreckage, 'and well-suited to such villainy.'

'Well-armed men passed through here,' Adelrich confirmed, studying the ground around the village, 'but nothing larger.'

'No statue,' Alaric muttered, trying not to look at the mound. 'So we return to the river.' The others followed him back, but it was a sombre group that focused almost obsessively upon their quest, avoiding images of the place they had just seen or the fate its people had doubtless suffered.

THEY HAD ALMOST reached the edge of the forest when they came upon a third village. 'Not again,' Dietz muttered quietly, and he saw several of his companions making similar requests. Even Kleiber paused in obvious prayer, and Dietz suspected the witch hunter was asking Sigmar to spare them the sight of another mass grave.

This settlement sat along the river, so close the water lapped up against the outer buildings, and that had been its salvation. As they rode in they saw signs of fire again, but several buildings still stood and a few were even serviceable. The river had doused the flames before they could spread along the waterfront and so had spared the town the same fate as its predecessors.

Not that this had saved it completely. The buildings furthest from the water had turned to ash and blackened wood, and several more bore both scorch marks and signs of violence. A few buildings had toppled as a result, creating a pile of wreckage near the village's centre. The remaining homes stood open and empty, their dark doorways staring reproachfully at the travellers as they rode past.

'Is anyone still alive in this land?' Alaric wondered out loud, smacking his fist against his thigh. Not that he liked the Baron von Drasche – far from it – but he had nothing against the man's people. Besides, no one deserved this. What had happened here? He turned to ask Dietz a question and saw that his friend had stiffened in his saddle. One hand was gliding slowly to the long knife at his belt and the other was stroking his horse's neck, keeping it calm. Glouste, that damnable tree-monkey, chittered once and disappeared into its owner's jacket. That, as much as anything, warned Alaric to be ready. Much as he hated to admit it his friend's pet had an uncanny sense for imminent danger.

Adelrich was already off his horse and moving silently towards the largest remaining structure, a small single-storey house whose thick wooden walls looked almost undamaged. The scout had his longsword in one hand, the other held open before him, and as he reached the building his free hand reached up and flattened against the door. Then he froze, going completely motionless for several seconds. Suddenly he shoved the door hard, reached in, and grabbed at something inside.

'Got you!' Adelrich shouted, yanking his arm back, and a wretched-looking individual with it. The man might have been young, but his hair was thin and oily, his face lined and flushed, eyes bulging above sunken cheeks, his skin pale. He wore little more than rags and yelped with fright as Adelrich hurled him towards the others.

'Don't kill me!' the man pleaded, dropping to his knees, and Alaric felt disgust – not towards this unfortunate, but whoever had instilled such fear in him.

'We won't hurt you,' he told the man, dismounting and tossing his reins to Dietz. 'It's all right.' That was a stupid thing to say, he knew, but as usual he had spoken without thinking. 'We mean you no harm,' he tried again, holding his hands out from his sides. 'Look, I'll leave my blade in its scabbard.' He wished he'd thought to disarm first, but it was too late for that now – he was sure if his hand ventured anywhere near his sword hilt the man before him would interpret this as an attack. Not that the wretch was any threat, but Alaric desperately wanted to know what had happened here, and this man was the only survivor they had found thus far.

'Alaric!' At Dietz's hiss he glanced back, and turned just in time to catch the water skin and biscuit the older man tossed him. 'Give him those.' It made sense, Alaric admitted – the man was clearly starving. He offered the food and drink to the man, who was still kneeling, hands up to protect his head. When the villager didn't move, Alaric inched forward and set the offerings on the ground a few feet away, and then backed away.

'Go on, eat,' he urged. The man glanced up, saw the food at once and snatched it up, cramming the entire biscuit into his mouth in a single motion and swigging water from the skin even before he had begun chewing. He swallowed convulsively, almost gagging, and spluttered a bit, spewing water about him, but at last he had forced the food down and sat back.

'More,' he demanded, and Dietz wordlessly tossed down several more biscuits and a second skin, plus a hunk of cheese. The villager gathered them up and rose unsteadily to his feet. He backed away, inching past Adelrich, who moved aside at Alaric's nod. When he reached the doorway,

however, the villager did not enter. Instead, he tossed the
food and the water skin into the building, and then pulled
the door shut behind him. They could all hear the sound of
hurried footsteps and a soft squeal of delight, followed by
slurping and chewing.

'My sisters,' the man explained, his back protectively
against the door, and Alaric felt like laughing and crying
all at once. They were almost twenty, all well fed and well
armed and mounted. He was one man, barely alive. Yet he
guarded the door as if he would strike them all dead
should they pursue his sisters.

'What happened here?' Alaric finally asked and the villager seized gratefully upon the change of subject.

'Soldiers,' he replied grimly. 'Rounded us up an'
marched us to the elder's house. Slaughtered everyone,
then tore the town down around 'em.' He puffed up
slightly. 'I saw 'em coming... was fishing. Hid my sisters in
the root cellar and climbed a tree. They didn't find me.'

'Was there plague here, boy?' Fastred asked kindly, and
at the word 'boy' Alaric looked again and blinked in surprise. Fastred was right – what he had taken for a man was
no more than a boy, perhaps fifteen summers! Even as he
realised this, the boy shook his head.

'Marauders, then,' Kleiber asked, leaning forward, and
Alaric was not surprised to see the boy cower from the
witch hunter. Even after weeks of travel together he found
Kleiber's zeal intimidating, but the boy shook his head
again.

'Did Chaos venture this far west, then?' Holst asked,
standing stock-still so as not to frighten the lad. 'Was it
orcs or goblins or the like did this?' The boy once again
shook his head.

'Soldiers,' he repeated, and Alaric knew he was not the
only one confused.

'Whose soldiers?' he asked finally, and the young villager gaped at him as if he were simple.

'The baron's, of course,' the boy said. 'Only soldiers
here.'

'Baron von Drasche?' Alaric repeated, and this time the boy nodded. 'But you said the town was plague-free.' He rocked back on his heels. 'Why would the baron send his troops to destroy your village?'

The boy shrugged. 'Undesirable, they said. "Cleansing the land," they said.' He glanced about warily, as if afraid the baron would hear him and punish him for speaking out of turn.

'I can't believe it,' Alaric muttered, no longer seeing the villager before him. 'Not even Gernot would–'

'Would what?' Dietz demanded, stepping close to him. Alaric hadn't noticed him dismounting, but realised now that all of them had done so, probably to reduce the boy's fear.

'Who is Gernot?' Fastred added, also approaching. The others gathered as well, all but Adelrich and Holst who stayed near the boy.

'Gernot is the Baron von Drasche,' Alaric explained finally, pleased he kept the bitterness from his voice. 'A nasty piece of work; he once complained that his lands were the dregs of the province and his people the refuse.' Alaric deliberately blocked out the argument that had goaded the young baron into such a statement. 'Apparently he has decided to correct the situation.'

'His soldiers destroyed all these towns?' Fastred asked, amazed, and the boy shrugged.

'Uxer, that's three days downriver, they left that one alone. An' they took Hans the potter from Merxheim, and Greta the weaver, an' a few others.'

'So he's actually dividing his own subjects into those worth saving and those to die,' Renke marvelled softly. 'Astounding!'

'No man has such dominion,' Kleiber agreed. 'All who live just lives are entitled to protection by their lords, and only the gods may smite them.'

'Oh, the baron follows the gods,' the boy said bitterly, speaking out for the first time. 'His soldiers burn offerings at every town. I heard 'em say they'll slaughter ten oxen when they finally bring the gypsies down.'

'The gypsies?' Alaric had been lost in memory, but now he glanced down at the boy. 'What have they to do with this?'

'They're the only ones left,' the village replied. 'Big band of 'em, been wandering through here a year or two now. The baron hates 'em, but can't get rid of 'em 'cause they just fade into the trees.' He shrugged. 'Guess with no more villages they won't have any place to hide.'

'Serves them right, too,' Renke snapped, his face twisted into a surprising snarl. 'Dirty thieves, the lot of them, good for nothing but mischief and disease.'

'They are an ungodly people,' Kleiber agreed as if that were enough offence to justify a slow, painful death. For him it probably was.

Even Kristoff was nodding. 'I've crossed paths with gypsies before,' he admitted quietly, 'and never had good come of it. They're crafty, certainly, and out for themselves. This baron is not the first I've heard who wished them gone from his lands.'

'That's no reason to hunt them like animals!' Dietz snapped, glancing over his shoulder to the boy and lowering his voice. 'Nor does it justify killing his own subjects.'

'I'll not argue that,' Fastred said, stroking his beard idly. 'But it is ultimately his land to govern as he chooses. Who are we to gainsay his choices?'

Kleiber and Renke both opened their mouths to reply, but Alaric spoke first to cut them off. 'Fastred's right – we have no say here. Nor is it our responsibility. We should find the statue, destroy it, and be gone.'

Slowly the others nodded. Alaric understood their anger, as he felt the rage pouring through his own veins, but this was neither the time nor the place. They had a task to complete. Perhaps afterwards he would return and have a word with Gernot – in private.

In the meantime, there was the boy to consider. Turning back, Alaric walked towards the villager, keeping his steps slow and his hands at his side. Finally he stopped just beyond arm's reach.

'What will you do now?' he asked softly, and the youth, who had nervously watched him approach, started at his voice.

'Nothin',' the boy replied finally, and Alaric almost laughed.

'No, I mean where will you go? How will you and your sisters survive?' At the mention of his siblings the boy's brow furrowed. 'Look, do you have a trade?'

At that the boy perked up slightly. 'I'm good with wood,' he boasted, tugging a small pendant from around his neck. 'Made it myself,' he bragged, removing it from its cord and handing it to Alaric. It was an owl and finely carved. The boy did have talent.

'Good, good,' Alaric said then, reaching for his pouch. 'Best if you leave here – make for Carroburg or Altdorf or one of the other cities, but outside this province. Understand?' The boy nodded. 'Take these coins–' He had his hand in his pouch already, but the boy shook his head and backed away.

'I'm no beggar,' he grumbled, and Alaric almost growled in frustration. He was trying to help! How would this poor wretch survive otherwise, him and his sisters alone and with nothing? He glanced over at Dietz, who looked pointedly at the pendant still dangling from Alaric's fingers. Then he glanced at the pouch and nodded his chin towards the boy.

Ah, of course. Alaric turned back to the youth. 'No, of course not,' he agreed cheerfully, 'but this pendant' – he held it up between them – 'is truly fine work. Will you sell it to me?' When the boy's chest puffed out he knew Dietz had hit upon the right tack. 'I can only imagine its worth to you,' Alaric continued, rummaging in his pouch, 'and I am sure you hate to part with it. I hope this will be sufficient recompense?' He realised as he said them that the boy might not understand the words, but judging from the gleam in his eyes he had followed the meaning. Alaric held up four gold coins and the boy snatched them from him, stuffing them into his tattered shirt.

'Fine then.' Alaric tied the pendant around his neck, adjusting the cord so the polished woodcarving hung neatly at the front of his shirt, and returned to his horse. 'Good luck to you and your sisters,' he called out, swinging into his saddle again. Then he turned and led the way from the ruined village. The others followed him, though he saw several of them glancing back from time to time, looking at where the boy still stood watch by the closed door. At one point Alaric thought he saw something fall from Dietz's saddlebags, and when he turned to his companion the older man shrugged innocently.

'Must not have tied it shut,' he said, but Alaric knew better. A moment later something tumbled from Renke's side as well, and then something from Adelrich's. Soon the way behind them was littered with food, rope, a knife, a blanket and several more coins. The boy and his sisters would have enough to get them to a larger city and perhaps enough for the lad to apprentice himself to a woodcarver as well.

PUTTING THE BOY from his mind, Alaric led his companions further along the river, wending their way towards the Grey Mountains. They had left the Reikwald behind and were in gentler country, rolling hills dominated by rich farmlands. Small stands of trees still appeared here and there, but much of the land was covered in crops, and from their horses they could easily see over vast stretches.

They reached another town a few days later, the Uxer the boy had mentioned. Just as he'd stated, this town had not been harmed and it seemed a tidy, active place.

'I can see why the baron would leave this place unmolested,' Kristoff commented as they rode through, admiring the neat houses and the bustle of activity all around them. 'It's certainly a credit to his name.'

'That it is,' Adelrich replied, rejoining them – the scout had veered off towards the docks when they approached. 'It has the last dock along the Hundleir.' He grinned in answer to Alaric's unspoken question. 'The gypsies the boy mentioned have a camp somewhere nearby.' He scratched his chin. 'Arrived in boats two months back, beached them and drove their wagons ashore, through town and out the other side. A month ago four of them sailed in and hauled a small cart onto the docks. Heavy, I hear, but covered in blankets. They wheeled it out towards the gypsy camp.'

'We might have known they would have the statue,' Kleiber commented. 'I only hope we have arrived in time to prevent them from sacrificing infants before it, as is their wont.'

'Those are only old tales,' Dietz argued, but the witch hunter sniffed dismissively.

'Old tales are borne from old truths,' he stated. 'The gypsies are a blight upon our world and all right-thinking folk despise them upon sight.'

'Prepare to brave your disgust then,' Alaric told him. 'We will need to find the statue ourselves, which means close contact with these gypsies, if they possess it.'

They left the town, resisting the urge to sleep on real beds and eat food someone else had cooked for at least one night. Fastred in particular looked longingly towards a long, low building that looked suspiciously like a tavern, and Dietz knew the large man was thinking of the ale and wine within. The very thought set his mouth watering, but he knew their mission came first. 'Perhaps we can drink to our success later,' he told Fastred as they rode away and the explorer nodded glumly. 'I'll buy,' Dietz added, and that cheered the other man up considerably.

ONCE PAST UXER they kept riding, though they slowed considerably. There had been no tracks in the town itself, or at least none to be distinguished from the general foot traffic. Out here, however, the signs of man and horse were less frequent and Adelrich had a better chance of noticing the marks they wanted. They were still within sight of town when the scout stopped them and indicated a faint trail amid the grass and mud.

'Many wagons,' Adelrich announced, studying the tracks, 'at least one month ago, possibly two or three.' He ran one hand, palm down and fingers splayed, over the marks. 'Frequent visits to Uxer,' he decided finally, 'but only in small groups.'

An hour later they crested a small hill and found themselves looking down upon a shallow valley. It was a wide, low stretch filled with trees spaced too evenly to be natural – Alaric guessed it might have originally been an orchard. Sunlight leaked through the gaps in the foliage and spilled upon the long grass, and upon the camp nestled there.

Alaric's first impression was one of frenzied disorder, but he revised that as he registered more details. The scene below was certainly a lively one, filled with constant activity, but his eyes began to see patterns in the way the people moved, as if they danced about one another. Music wafted up to them, enhancing that notion of a dance, and in fact he saw people stepping in time to the melody. Strange covered wagons were ranged among the trees, almost hidden in the shadows, but the people who owned them were impossible to miss, their brightly coloured clothing producing flashes of brilliance as warm as the flames from their small cookfires. Horses grazed near each wagon, evidently tethered to their masters' homes.

'Gypsies,' Renke whispered, the name almost an insult from his lips.

'Indeed,' Kleiber agreed, 'and like as not, the recipients of the abomination we pursue.'

Dietz looked ready to protest, but stopped and nodded instead. 'Probably true,' he finally agreed. 'Let's go find out.' He kicked his horse into motion, cresting the hill and trotting down towards the gypsy camp.

CHAPTER SEVEN

'DAMN AND BLAST!' Muttering one of Dietz's favourite curses, Alaric prodded his own horse forward and raced after his friend. The others followed right behind and they all reined in together at the bottom, mere yards from the startled gypsies.

'What were you…?' Alaric's question died on his lips as he glanced around. A moment ago these people had been laughing and dancing without a care in the world. Now they had somehow moved to surround the travellers, and in each hand he saw a knife, a whip, an axe, or even a sword. A low murmur had sprung up as well and it was growing louder.

'Oyega, Roma,' Dietz shouted, and the tension stilled. He looked down at the gathering gypsies, glancing from face to face and finally settling on one, an older man with a shock of white through his otherwise black hair and golden hoops in each ear. 'Zeo?' Dietz asked him.

The man nodded and stepped forward, openly sheathing the dagger he'd been holding. The tension dropped still further, and another buzz spread through the crowd, though to Alaric this one felt different – not hostile at all, more curious and slightly excited.

'Conocinti,' Dietz continued, gesturing at himself and the other riders. Then he held up a wineskin – not water, Alaric noted, and wondered where his companion had been hiding that. 'Spartirimos vini,' he said, and took a swig, then offered the skin to the gypsy.

For an instant no one moved as the earringed man studied Dietz. Then he reached up, accepted the skin, and took a hefty swallow. Wiping his mouth with the back of one hand, he beckoned for Dietz to dismount, which he did. Still the gypsies stayed silent and the travellers held themselves ready. Then the gypsy grinned and embraced Dietz. The air around them exploded with shouts and laughter. Weapons vanished and the other riders found themselves dragged from their horses and offered warm bread, cold water, strong wine and fresh fruit.

'Your accent,' Alaric heard the man asking Dietz as they were led into the centre of the gypsy camp. 'Estalian?'

Dietz nodded. 'I met them in Middenheim. Their daughter Rosali and I were – close.' Was it just the dim light or was Dietz actually blushing?

The man he had called Zeo laughed and clapped him on the back. 'Good, good! Tonight you are one of us, in honour of Rosali. Come!'

'A girl taught you gypsy speech?' Alaric asked quietly as he and Dietz brushed past one another on the way to the central fire.

'Among other things,' was the short reply.

It proved to be an interesting evening. The gypsies were true to their Zeo's word, welcoming the travellers like longlost cousins. That meant a feast, with music and dancing, and much wine, but it also meant no standing on ceremony – Fastred was handed a basket of fresh rolls and pushed towards the circle to hand them out, Renke was wrangled into filling goblets with wine, and even Kleiber was pulled into helping with the meat, a boar hanging on a spit over the fire. Alaric found himself chatting with several of the gypsies and enjoyed the opportunity to meet them, find out more about their culture, and learn their language. Fastred and Kristoff seemed to feel the same. Holst, Adelrich and the soldiers stayed wary, though they gladly accepted the gypsies' hospitality and willingly helped when asked. Kleiber and Renke were still visibly uncomfortable in the crowd, though Renke did his best to hide his disapproval. The witch hunter did not bother masking his contempt, but that only made him a target for several young, pretty lasses who took turns trying to sway him to think of them more favourably.

Zeo – Alaric learned that the word meant 'uncle' and was the honorific given to the band's leader – sat between him and Dietz, and alternately questioned them, told them stories, and offered them food and drink.

'We come here during summer,' Zeo told them over spits of roast meat, 'avoid the swelter. The townsfolk know us. They come in evenings, we read fortunes and sing and dance, and they give us coin and food.' He frowned. 'Not lately, though. Lately they stay away, don't look at us when we pass. Some won't sell to us, say we steal babies.' He snorted. 'Why steal them? People give us their children all the time, no need to steal!'

Dietz nodded. 'The baron has been spreading lies,' he suggested quietly, and Alaric knew he was probably right. It would be typical of Gernot, inventing falsehoods to turn the people against these wandering entertainers. He had heard many stories of gypsies himself, but had never met them, and he was both fascinated and delighted to find that many of the darker tales had been lies as well. These people were open and honest and playful, though he knew Dietz's words had helped that. Their language and clothing were colourful, and their grace and rhythm daunting, but he could no longer see them as dangerous.

Apparently Dietz's pet felt the same way. Shortly after they sat down Glouste emerged from Dietz's jacket, producing a shout of surprise and delight from Zeo and several others. The tree-monkey crept out onto her master's shoulder and looked around, nose twitching as she sampled the rich smells of food and wine, and warm bodies in motion. Finally she accepted the morsel Dietz held out, and then licked her lips, whiskers twitching eagerly, and nudged his cheek for more.

'Alberi volpini,' Zeo marvelled, holding out one hand palm up, a shred of meat upon it. Glouste examined him carefully, and then the meat, and then the man again before finally accepting the offering. She butted his hand with her forehead in thanks. 'It means "tree fox",' he told Alaric, who had been about to ask. 'I have heard of such, though never have I seen one myself. Like the ferret, yes?'

'This is an Indyan tree-monkey,' Alaric corrected, and to his surprise the gypsy roared with laughter.

'Scimi?' Zeo repeated to the others around him, still laughing, then shook his head. 'No, my young friend, not scimi.' He patted Glouste's head cheerfully, causing her to purr and butt his hand again. 'Closer to volpini the fox, than the monkey, this one.'

Alaric bristled. How dare this ignorant nomad doubt his classification? 'I tell you it is a tree-monkey,' he repeated. 'We found it in Ind.'

'Ind?' Zeo shook his head and fired off a rapid question to one of the others nearby, a man whose hair and short beard were streaked with white. The second gypsy replied, and Zeo nodded. 'Yes, we have heard tales of that land from cousins. They talk of strange creatures walking and climbing, and flying in those jungles.' He shrugged. 'I do not know that place, but I tell you what I do know. This charmer is no scimi.' He gestured at Glouste's paws, planted securely on Dietz's shoulder. 'The diti, the fingers, the paws, are wrong. The testi, the head, is wrong. The codi, the tail, is wrong.' He smiled, still stroking Glouste's head. 'We Roma know scimi well. This is no scimi.'

As the gypsy leader talked, Alaric calmed down and sat back, thinking hard. He had assumed Glouste was a tree-monkey – he had heard of them from the sailors when they had first docked in Ind, but what Zeo said made sense. Glouste was not built like any monkey he had seen before, and did resemble a fox more with her pointed face, dainty paws, and thick tail. Finally he nodded.

'You are right,' he admitted, deliberately avoiding Dietz's triumphant smile. 'She is no scimi.'

'Hah!' Zeo clapped him on the back and handed him a full goblet of wine. 'You are wise, but admit mistakes. This is good! This is how to learn!' Alaric accepted the wine with a smile and raised the glass in a silent toast before drinking. The gypsy was right – accepting knowledge from others was the way to learn, and clearly the Roma knew a great deal. He found himself wishing they could stay with the gypsies, travel with them and learn from them, but Zeo had said 'this night' and some instinct told Alaric not to push their hospitality. Besides, there was still the statue to consider.

HOURS LATER, DIETZ noticed his shoulders felt bare. It took a moment to realise why.

'Glouste?' He looked around, but saw no sign of his pet. The Roma had taken to her immediately and had spent the evening feeding her and playing with her, so it was no surprise she had wandered off. Most likely, she was playing with several of the gypsy children, or being brushed by one of the older girls. Still, he could feel the effects of a full belly and a great deal of wine, and decided to use the excuse to stretch his legs. Zeo and Alaric were talking about mountain travel and barely noticed when he stood and walked away.

'Glouste?' His other companions were scattered about the camp – Renke and Kleiber sitting together stiffly, Fastred chatting with one of the gypsy elders, Kristoff apparently haggling with a few young men, Holst and his men pretending they were not amused by several children's antics, and Adelrich flirting with a pretty lass. None of them had seen his pet – he could stop thinking of her as a tree-monkey, at least, and liked Zeo's description of a

tree-fox much better – but promised to alert him if they
did. He wandered on, through the camp, asking here and
there after Glouste. Several had played with her or fed her,
or petted her that night, of course, but none had her now.

'She was playing with Zisi last,' one little girl told him
sleepily, 'over there.' Her lazy gesture indicated a wagon
near the edge of the gypsy's camp. Dietz thanked her and
her mother and followed her directions.

'Glouste?' A soft chittering caught his attention and he
peeked into the wagon. Like the other gypsy wheeled
homes the walls had many compartments and the floor
was lined with heavy quilts. A little girl lay asleep there,
Glouste still curled up in her arms. When she saw Dietz the
tree-fox slithered free, nuzzled the sleeping girl one last
time and hopped over to him.

'I'd wondered where you'd got to,' he whispered as she
climbed up his arm and settled about his shoulders again,
nudging him behind the ear. He scratched between her
ears as he let the wagon's flaps fall shut and turned to head
back to the fire. A wisp of white caught his eye, however,
and he turned away instead, looking out from the camp
towards a small grove of trees just beyond. Was there
someone there?

'Hello?' No one answered, but the image had piqued
his curiosity. Still scratching Glouste he walked away
from the wagons and into the night. The trees immediately swallowed the last vestiges of camp noise, bathing
him in cool silence, and his feet on the grass and fallen
leaves made a faint crunch that was all too loud amid the
quiet.

The grove was not large, maybe fourteen trees in all, and
had a natural clearing at its centre, perhaps ten feet across.
In the middle, he saw as he slid between the trunks, was
the white he had glimpsed from the wagon. Only up close
it was less white than pale yellow, the colour of old bones,
and it loomed above him, wings flared, tail jutting out,
face leering down.

The statue.

'Damn and blast,' he muttered. Feasting with the Roma had all but driven their quest from his mind. Only now did he remember the tracks Adelrich had found and the story from the old fisherman the scout had met in Uxer – that the gypsies had brought something large and heavy back with them. Now he knew what that was.

Backing away quickly, Dietz all but ran as he stumbled out of the grove and back to the camp. He had to tell Alaric as soon as possible.

Unfortunately, his employer was still conversing with Zeo.

'Ah, you found her!' Alaric said as Dietz returned and crouched next to him. 'What did you call her?' he asked Zeo. '"Alpiri volbini"?'

'Alberi volpini,' the gypsy leader corrected gently.

'Ah yes.' Alaric's loose nod indicated just how much he had drunk. 'Alberi volpini.' Still, Dietz knew he had to reveal what he had found.

'I've seen it,' he hissed in Alaric's ear, causing the younger man to lean away and look up at him blearily.

'Found what?' he asked far too loudly.

'The statue,' Dietz replied, and Alaric's face drained of colour. Zeo, sitting right beside them, overheard their whispered conversation.

'Statue?' He nodded. 'Ah, you mean our deo statua, our icon.' Rather than being offended or wary he seemed proud. 'In the grove, yes?' he asked when Dietz did not respond.

'Yes,' Dietz admitted. He was surprised the gypsy would tell them about it so openly.

'Ah, it is a great thing,' Zeo said happily, sipping his wine again. 'We find it in town, yes? Near two rivers?' He had to mean Merxheim, where the Reik and the Hundleir met. 'No one there, so we take.' He shrugged. 'And we bring back here.'

'Why would you want it?' Fastred had heard them speaking and approached, sitting down heavily across from them. Dietz saw Renke and Kleiber coming closer as well,

and Holst gathering his men. He was not sure where
Kristoff and Adelrich were, but suspected they would
notice their companions grouping and would join them
shortly. Something in him found comfort in that.

Zeo seemed surprised by the question. 'Why, it is Strygoi,
of course! Perhaps Ushoran himself!' Dietz felt his blood
turn cold at the name and the shock must have shown on
his face, since the gypsy leader turned to him and nodded.
'You understand, yes?'

'Yes.' Dietz forced himself to nod. 'You are Strigany.'

'What is that?' Alaric asked, leaning forward, as Zeo nodded in turn. 'What does that mean?'

'We are kings,' Zeo told him proudly, gesturing towards
the ragged wagons as if they were palaces. 'Our people
ruled long ago, the Strygoi. We scattered when the orcs
came,' here he paused to spit upon the ground, and the
other gypsies did the same, the practiced motion suggesting a ritual, 'and wander ever since, but still our blood is
that of kings.'

'And Ushoran?' Dietz wished he could shut Alaric up,
but he knew better. The young man was a Reiklander, and
as insatiable for knowledge as his kind was said to be for
drink. Fortunately, the gypsies had not taken offence yet.
In fact Zeo seemed happy to tell of their proud past.

'He was our king,' Zeo said reverently. 'Our deo, our god.
He ruled many lifetimes and protected Strygos from harm.'

'He was a vampire!' All heads turned as Kristoff staggered into the circle, his wobbling gait showing he was
far-gone in drink. Dietz felt his stomach lurch – he had
hoped the trader would provide a voice of reason, but
clearly Kristoff was too drunk to mind his words or guard
his thoughts. 'I've heard the tales,' the trader continued
loudly. 'Ushoran, Lord of Masks! He preyed upon the weak
and turned his followers into bloodsuckers as well!'

'No, no,' Zeo protested, though he had begun to scowl.
'Not Vorkudlak, as you say. Not a vampire. Ushoran drew
his strength from the land!' More Strigany were listening,
and moving closer, and Dietz wondered where the genial

atmosphere had gone. Why had the air gone so still and cold? And where had all the gypsies found blades?

'Daemon worshippers,' Kleiber stated coldly, drawing himself up to his full height, his hat casting daggers of shadow upon the ground. 'You are praying to that abomination of a statue and offering it the blood of the children you have stolen!'

Now Zeo was on his feet as well, and Dietz and Alaric rose beside him as the Strigany's scowl turned to a glare. 'You insult us! You demean us! You taint our hospitality!' Zeo's hand had closed upon his dagger hilt, and Dietz knew if he drew the blade it spelled their death. Alaric apparently knew it as well and hurled himself between the two men, facing Zeo, his own hands raised and empty.

'Zeo, no!' Alaric pleaded, calling up the words he had learned earlier tonight. 'The vini speaks, not the man! He is not accustomed to such strong spirits. He is,' he paused, hoping Kleiber would never understand, 'gracili de vini, uni fanciulli.' If the witch hunter ever learned he had just been called a child and a weakling Alaric's own life would be over as well, but the statement made the gypsies pause.

'Gracili?' Zeo repeated, still glaring at Kleiber, who stared back.

'Si,' Alaric insisted. He gestured towards Kristoff and Renke as well. 'Them also.' He nodded towards Dietz and Fastred and Adelrich, the ones who had not insulted their hosts. 'These are uomini, benportanti.'

Zeo relaxed and flexed his hand, releasing the hilt. 'Si,' he grunted, giving Kleiber one last look before turning his attention to Alaric. 'Yes, you are right. I see.' He nodded. 'We have shared wine, broken bread. Tonight you are Roma.' He glanced around and saw how close his people had gathered. 'Tonight they are Roma,' he said again, the steel of command in his voice, and they backed away, the weapons vanishing from their hands. 'But do not stay,' he warned Alaric softly as he settled onto the ground again and reached for his cup.

Heeding his advice, Alaric waited less than an hour before rising again to his feet.

'We must depart,' he told the gypsy leader, doing his best to sound regretful. 'Thank you for your hospitality, your *amicizi*.' He bowed low, though he kept his eyes upon Zeo's face as he had seen several gypsies do that evening. 'May your people run free and proud always.'

Zeo rose to his feet as well, with the boneless grace of a much younger man. 'May the wind be at your back and the ground smooth beneath your feet,' he replied, favouring Alaric with a slightly smaller bow as befitted a noble guest. He inclined his head to Alaric, Dietz, Fastred, and Adelrich. 'You are welcome among our wagons.' He pointedly ignored Kleiber, Renke, and Kristoff, who had the wisdom not to object to the slight. Dietz made his goodbyes as well, as did the others, and several gypsies brought their horses. Then they mounted and rode out.

'That was too close,' Dietz muttered when they were safely over the hill beyond the camp, and Alaric nodded.

'Was what he said about his people true?'

Dietz nodded warily. 'Aye, but so was what Kristoff blurted out. The Strigany were the gypsy rulers, long ago when they lived in Strygos, but Ushoran, their king, was a vampire right enough. Many of his chieftains were as well. They all died when the kingdom fell, but the Strigany are still feared by the other gypsies. They have dark powers, some say.'

Kleiber stirred, and Alaric glared at him, expecting the witch hunter to denounce their recent hosts. Instead the fanatic surprised him. 'I saw no sign of heresy,' he admitted, 'only generosity and warmth.' He actually looked embarrassed, which Alaric was sure was a first. 'Perhaps their worship of the statue, wrong though it is, is merely misguided and not truly evil.'

'I shouldn't have said what I did,' Kristoff agreed, rubbing the back of his neck sheepishly. 'I must have had too much to drink, and all I could think about was the last time I encountered gypsies – I traded with them and they robbed me blind.' He chuckled. 'It was my own fault, too. I was careless and cocky and got what I deserved.' He grimaced. 'I let old grudges get the better of me back there, and nearly got us killed.'

'Nearly I can live with,' Dietz replied, and Alaric laughed. His laugh died away, however, as they crested another hill – and found a score of spears jutting up at them, grim-faced soldiers behind the shafts.

CHAPTER EIGHT

'OFF THOSE HORSES, gypsy scum!' one of the soldiers shouted, poking his spear towards Alaric, the lead rider. The soldier wore mail with a tabard depicting a black ram, the von Drasche arms, and the gold slashes on his sleeves. His helmet marked him as a sergeant.

Alaric straightened in his saddle, suddenly every inch the noble. 'How dare you?' he demanded with such vehemence the soldiers backed away a pace, their spears dipping. 'I, a gypsy? Are you blind as well as daft? Move aside at once, sergeant!'

The soldier squinted at him in the dim starlight, taking in Alaric's fine but dusty clothing and lingering on the rapier at his side. He eyed the rest of the group as well, not missing Kleiber's distinctive garb or Holst's military bearing. Finally he stepped back another pace and raised the spear so that its butt rested on the ground.

'Apologies, m'lord,' he said, inclining his head. 'Orders are to stop anyone seen near those bandits' camp. No exceptions.'

'What do you mean to do with us, then?' Alaric demanded, leaning back in his saddle as if the answer barely mattered. Even Dietz, who had worked for the young man for more than a year, was impressed. He had seen traces of Alaric's noble upbringing all along, but had never seen him play the bored, arrogant, useless lord so fully and so convincingly.

The sergeant was also at a loss. 'We'll need to report to the baron for orders,' he decided finally, and Dietz noticed the soldier glancing towards Uxer behind him.

'Is the baron in residence?' Alaric asked, not missing the look. 'Fine then,' he continued when the sergeant nodded. 'You will inform him that Alaric von Jungfreud sends his compliments and is passing through on urgent business.' When the soldier, who had gaped at Alaric's name, didn't move, Alaric tapped the man's spear with his foot. 'At once, sergeant.'

'Yes, sir.' The sergeant snapped out of his shock and turned away, whispering to several of the soldiers as he did. Ten of them stayed behind, arrayed before the travellers, but standing relaxed and leaning on their spears. The other ten, with the sergeant, marched quickly towards the town, disappearing into the night.

'Now what?' Dietz muttered, and Alaric shook his head. 'I doubt he'll let us pass unmolested, but he won't dare harm us, either.' He sighed. 'I'll probably be forced to speak with him.' He turned to include the others in their conversation. 'Just stay close and let me handle this. The baron and I are old acquaintances, and though he may not like finding me here he'll be hard-pressed to interfere.'

Less than an hour later the sergeant returned. 'The baron extends his greetings,' he informed Alaric, still breathing heavily, 'and asks you and your companions to grace him with your presence.' The soldiers who had returned with him surrounded the travellers, indicating this was not really a request.

Alaric simply inclined his head, ignoring the soldiers completely. 'We would be delighted to accept,' he told the sergeant, and urged his horse forward, moving into the lead as if visiting the baron had been his idea all along. The sergeant jogged to catch up and the rest of the party followed along, the soldiers marching on either side and several behind.

Uxer had only one small inn, an unimpressive two-storey wooden structure across from the tavern that Fastred had stared at so longingly. There were, however, three handsome stone houses, set well back from the riverbank, and it was to the largest of these that the sergeant led them. Evidently, the baron had displaced one of the town's leading citizens to satisfy his own comforts. The sergeant's men held their horses while the travellers were escorted inside and into a handsome sitting room. Their host was waiting for them.

'Alaric von Jungfreud! Welcome, welcome!' Gernot, the Baron von Drasche, was a short, stout man with long, greasy blond hair, watery blue eyes and a sparse beard. His gilt mail and tunic were handsome but ill-fitting, and an ornate rapier banged against his leg as he strode forward. Alaric, by contrast, looked every inch the nobleman as he bowed to the baron, tall and slender and good-looking even in his travel-stained jacket and breeches.

'Baron, it has been far too long.' Alaric indicated the others. 'Allow me to introduce my companions.' When the baron nodded, he continued. 'Dietrich Froebel, my assistant.' Dietz did his best to bow. The others bowed as well when they were introduced, and Dietz saw the baron's eyes narrow as he registered each traveller's affiliation.

'Quite an assortment, Alaric,' he said finally, stroking his beard in what was certainly meant to be an impressive gesture, but which came across as desperate vanity. 'What are you all doing here in my lands?'

'Business for the crown,' Alaric replied smoothly. 'I'm not at liberty to discuss it, I'm afraid.' It wasn't a complete lie, Dietz mused – Todbringer, who was an elector count and therefore a servant of the Emperor, had sent them.

The baron tugged at his beard angrily, but Alaric had guessed correctly – the minor noble did not dare interfere with a plan of the Emperor's.

'And you,' Alaric asked, idly smoothing his jacket front. 'What brings you to this corner of your lands?' He glanced about them at the wide stone room with its fine woven rugs and polished wooden furniture. 'Surely your manor is more comfortable?'

Watching the two men, Dietz was reminded of a sword fight he'd once seen. The combatants had both been skilled men, and it had been a nasty fight, but they had remained civil the entire time – even when one had gutted the other. This felt much the same. Despite the smooth voices and relaxed postures he could tell these men despised one another.

'I am dealing with a disturbance,' the baron replied as casually as he could through clenched jaws. Then he smiled. 'Perhaps you can help. I understand Sergeant Vilne found you riding just beyond town?' Alaric nodded. 'I wonder, then, if you have seen a gypsy camp anywhere nearby?'

Dietz knew Alaric was considering his answer carefully. He remembered what the boy had said in the wrecked village, that the baron was determined to destroy the gypsies. Given a choice, he would choose even the Strigany over this oily little man any day. So would Alaric, he was sure, but the statue was more important than personal feelings.

'Yes,' Alaric admitted finally. 'We did see it. We were their guests, in fact.'

'Ah, excellent,' the baron said, a nasty gleam in his eye. 'Then you can show us where it is.'

For an instant Dietz wondered about this. The camp had been well concealed within the trees, true, but surely the baron had enough men to comb the woods and find the wagons? Then he understood. Yes, the baron could find the camp without their help, but he wanted to make Alaric assist him. It was a petty attempt at control, ill-becoming a noble and particularly one who held power over lands and people. Perhaps it was not surprising given the few hints Alaric had made before about the baron's character.

Finally Alaric sighed. 'Very well.' He glared at the baron. 'I will not be party to your bloodlust, however. My companions and I will guide you to the camp, but we will not take part in any attack.'

The baron's expression turned sly. 'What's wrong, Alaric? Still no stomach for fighting? Your father must be so disappointed.'

For a second Alaric's eyes flashed, his muscles tensed, and his hand reached for his sword. Dietz saw this, and also saw the glee on the baron's face. He wants Alaric to attack, Dietz realised, so he can kill him. He didn't dare interfere openly, but he nudged a candlestick beside him so that it toppled to the floor with a loud crash.

Alaric glanced up.

'Sorry,' Dietz muttered, trying to look and sound contrite. 'How clumsy of me.'

The momentary respite was enough. Alaric forced his hand to open, and turned his back upon the baron instead, though it clearly took all his will. The baron, for his part, growled in frustration and glared at Dietz, then laughed.

'After you,' he said pointedly, bowing towards the front door, and followed as Alaric strode through. Dietz hurried behind them, making sure the two nobles were not alone at any point.

Soon the travellers were mounted again and riding back the way they had come, the baron and his men beside them. Dietz counted ninety soldiers, all in full armour, and the sergeant had left ten behind on the hill. One hundred soldiers, just to handle a gypsy camp? This would not be battle – it would be a slaughter.

'ARE YOU CERTAIN you won't join us?' Baron von Drasche asked with a nasty grin as they halted, hours later, upon the hill above the gypsy camp. 'I promise to leave at least one for you to skewer – an old lady, perhaps, or a young child?' He was goading Alaric again and laughed when he received no reply. Instead the baron signalled his men and charged down the hill, weapons at the ready. Dietz was relieved to note that the baron, so intent upon the upcoming slaughter, had not bothered to leave anyone to guard them. He expected Alaric to lead them away as soon as the baron had vanished from sight, and his employer did wait until then to move, though the direction he chose was unexpected.

'Come on,' Alaric hissed to Dietz as soon as the soldiers were gone, kicking his own horse into motion, but heading down the hill instead of back over it. Dietz spurred his mount along on pure reflex, though shock almost overtook him.

'We're not helping?' he protested, and was relieved by the revulsion he saw on his employer's face.

'Of course not,' Alaric snapped, 'but I'm damned sure not letting that ass butcher children. Hurry!'

Adelrich and Fastred joined them and together the four raced down the hill, veering to one side as they rode. Despite their speed, the baron's men had a good head start, and were already entering the camp from the front as Alaric led his three companions around the back. They reached the far edge of the gypsy camp, closest to the statue's grove, and leaped to the ground by the rearmost wagons even as the first sounds of battle reached them.

'Wha–?' One of the gypsies they had seen earlier, a young woman with long dark ringlets, emerged from the wagon, a dagger in one hand, and peered at them through bleary eyes.

'The baron is attacking!' Alaric told her quickly. 'You and your children need to flee at once. Go!' As if to punctuate his statement another gypsy, an older woman who had offered Dietz a second helping of stew earlier that very night, staggered out of the trees towards them, blood streaming down her face. Even in the dark Dietz could tell there was something wrong with the shape of her head. She collapsed before any of them could go to her, pitching face-forward into the dirt, and did not move again.

'We can't just go,' said the man who had appeared from the wagon beside the young woman, hefting a thin curved sword as he dropped from the wagon bed. 'We cannot leave our kin.' The sounds of fighting, cursing and dying were clearly audible, ringing through the woods, and the man was eager to run to his family's aid.

'Then you'll all die,' Adelrich said bluntly, shoving the man back. 'Get your children out of here!'

'Wait!' Dietz stopped them and peered into the wagon, where the same little girl he'd seen curled up with Glouste now eyed him warily. 'Zisi, you and the other bambini have a signal, yes? A private whistle?' She nodded, eyes wide. 'Good. Use it now. Summon them here.' She glanced at her father, who nodded, and then she skittered to the front of the wagon. Pursing her lips, the girl emitted a short, piercing tone and then a second one, followed by a slightly longer one, the sounds carrying even through the din of battle. Within seconds they heard soft footsteps and then the children began appearing from the darkness of the camp. Most were only partially clothed. Several had wounds, clear evidence that the baron's men had progressed beyond simply fighting the gypsy men, and were now attacking the women and children as well.

'Take them all,' Dietz told the couple. 'You are now Zeo,' he pointed out to the man. 'And you,' he told the woman, 'are Nona, the matriarch. In these children your people will survive.' The couple glanced once more towards the clearing, wincing at a particularly loud cry that ended abruptly. Finally they nodded and hustled the children into the woods, pausing only to clasp each of the men's forearms in thanks. Then they were gone.

'What about the wagon?' Fastred asked, but Dietz was already striding to the next one. Three young men, clearly brothers and little more than children themselves, and a woman not much older had been watching from behind their door curtain and gave up all pretence as he approached, tossing the curtain aside and hopping lightly down. Dietz wondered for a second why they were not fighting or fleeing, and then saw just how young they truly were and guessed their parents had ordered them to stay hidden.

'You are conocinti,' one of them said, clasping Dietz's forearm firmly. 'Thank you.'

Dietz shrugged. 'Thank me by pretending that wagon is yours,' he replied, indicating the now-empty wagon behind them. 'If the baron realises it's empty he'll send his soldiers to scour the forest for them.'

The gypsies nodded and the woman and one man took refuge in the last wagon while the other two returned to their own home, each of them clasping weapons and ready to die guarding the children's escape. Judging from the sounds that still filtered through the trees, it would probably come to that. Realising they'd done all they could, Dietz and Alaric remounted, Fastred and Adelrich behind them, and turned their steeds back towards the small grove. Kleiber, Kristoff and Renke had reached it before them, and they arrived to find the witch hunter standing over a pile of rubble, his pistol still smoking – the sounds of battle back in camp had masked the gun's report.

'It is done,' he told them, holstering his pistol, and after a quick glance they nodded and kicked their horses back into gallops, returning to where Holst and the soldiers still sat atop the hill.

'We should leave now, while the baron is occupied,' Renke suggested uneasily, but Alaric shook his head.

'I know Gernot, and he requires an audience. If we leave now he may send men after us out of spite. Better to wait here, applaud his "victory" when he returns, and then depart with his blessing.'

The others nodded, though Renke looked pale at the thought of more delays. As they waited, forced to endure the cries from below, the small man manoeuvred his horse beside Alaric's.

'I need to speak with you,' he whispered, and Alaric noticed he was sweating despite the cool night air.

'What's wrong?' he asked, shifting his horse closer to the geographer's, but Renke shook his head.

'Not here,' he said. 'Some place private. Soon,' he added through clenched teeth, but Alaric's reply was halted by the sound of approaching hooves. He nodded and turned to face back down the hill, where the baron and several soldiers were departing the increasingly silent gypsy camp. Not all the soldiers were there, and for an instant Alaric hoped the gypsies had acquitted themselves well and taken a few of the baron's men with them, though he knew the soldiers were not to blame for their master's cruelty. Then other noises drifted up from the gypsy camp, sounds of equal violence, but different methods, and his face tightened. No, the men who had stayed behind deserved a far better fate. If only he could provide it.

'That's done then,' the baron announced with obvious satisfaction, holding his sword up so the blood along it was clearly visible in the moonlight. He wore an expression Alaric recognised from days past, his eyes heavy-lidded and his mouth slightly open like a cat scenting fresh cream. It was a look of extreme satisfaction.

'Finally!' The studied contentment dropped away, replaced by a look of outright lust. 'I've wanted those gutter-rats gone for years!' he confessed, shocking Alaric with his candour. 'I knew someone would object if I killed them, though – weak-hearted fools!' He grinned at Alaric, sending a chill through him.

Gernot knew better than to speak openly about such things, especially in front of strangers. Either his easy victory had made him careless – or he had other plans. 'Good thing the Chaos invaders swept through, eh?' he continued, approaching Alaric and resting his sword easily across his saddle. 'Anything can be justified as a defence against daemon-worshippers – or an attack by them.' Those last words carried more emphasis and Alaric recognised the inevitable. Still, he had to attempt the bloodless route first.

'Indeed,' he replied coldly, and then faked a yawn. 'Well, now you're done I'm sure you'll wish to return to your manor. We've our own business to pursue, so we'll be on our way.'

'Yes, yes,' the baron answered, moving his horse in front of Alaric's and eyeing him coldly. 'Such a shame you cannot stay longer.' He leaned in slightly, as if sharing a confidence. 'You'll not mention this to anyone, of course?' He resumed his pose of the careful, diplomatic ruler. 'These are troubled times for our Empire, what with the rebuilding and the continued incursions. Now is a time for all patriots to unite, to stand together to protect our lands and our peoples.' He had the audacity to look solemn. 'Surely one man's attempts to rid his land of undesirables, to improve the quality of life for his people, is of no one else's concern? It would be best not to trouble others with such petty details when so many larger issues remain at stake.'

'I'll not say a word,' Alaric assured him blandly. Meanwhile his hand had slid to the hilt of his rapier and he shifted in his saddle, using the noise to mask the sound of the blade loosening in its scabbard.

'Quite,' the baron replied. He leaned back again and assumed a look of deep consideration. 'I know you for a man of your word, Alaric,' he admitted finally. Then he sighed heavily. 'Still, your companions – I don't know them, and if they talked my reputation might suffer.' He made a great show of thinking again, and then shook his head and gestured with his bloody sword. 'Now I think on it, far better they don't get that chance. Or you.' He grinned. 'Kill them all,' he called out, and kicked his own horse towards Alaric.

Dietz had expected a betrayal, as had the others, and they had their weapons drawn before the soldiers reached them. He slashed one across the face with his knife, sending the man tumbling backward with blood spraying from his cheek, and blocked another's sword slash before laying open his forehead on a return stroke. Kleiber had reloaded his pistol while they had waited, and now the gunshot echoed through the valley as a soldier plummeted from his horse, a smoking hole in his chest. The others laid about them with their swords and daggers, and Fastred's crossbow twanged as a soldier fell with a bolt through his sword arm.

'Shoot the horses!' Holst shouted, and his soldiers' bows twanged as arrows blossomed in the legs and chests of the soldiers' mounts. It was a clever tactic – the men were heavily armoured, but their horses were not and the wounded beasts reared in pain, knocking other soldiers to the ground and trampling more as they fell. Alaric had blocked Gernot's charge and delivered a stinging cut to one cheek before a soldier's mount collided with the baron's, sending him tumbling down the hill and leaving Alaric alone to assess the situation. He saw at once that they were badly outnumbered, but they were also more alert and he recognised the opportunity.

'Head for the trees!' he shouted, kicking his own horse into motion and barrelling down the hill and into the trees beyond the gypsy camp. The others followed, most of the baron's soldiers too busy calming their mounts or avoiding panicked hooves to give chase. A short time later the travellers stopped amid the trees to catch their breaths, well away from the baron's men and well hidden.

'Everyone here?' Alaric asked softly, and one by one the others responded. 'Anyone hurt?' Several of them had minor cuts or scrapes and one soldier had a nasty leg wound, but the baron's men had been using spears and swords and had been hampered by fighting at such close quarters. Renke did not respond to the question, and when Adelrich nudged him the smaller man pitched forward, toppling from his saddle and landing hard upon the ground.

'Damn and blast!' Dietz was out of his saddle in an instant, Kristoff and Fastred right behind him. 'He's been stabbed,' he reported to Alaric a moment later, 'badly.' The three men worked frantically, but after a few moments

their patient gave a rattling sigh and died, his body jerking
beneath their hands. They backed away, falling silent, and
gave him a respectful moment before wrapping his body
in cloaks and tying it to the back of his horse. Then, sombre, they mounted their steeds and rode on.

'We'll take him back to Carroburg,' Alaric said softly
when they finally made camp at dawn. 'The Imperial Geographic Society had a man there, Renke visited him briefly.'
He glanced towards the body, now stretched on the
ground with torches around it to keep any animals at bay.
'His maps can go to them, as he'd have wanted.'

'There's something–' Dietz started, and then stopped
and glanced around. 'His wound,' he continued more quietly, making sure the others could not hear him.

Alaric grimaced. 'I owe Gernot that,' he said bitterly.
'After this is done I'll make him pay.'

Dietz shook his head. 'That's not what I meant.' His
voice dropped so low Alaric had to lean in to hear. 'Renke
was stabbed.'

'That's what you said, yes.'

'Not a sword stab, though: by a dagger.'

Alaric started to form a question, but stopped at the
older man's nod. Dietz had grown up rough and knew
knife fighting well. If he said it was a dagger blow then that
was the weapon used.

'Furthermore,' Dietz added. 'It wasn't from the front or
side.'

He fell silent as Alaric pondered this – a dagger from
behind? The baron's men had fought with spears and
swords, not daggers. And even in the tumult he doubted
any would have been at Renke's back. Which meant– His
eyes widened, and Dietz nodded.

'The baron didn't do this,' he agreed softly. The two of
them glanced around at their companions: Kleiber,
Kristoff, Fastred, Adelrich, Holst and his soldiers.

One of them had killed Renke. But why?

CHAPTER NINE

THEY SET OUT at dawn, riding hard to stay ahead of the soldiers von Drasche would certainly send after them. That night Adelrich scouted along the River Hundleir until he found a place narrow enough for them to cross. The others busied themselves repacking their gear, adjusting bags and packs on top of their saddles instead of alongside to keep them dry during the crossing. Everyone avoided glancing at Renke's horse, or the tightly wrapped figure bound across its saddle.

When Adelrich returned he led the way towards the riverbank, and one by one the men guided their mounts into the water, alternately walking and swimming across the cold, swift Hundleir. Finally Adelrich dragged himself onto the opposite bank, the last of the party to cross, and they all collapsed on the grass, grateful to be beyond von Drasche lands at last.

They did not lie about long, however. Within the hour Alaric had roused the others and, adjusting their gear a second time, they mounted up and rode away. The forest here was thicker, but Adelrich possessed an uncanny sense of direction and kept them riding north-east, towards the Reik. At last they emerged near the town of Arzbach, not far from Carroburg itself. Dietz negotiated passage on a river barge, and soon they were on the water again. It was as peaceful as the boat ride they had taken to reach the Hundleir, though now for different reasons. By evening they had passed back through Carroburg's gates, and led their mounts quietly through the streets, ignoring the obvious questions on the faces of everyone who saw them and their grisly burden. Renke had kept meticulous notes of their journey, including the address of Carroburg's chapter of the Geographers' Guild, and they headed there immediately, wending their way through the city's many layers.

Carroburg's resident geographer, a tall, florid man named Hanser, showed genuine grief at the sight of Renke's body. He took the little geographer's maps and notes with reverence, and promised to treat them with the care they deserved. He also offered to make arrangements for Renke's burial, and the travellers were only too happy to leave their fallen companion with him. They left soon after.

Fastred secured rooms for the night while Adelrich saw to the horses and Kristoff inquired about ferries farther down the Reik. That left Dietz, Alaric, and Kleiber to find supplies. They spent the rest of the day examining, tasting, haggling, buying and carrying back various packages, forcing themselves to concentrate on these everyday activities. By evening, when they gathered in the common room of the inn where they were staying, Adelrich had found a boat leaving two days later for Nuln and booked them passage.

The next day was far too idle for anyone's good. Left to their own devices, no one could help thinking about Renke and his death, and the maps he would never finish. These thoughts haunted Dietz and Alaric in particular. Someone had killed Renke, someone in their own party, but why?

'He didn't have anything of value,' Alaric pointed out the second night, when he and Dietz were checking on the horses, 'or anything to steal. So why kill him?'

'No disputes with the others?' Dietz wondered aloud, and sighed when his employer shook his head. 'I know. I am only trying to figure this out. Why kill Renke?'

'He must have learned something,' Alaric decided. 'Something too dangerous to risk getting out. So whoever it was killed him to keep him quiet.'

'That could be, but who?' Dietz ran through the other party members in his head. 'Kleiber? He'd simply execute anyone who stood in his way and call it righteous. Kristoff? I cannot see him resorting to such methods. Fastred? He's so free with his stories I cannot imagine he has anything to hide? Adelrich?' Dietz's mind shied away from the notion of his friend as a killer. 'No, he wouldn't do that. Holst? What could a guard captain say or do that would be worth killing a man like Renke?'

'It makes no sense, I agree.' Alaric shook his head. 'But someone did this. We'll have to be careful.'

They boarded the barge the next morning, and it was all Alaric could do not to stare at each of his companions in turn. Dietz had an easier time pretending unconcern – he had grown up hard and had often been forced to play at friendship with people he detested or even feared. If the others noticed their new distance no one mentioned it – they all concentrated on boarding and stowing gear and getting out of the sailors' way. Everyone particularly avoided the barge pilot, fully aware that Renke would have been there pestering him for a look at his river maps and a description of their intended route.

IT SHOULD HAVE been a pleasant journey. The Reik was smooth and quick, the weather pleasant, the barge not too cramped, the food fresh and mostly edible, the crew boisterous. They should have enjoyed the chance to sit and relax and watch the banks slide past. Instead, Kleiber spent his time polishing his weapons or praying, Kristoff and

Fastred alternated sleeping, drinking and playing cards, Holst drilled his remaining men without pause and Adelrich whittled fixedly on a chunk of wood. Dietz took up a similar practice just to keep busy, carving a block into some shape he could not yet see, which left Alaric to pace and think, and brood.

Three days later they docked at Nuln and clambered out onto the weathered pier. Alaric paid the barge captain the rest of his fee and the others stretched their legs and walked the horses down to the shipyard proper, glad to be back on solid ground. Their respite was brief, however.

'I've found us another boat,' Adelrich told them over dinner that night in one of the quieter, cleaner inns. 'This one heads along the Upper Reik and then around. They can get us within a day's ride of Grenzstadt.' Everyone nodded – even without Renke they knew Grenzstadt guarded the western end of the Black Fire Pass.

The second barge ride was less pleasant than the first. Everyone staked out a space alone and stayed there throughout the trip, barely acknowledging the others. Finally Alaric had had enough.

'All right!' he shouted, getting everyone's attention. 'This is pathetic! Look at us, huddling in our corners like sulking children! Is this what Renke would have wanted?' He hated to use their dead friend's name so brusquely, but knew it was the only thing that might work. 'Would he have approved? This is no longer just about doing what's right, or about protecting the Empire – now it's about making Renke's death mean something!'

Everyone stared at him, shocked, until finally Fastred nodded. 'You are right,' the big man agreed. 'We are all behaving poorly out of grief and frustration, but that is the last thing we should let govern us.'

Suddenly the tension was gone. Everyone gathered by the barge's low prow and shared food, ale and water, talking and joking again. A pallor still hung about them, but it had thinned, and Alaric thought he could sense Renke nearby, nodding his approval. The last thing the little cartographer would have wanted was to jeopardise their mission.

The day after, the barge reached a fork in the river. One branch continued south while the other curved back to the north-east. They followed the latter, skirting the base of the mountains as the landscape turned more bleak, steeper and filled with rock instead of grass and earth. Two days later the barge put in at a small town and they stepped off. This was as far as it would go – past this point the river rose dramatically, narrowing and becoming much quicker, with no room to manoeuvre. The river barge would never survive such a journey.

'Still, it got us here,' Adelrich pointed out as they watched the boatmen poling the barge back into the current. 'That's saved us a week or more.'

'Aye, and the horses are well-rested,' Dietz added. 'They've had a hard journey already, no sense making matters worse by overworking them.'

After buying salted meat, flat bread and dried fish to replenish their stores, the travellers rode out. They followed the river around, moving quickly, but not at breakneck speed, and after two days in the saddle they spotted a large, solidly built town up above, set before the lowest of the mountain peaks.

'Grenzstadt,' Adelrich confirmed, looking up at it. 'Behind it lies the Black Fire Pass.'

As it turned out, they did not even enter the town. Grenzstadt was set below the entrance to the pass and a wide, rough path led around it to the guard post there. They took the more direct route and walked their horses up to the guards, who had seen them coming and were waiting for them by the heavy wooden barricade. Kleiber's status as a witch hunter, combined with Holst's military papers and Kristoff's trading privileges, got them past the barricade and into the pass itself. They also asked the guards if a heavily laden wagon had passed this way two or more months ago, and the captain confirmed the presence of such a vehicle. They were heading in the right direction.

The Black Fire Pass proved very different from their expectations. Dietz knew the stories, that here Sigmar had held back the final attack of his enemies and forced them back beyond the mountains, protecting the lands that became his Empire. He had assumed the pass was merely that, a narrow channel cut through the mountains. Instead they passed beyond Grenzstadt to the mountain itself, up a wide path, and into a small valley worn between two cliffs. The ground was uneven, forming small hills of solid rock in many places, with other passages branching off on either side. The cliffs above were not smooth either and bore ledges and crevasses all along their lengths.

'You could hide an entire army in here,' Holst remarked as they rode, which did nothing to increase their comfort. As soon as they reached the valley he deployed his soldiers around the others, with Adelrich in front and several guards on either side and behind. Swords were kept loose in their scabbards and spears in hands, and Dietz knew they were all thinking the same thing. This was an ideal place for an ambush.

A few moments later they topped a rise to find Adelrich waiting, sword in hand. The reason for his unsheathed weapon was readily apparent as they glanced beyond him. The path narrowed below them, flattening into a small ledge at the bottom before rising again on the far side of the valley. High walls loomed alongside, chipped and notched by many caves, nooks and trails. This spot *was* ideal for an ambush, and judging from the corpses they saw littering the ground below, one had already occurred.

'Soldiers,' Adelrich confirmed as they rode down the slope and threaded their way between the bodies there. 'Dead less than a day.' He gestured towards one man who had been cut almost in half. 'An orc axe, by the looks of it.' His hand tightened on his sword hilt. 'A warband did this.'

Holst's men tightened around the others, spears raised as everyone glanced about: an orc war party here? No wonder the Grenzstadt captain had not wanted to let them pass. How long had he been blocking this pass against the invaders? And why hadn't he warned them of the danger?

While everyone looked this way and that, Adelrich was still, eyes distant as he listened intently to the sounds beyond their own horses. 'Someone is coming,' he declared finally, leaping into his saddle. 'A great many someones.'

'Defensive positions!' snapped Holst, and his men surrounded the travellers, spears bristling outward. Fastred raised his crossbow, Kleiber his pistol, and Adelrich his bow, while Alaric and Kristoff drew their swords and Dietz his knives. For a moment nothing moved save the wind whistling through the rocks above. Then they all heard what Adelrich had, the clump of many feet marching closer.

The sound grew and they tensed, ready to fight. Then, not ten feet away, shadows appeared from a small passage in one wall. The shadows stretched towards them as the figures casting them grew closer, reaching the valley itself.

The entire group sighed in relief at the sight of men in Empire armour, soldiers, much like the ones at their feet.

'Stand down!' a voice bellowed, and Holst nodded to his men, who raised their spears and set the butts against the ground. Weapons were lowered as more soldiers appeared, surrounding them.

'Identify yourselves!' the man shouted again, and now Dietz could distinguish a man among the soldiers wearing a plume in his helmet, a sergeant like Holst.

'Alaric von Jungfreud–' Alaric began, but was interrupted, by Holst, surprisingly.

'Farlun Holst, Sergeant, Middenheim Count's Guard,' he declared crisply, stepping forward to confront the other sergeant, 'escorting important personages into Black Fire Pass on vital business of the elector count and the Empire. Request permission to meet with your commanding officer!'

The other sergeant nodded. 'Follow me!' His men formed up around him, and at a gesture Holst's did the same for him and the travellers. They followed the Empire soldiers down the narrow pass from which they had emerged, two separate groups close together. Adelrich eased his horse up beside Alaric as they rode.

'He didn't intend it as a slight,' Dietz heard the scout say softly. 'Holst figured the other sergeant would respond better to him, that's all.'

Alaric laughed lightly. 'I took no offence, I assure you,' he replied. 'If I thought it would help I'd happily let Holst do all the talking all the time!'

'No you wouldn't,' Dietz commented from behind them, chuckling at the look on his employer's face. 'I know you – after half an hour you'd start lecturing on something, anything.'

Alaric laughed with him, a touch ruefully. 'Perhaps you're right,' he admitted. 'I have such an excellent voice it's hard not to use it often.' They all laughed, and the mountains suddenly seemed less overwhelming.

THE EMPIRE COMMANDER, Meinard Haas, was a short, stocky man with thick red-brown hair and a short bushy beard. His camp sat in a wide clearing at the end of the pass and the tents were laid out with proper military precision, arrayed around his own command tent. The sergeant escorted Alaric and the others to the front flap, announced them, and then stepped aside to let them enter. He had confiscated their weapons upon entering the clearing, however, and had detained Holst and his men by the outermost tents.

'Commander,' Alaric began, stepping inside and bowing. 'Alaric von Jungfreud, at your service. We are here on urgent business from Elector Count Boris Todbringer of Middenheim.'

Haas nodded back. 'Captain Verten allowed you entrance to the pass, so I assume you have legitimate business here. What can I do for you?' He remained standing and did not offer them places to sit, or anything to eat or drink.

'We seek a wagon,' Alaric explained. 'It came from Middenheim some months ago and was heading here, bearing a single large, heavy, covered object. Captain Verten remembers allowing it through.'

'I've not seen anything like that,' Haas replied, 'nor do I care. I have other concerns.'

'The battle we stumbled upon?' Fastred asked, and introduced himself when Haas glanced his way.

'Yes, that,' the commander admitted, 'and more, if you had gone over the next rise you would have found battle for yourself. Sergeant Druber informs me an orc war party was waiting just beyond for a second ambush.' He laughed at Alaric's involuntary shudder. 'Hardly a pleasant outing, is it, lad? This is war you've stumbled across.'

'War?' Kristoff spoke up from one side. 'I thought the Empire held this pass?'

Haas shook his head. 'We did – until the Storm of Chaos. Orcs flooded through here and down into the Empire beyond. After the war many fled back this way.' His face wrinkled in disgust. 'Grenzstadt couldn't hold them off, not enough men.' The last three words were said with a snarl, and Alaric realised the disgust was not aimed at the town and its soldiers, but at the rulers who had left it too weak to defend itself. 'We've been sent to clean up,' Haas added heavily, 'but too late. The orcs have had time to organize. The various bands are united now under one leader – he must have killed his rivals. Now he's got a proper warband behind him and they hold the pass. We've been picking away at them, but they're strong and they've had time to entrench.' He paused and glanced up at them again, a strange look fleeting across his face. It was almost embarrassed, and Alaric realised the commander had said more than he'd intended. The moment passed and Haas was all business again as he walked right up to Alaric, his voice gruffer than before.

'Now,' he demanded, glaring up at Alaric. 'Why are you really here?'

'I told you, we're after a wagon–' Alaric began, but the commander cut him off.

'So you say, but I've not seen anything like that here.' His eyes narrowed. 'We've had looting, though, someone prowling among the dead, stripping their valuables.' He eyed Alaric and the others. 'You lot are a motley crew – look like you've been living hard. Are you scavenging among what's left of my men?'

'How dare you?' Kleiber began, red-faced, but Dietz and Fastred grabbed his arms and kept the witch hunter from launching himself at the Empire commander.

'I understand your outrage, commander,' Alaric said carefully, keeping his face and voice calm, 'but I can assure you we did no such thing. You are welcome to search our belongings if you like. You can also send a man down to Captain Verten, who can confirm that we rode through Grenzstadt yesterday morning. We came from Nuln by river barge, and that too can be confirmed. We are here for that wagon, not to desecrate the dead.'

Haas continued to glare at him for a moment, and then stepped back. 'Aye, it's easy enough to prove what you say,' he admitted. 'I apologize. My men are dying about me and even their bodies are not safe.' He suddenly looked very tired, and gestured them towards the rough stools scattered about his tent, no doubt for strategy sessions. After they'd all sat down, Haas sank onto one himself and, producing a wineskin from a small table, offered it around.

'How important is this wagon?' he asked finally.

'Very,' Alaric replied, and the others nodded.

'The fate of the Empire itself may rest upon our mission,' Kleiber intoned, and Haas glanced at Alaric for confirmation.

'That may be overstating it a little,' he admitted, 'but only a little. We have to locate that cargo and destroy it, commander.'

Haas grimaced. 'That might not be so easy. This entire pass is riddled with hidey holes. We'll never be able to find it.'

'It will be somewhere bloody,' Dietz pointed out, and Alaric nodded.

'That's right,' Fastred agreed. 'They're placed to receive sacrifices. Most likely it will be near the site of a battle, or perhaps in the orc camp itself.'

'My scouts have not seen anything unusual in the orcs' camp,' Haas said, 'but they weren't looking for much beyond the enemy's numbers and placement.'

'I can scout it,' Adelrich offered, rising to his feet. 'If your men can direct me, I'll go at once. I know what we seek.'

'They'll kill you if they find you,' Haas warned, but the scout shrugged.

'Every mission is like that,' he pointed out.

Alaric did not like the idea of sending Adelrich alone, but he knew better than to argue. The scout had demonstrated time and again his speed and stealth – no one else could keep up with him, and one man stood a better chance of evading notice than three or four.

'All right, go,' he decided finally, 'but be careful, and do not venture any closer than you have to.'

Adelrich laughed. 'What, I'm not to wander among the orcs without good reason? Don't worry. I'll stay as far back as I can.'

Haas stood and joined him at the tent flap. 'Druber!' The sergeant appeared at once. 'Guide this man towards the orc camp,' he instructed, 'and give these men back their weapons.' The sergeant saluted and marched off, Adelrich right behind him.

'Now,' Haas continued as he returned to his stool and accepted the wineskin back from Fastred, 'while we wait, tell me what transpires in the world beyond.'

IT WAS HOURS before Adelrich returned. Haas had proven a decent host once convinced of their sincerity, and had provided them with plain but decent food, cold mountain water, and several tents whose former owners no longer needed them. Most of the party had taken the opportunity to get some rest, but Dietz sat outside, watching for his friend's return, Glouste curled in his lap.

'Couldn't sleep?' Adelrich asked as he appeared out of the shadows, making Dietz jump and then yelp, as Glouste registered her displeasure by digging sharp claws into his thigh. 'Sorry,' the scout added with a laugh, sinking to the ground beside him and accepting a full water skin.

'Anything?' asked Dietz, slapping the tent behind him to wake Alaric. He continued until he heard movement within. A moment later his employer had emerged, bleary-eyed, and was sitting beside them. Kristoff and Fastred had also heard the commotion and were out a moment later. Adelrich waited until everyone was present before replying.

'Nothing,' he admitted. 'I found the camp easily enough, thanks to Druber's scouts. They've got a large force here, perhaps as large as those beastmen back in the Howling Hills.' The others winced at the thought of that many orcs arrayed against them. 'No sign of the statue, though, and they don't use tents so it couldn't have been hidden inside.'

'Could it be hidden in a crevice nearby?' Alaric asked, and the scout shrugged.

'Could be,' he admitted. 'I couldn't search them all, not without risking discovery myself. I didn't see anything, though, and no signs of its being dragged that far down the pass.'

'We know it's here,' Dietz pointed out, 'somewhere.'

'It would be somewhere important,' Fastred commented, accepting the water skin from Adelrich. 'Somewhere they could offer it sacrifices.'

'They might have moved it, though,' Kristoff said, ignoring the others' groans. 'Well, they might. Either because they feared discovery or because they found a better location.'

'It hasn't left this pass,' Adelrich asserted. 'I'm sure of it. Haas would have noticed if they'd carried it across to the other side, and they wouldn't bring it up here and then carry it back into the Empire.'

'I agree,' Alaric said finally. 'It's here somewhere. We just have to find it. We'll search every pass if we must, but we will find it.' He glanced around, noticing the fatigue on everyone's face. 'We'll start tomorrow.'

CHAPTER TEN

THE NEXT MORNING they woke with the dawn. All around them the Empire soldiers were rising, washing, eating, relieving themselves, and receiving orders for the day. Alaric gathered his companions off to one side and they discussed their own plans over the meagre breakfast Druber had provided.

'We'll need a map of the area,' he pointed out, and continued briskly to get past the dismay he felt and saw in the others as well. Renke would have loved the Black Fire Pass, with all its side passages and tunnels. 'Holst, ask Druber for one – he's more likely to give it to you.' Holst nodded. 'Adelrich, we'll need to start scouting the rest of the pass. Speak to Haas's scouts and tell them what we're seeking – not why, just a general description. That way if they see it we'll know.' Adelrich nodded. 'The rest of us can search as well. We'll cover more ground if we spread out, though we'll stay close enough to hear one another shout. I don't want anyone getting jumped by orcs.' He thought about it. 'Adelrich, I'll want you checking upper passes we can't get to. We'll watch the ground.' He glanced around. 'Right, then?' They all nodded. 'Good. Let's get to it.'

The day passed slowly, as did the next. They learned a great deal about the Black Fire Pass, about its cracks and gaps, and tunnels and caves, and cliffs and ledges. They learned to hate the sight of the cold stone around them and the feel of the wind dipping down into the pass, and the chill of the rock below them when they slept. They learned to tolerate Druber's short answers, and dry biscuits and over-salted beef. They learned to respect Haas's tactical sense and his concern for his men. They also learned that, though the Black Fire Pass had thousands of hiding places suitable for the statue, not one of them held anything of interest, at least none of the ones they had yet found.

As the second day wound down, one of Haas's scouts burst into the camp, barely slowing as he dodged between soldiers and ran for the command tent. Alaric and the others had just returned themselves and were telling the commander their lack of success when the scout appeared at the tent flap.

'Sir!' The man stood at attention until Haas waved for him to continue. 'The orcs are on the move, sir!'

'How many?' asked Haas quietly, turning his attention towards the map spread across the one large table in his tent. It showed the Black Fire Pass and had the orc camp clearly marked, with a mass of lead pellets representing the enemy.

'All of them, sir!'

That got Haas's attention. 'What?'

'They're all on the move, sir! The entire camp!'

'The full warband is moving?'

'Yes, sir!'

A rustle at the tent flap drew their attention, and Sergeant Druber stepped in. 'Just heard, sir. Other scouts confirm it. Entire warband mobilised.'

'Show me,' Haas commanded, and sergeant and scout both stepped to the map. Alaric and the others followed.

'Travelling back towards us,' the scout explained, cupping his hand around the pellets and sliding them down through the Black Fire Pass. 'At their current speed they'll be here by midnight and here by dawn.' He indicated two spots on the map. Druber glanced at the locations and nodded his agreement. Haas considered, then selected one pellet and set it on the further location.

'We will take them here at first light,' he stated. 'Druber, prepare the men. We attack with full force at dawn.'

Druber saluted and he and the scout left. Haas watched them go and his eyes trailed across Alaric, and then returned to him. 'You and your men as well.'

'What?' Alaric stepped up to the map. 'Commander, I appreciate what you're doing here, but we have our own mission to complete.'

Haas shook his head. 'You've found nothing, and may never find anything. I know how easily things can disappear in this pass. I need every man I can get tomorrow, and that includes yours.'

Alaric started to protest again, but Dietz stepped up beside him. 'If the orcs have the statue, they'll be carrying it with them,' he pointed out, causing his employer to pause. 'They wouldn't leave it behind.'

'And what if they already have it hidden somewhere safe?' Kristoff asked.

'Then we can find it at our leisure after the battle,' Adelrich replied. 'It would be far easier to search if we weren't looking over our shoulders every instant.'

Alaric considered this for a moment. 'We are not soldiers,' he pointed out, deliberately ignoring Holst off to the side. 'We can handle ourselves in a fight, certainly, but we are neither trained nor equipped for war.'

Haas frowned, and then nodded. 'Fair enough. I'd ask that you guard this pass here, then.' He tapped a spot on the map, indicating a route that branched off from their selected location. 'Make sure no one sneaks up on us from that side,' he continued. Then he glanced back up at Alaric and shrugged. 'You will be off to one side and may have to do nothing more than scare off any orcs that look your way. Your presence will free up my men to concentrate on the attack.'

'Well, in that case,' Alaric bowed, 'we are at your service, commander.' He straightened up again. 'We will march with you at first light.'

'Good.' Haas favoured him with a small smile. 'I know this is not why you're here, but I appreciate your aid. Afterwards, assuming we are the victors, you will have my full support for your mission.'

Alaric nodded, then led the others from the tent. 'Searching would be far faster with so many more eyes,' he admitted as they returned to their own tents to gather their gear. 'Assuming we survive.'

DIETZ SLEPT FITFULLY that night, and was still shaking the sleep from his head the next morning as they gathered alongside Haas's troops. He had never fought in a war before – fought, yes, even killed, but never marched. The fact that they were only guarding a side passage did not change the fact of riding into a major battle, and he knew they could find themselves in combat at any point. The idea of confronting so many enemies, so openly, unnerved him, and he could see many of his companions felt the same. Alaric was paler than usual and holding himself with brittle dignity, clearly unwilling to show his fear. Fastred was less concerned with appearances, the big man grumbling about foolish obedience and the idiocy of sending untrained men to their doom. Kristoff was quiet, though he held his reins so tightly Dietz thought they might snap, and Adelrich could not sit still. Only Kleiber showed no trace of concern.

Holst and his men were calm, of course, but they were trained for this.

'Not my kind of fight,' Adelrich admitted to Dietz as they rode out behind Haas's soldiers. 'Scouts aren't usually deployed for a stationary defence – we're better at striking from a distance and from cover, and then fading back to let the heavier troops mop up.' He laughed. 'I keep wanting to duck up a trail and hide.'

'So do I,' Dietz said, knowing how his friend felt, 'but Haas is no fool. He won't throw lives away. He has a plan.'

Dietz's words proved prophetic. Upon reaching the designated area, a space where the pass widened considerably, Haas called his men to a stop and began placing them to face the approaching warband. He acted without hesitation and it was clear that he had planned each placement well in advance. He sent the scouts up the cliffs on either side to rain arrows down upon the orcs. One contingent was placed in a shallow ravine along one side with orders to close in once the orcs were past, cutting off their escape. Alaric, Dietz, and the others on horseback were stationed across the mouth of a narrower path cut into the opposite wall.

Haas gathered everyone together, surveying them calmly. He turned towards the scouts. 'You will fire as the orcs reach this point, halting them in their tracks.' His gaze moved to Sergeant Druber, who was sitting beside Alaric and leading their mounted soldiers. 'You will lead the charge,' Haas told his sergeant bluntly. 'Stay well back and out of sight. When you hear the archers firing, race back here and into the enemy's midst. Do not stop – just cut through to the back. Then wheel around and strike from behind. We will strike from the front, forcing their attention back to us, and then the secondary force will hit from behind on the opposite corner. They will be divided, confused, and unsure where to focus. We will constrict and crush them between us.' He looked over to Alaric. 'You and your companions will hold this pass and prevent anyone from attacking us through it. Go with Druber and stay out of the way. Then move to the mouth of the pass once he charges.' He swept his gaze across the assembled men. 'Understood?'

'Yes, sir!' the men thundered back.

Haas nodded. 'Good. To your positions, men, and remember, we fight to protect the Empire!'

'It's a good plan,' Alaric commented as he followed Druber, who led him, Dietz, Kleiber, Kristoff, Fastred, Holst and his men to their assigned position. 'Takes advantage of his assets and maximizes the enemy's confusion; very efficient.'

'Will it work?' Dietz asked, reminded again that his employer had received military training from childhood. He was disappointed to see the look of resignation on the younger man's face.

'No,' Alaric sighed. 'The warband is too strong. Haas will damage them, certainly, and slow them, but he lacks the numbers to defeat them.'

'Then his men ride to their deaths?' Kristoff asked softly, an odd note in his voice.

Alaric nodded, shook his head and shrugged. 'I don't know. The attack will fail, unless something shifts the odds. But will they survive? Who can say?'

'Sigmar will defend us all,' Kleiber insisted, and Alaric laughed, though not meanly.

'Perhaps he will,' Fastred said, almost pleading. 'After all, this is the site of his greatest victory. If his spirit defends his people anywhere, it is here. Perhaps he will protect us.'

'Perhaps,' Alaric agreed lightly, almost too easily. 'We shall see.' Then they were in place and all conversation ceased as they calmed their horses, loosened their weapons, and readied themselves for battle.

THE TIME STRETCHED on, each second agonizingly long, yet it was less than an hour before Alaric heard the stomp of heavy feet and the deep pounding rhythm of a war drum. During that time he had closed his eyes and tried to recall everything he had learned as a child, every lesson his father and cousins, uncles and brothers had drilled into him. Despite Haas's claim, he knew they would probably see combat themselves before the day was over, and the old training might finally prove useful, he thought as he dredged up long-forgotten instructions. *Breathe slowly and carefully. Relax your hands and shake them to keep them loose.*

Grip your horse with your knees, not your ankles and strike for the head and neck. Watch their eyes, not their hands. Think one move ahead. It all blurred together, making his head swim, and he was almost grateful when the drumbeat pulled him back to the present. Opening his eyes he glanced beside him and saw Dietz there as always, the large axe Druber had provided clenched in both hands, Glouste safely tucked within his leather jacket.

'This is it,' Dietz said quietly, and Alaric could hear the near panic in his voice.

'No it isn't,' he said, trying to keep his own voice from shaking. 'We still have that statue to find, remember? And I've got those marks from that temple to translate. I can't die before I've figured them out.'

His companion laughed as he'd hoped. 'You would stave off Morr himself with that, wouldn't you? "I can't go yet, I haven't solved that riddle!"'

'Of course,' Alaric replied, feeling better for helping his friend. 'He's a careful god, he'd understand.'

Whatever Dietz might have said in reply was drowned out by the sound of grunts, shouts and bellows, mixed with the beat of the drum. The orcs were near. Then the air was filled with a rushing sound like a heavy rain, and Alaric knew the scouts had launched their arrows – louder shouts and shrieks and the cessation of the drum confirmed they had struck.

'Let's go!' Druber shouted, kicking his horse to a gallop and drawing his long sword as he dashed from the side passage. His soldiers were with him and Dietz and the other travellers followed close behind, but Druber was ahead by half a length as he barrelled out from the path and back into the valley.

The sight there almost stopped Alaric cold. The entire warband was arrayed before him. He had seen orcs before, but nothing like this. At least three hundred of them filled the valley, decked in mismatched plate, chain and leather, skulls and chains draped about them. Feathers and tattered cloth, and what looked like flesh waved above helms

and caps, and the air was filled with spear tips, axe heads
and swordblades. Many of the orcs had painted their thick
hides with blood and mud, and other mixtures, creating
red, brown and black patterns against their green skin.
They were hideous, nearly as tall as a man, but far wider,
with heavy, bestial features and long hairy arms ending in
oversized, clawed hands. Many of them were milling
about, uncertain, staring at the arrows protruding from
many in their midst, but their weapons were still firmly
clasped, and even as Druber sped towards them the orcs'
grunts turned from surprise and pain to rage.

Then the sergeant was upon them. 'For the Empire!' he
bellowed, lashing out with his blade and carving an orc's
head from its shoulders. His horse kicked another in the
chest, knocking it aside so it slammed into two more and
bore them to the ground. Orcs were everywhere, closing in
on Druber, but then the first of his men reached him, cutting down an orc from behind, and the rest of the
mounted soldiers were soon forming a tight cluster in the
midst of the confusion. The soldiers laid about them with
swords and axes, hacking through orcish spears before the
weapons could be brought to bear.

They formed a spear of their own, Druber at the tip, and
they pierced the orc ranks and drove through to the other
side, though Alaric did not realise it until the sergeant and
his men had gone a full length past the last orc. Then Druber was wheeling about, turning his steed back towards the
orcs. Many of the creatures had turned, following the
horses' path, and were now regrouping to face them, bellowing curses and brandishing weapons eagerly.

Then a shout was heard off to the other side and from the
front: 'For the Empire!' And Haas's men attacked. Alaric felt
strangely elated as he watched Druber kick his horse back
into a canter and return to the fray. His eyes drifted across
an orc who seemed larger than the rest, and after a second
Alaric's brain registered the difference. The orc wasn't larger,
but simply closer. It was heading right for him, and now he
realised at least twenty more were right behind it.

'Get ready,' he called to the others, drawing his rapier, though his words were barely more than a whisper. Not that it mattered, as they had noticed the approaching orcs as well.

'Aaagh!' Alaric shouted as the orcs reached him, though it came out more as a yelp. He slashed the first orc across the throat, its blood fountaining upward as it crumpled to the ground, a look of surprise slowly reaching its face. A second one was right behind it, and Alaric blocked a heavy axe blow that made his sword shiver and his arm shake. He couldn't parry many other blows like that and his heart sank as the other orcs clustered closer, raging to reach him and tear him from his horse. Somewhere he thought he heard Morr laughing. Then he heard a surprising bellow behind him and felt more than saw a familiar presence at his back.

'Ulric!' It was Dietz, shouting like a true berserker and lashing out with the axe as he drove his own horse up alongside Alaric. Together the horses barrelled forward, kicking, biting and shoving, and the orcs fell back before them.

'Sigmar!' came a thundering cry behind them, and Kleiber was there, longsword clasped in both hands. His blade flashed about him as he rode, carving through orcs, and for an instant Alaric thought Sigmar would indeed be proud of the witch hunter's prowess and devotion. Fastred was beside him, just far enough away to stay clear of the sword, and he was firing his crossbow at any orc in his way. Holst and his men brought up the rear, spears levelled to impale any orc within range. The orcs faltered, their momentum gone, and Alaric took advantage of the pause to skewer another through the throat. More than half the attacking force was dead already and they made short work of the others, until finally the pass was empty of foes again. Alaric rested his sword arm across the front of his saddle and leaned forward, forehead against his horse's neck.

'Well, that worked better than expected,' he admitted quietly.

FOR A TIME, everything was confused. Dietz remembered
watching the charge cut through the warband and emerge
on the far side. He remembered Druber turning back
towards them and attacking again, only with the rest of the
Empire soldiers striking from the other side. The orcs were
distracted, confused, just as Haas had planned. Their ranks
broke, each orc fighting for himself, and Druber vanished
in their midst, though from time to time Dietz caught
glimpses of him.

Then a handful of orcs decided either to flee the fight or
to circle around and attack from the side. They made for
the pass, the very same one where Dietz and the others
waited, and suddenly he was no longer a bystander in this
war, but an unwilling participant. The orcs mobbed them,
bellowing, grunting and howling, and Dietz lost track of
the others, concentrating upon his borrowed axe and his
horse, and whichever orc appeared before him. When a
hand landed on his shoulder he shook it off. It landed
again, and again he pulled free. Then it reached for his
reins and he swung about, axe at the ready – to find Fastred there, crossbow in his lap, a shallow cut on one leg
and a look of concern upon his face.

'Put that down,' the explorer insisted, and Dietz let the
axe sag to his side, realising that most of the orcs were
already dead. He watched as Kleiber and Kristoff dispatched the last two.

'We won,' he said in a daze.

'Never mind that,' Fastred told him. 'Look.' He gestured
towards the mouth of the pass and beyond, where Haas
and his men were still battling the bulk of the orc warband. The Empire soldiers looked to be holding their own,
but Dietz could see that the orcs were still strong as well.

Dietz nodded. 'Yes, so? It's a war. We're in it.'

Fastred shook his head. 'No, look at the ground.'

Dietz looked again, trying to see the ground through the
feet and hooves, and flashing blades. 'It's rock. So?'

'Look at the blood.'

There was blood everywhere. It sprayed in droplets, gushed in torrents, flowed in rivulets – wait. He looked again, trying to follow that last sight. Yes, the blood on the ground near them was flowing in a clear stream, away from their narrow passage and towards the front of the fight. Quickly he edged his horse forward a few steps, still watching. Now he could see more of the battle site and he studied the ground as much as he could from his vantage point. After a minute he was sure. The blood along the side was also pooling and flowing, towards the middle. The other side was the same, at least as best he could tell from here, and at last he glanced up at Fastred.

'It's all flowing towards one spot.'

'Yes.' The portly explorer nodded. 'I downed an orc – good shot, right in the throat – and saw it rushing past him as he fell. Then I noticed another stream of blood, a little way away, angling in the same direction.'

Dietz met the other man's eyes and knew they were thinking the same thing. 'The sacrifice.'

Fastred nodded. 'The orcs drew Haas out to this spot. They wanted the fight here – that's why they reached this point at dawn, knowing he'd prefer to attack then. They're feeding the statue.'

Dietz glanced around, searching for signs of their friends. 'We need to gather the others.'

'What about the war? We were told to guard this pass.'

Dietz shook his head. 'We did our part. It's up to Haas now. We need to concentrate on our own mission.'

IT TOOK SOME time to gather the others because a second group of orcs had charged them while Dietz and Fastred were off to the side, and they turned back to find their friends locked in battle once more. Kleiber was gleefully slaughtering orcs and only permitted himself to be dragged away when Dietz told him the statue was nearby. Alaric was easier to convince, but harder to reach; he was in the centre of the conflict, and only Holst's presence nearby had kept him from being overrun. Adelrich was up on the cliff, but picked his way down as soon as he caught sight of Dietz signalling him. Kristoff was fighting furiously just beyond the passage, orcs on all sides, and it took Kleiber, Dietz and Holst to drag him clear. Finally they had killed or driven away the orcs and pulled their horses off to one side, where Fastred explained what he'd discovered.

'That's it!' Alaric was thrilled. 'It's got to be!' He turned to Adelrich. 'If the blood's flowing down, the statue has to be beneath. That means they got it down there somehow. We need to find the way in.'

'It could be anywhere along either side,' Kristoff pointed out.

'It could,' Alaric agreed, 'but let's hope not. We have to find it before it receives enough blood to open the portal.' He glanced at Fastred and Adelrich. 'You two know more about rocks and paths than the rest of us combined. Is there any way to narrow it down?'

Fastred thought about it. 'The rock is the same on both sides,' he commented, 'so that's no help. This type of rock often develops cracks and caves, so there may be many such openings around here, but not all of them will lead to the right place.' He shrugged. 'I suppose that's not particularly useful.'

'It's honest,' Alaric reassured him, 'and it's better that we know our real chances.'

'I've seen several openings along these cliffs already,' Adelrich added. 'Most of them stopped just beyond the surface, though, so at least we can eliminate many of them easily.' He glanced up along the sides of their passage, and then out towards the main pass, where the battle still raged. 'I suppose I'd best search along here first. If it isn't here we'll have to venture out and check the cliffs as best we can.'

Alaric nodded. 'We'll do our best to cover you,' he assured the scout. Adelrich nodded and clambered up the rough side of the passage until he reached the top. He perched on a small ledge and began examining that side. After perhaps an hour he climbed back down.

'Nothing here that leads deeper than a few feet,' he told the others. 'It has to be out there somewhere.'

'All right.' Alaric kicked his horse into motion, walking it towards the passage entrance. 'Let's go.'

The others followed him and they eased their way out into the pass. Once they were a few feet out, Adelrich slipped out behind them and began searching the cliff on that side. He examined every opening he found, ducking his head in when necessary and twice disappearing inside before returning. Each time he shook his head. The others stayed as close behind him as they could, skirting the larger battle and picking off any orcs who ventured near them.

A short way beyond the battle, back the way the orcs had come, Adelrich was heading towards a crack when he saw an orc emerging from another gap a little farther down. Quickly the scout pulled his bow, strung it, nocked an arrow and fired, taking the orc in the throat. Before the body had fallen, Adelrich raced towards it and disappeared into the rocks where it had emerged. A moment later he reappeared and waved the others over.

'It's a cave,' he told them when they reached him, standing half inside a wide crack. 'It goes down and around, probably beneath the valley floor.' He grinned. 'Signs of something heavy being dragged along.'

'Let's go.' Alaric hopped down from his horse and slapped its flank, sending it racing down the pass past the cave. He hoped all the orcs were already here, leaving none to molest his poor mount as it fled. The others followed suit, their horses eagerly taking the opportunity to flee the battle so close behind them.

The passage was so narrow that Kleiber and Fastred had difficulty squeezing through in places, though Dietz pointed out orcs would have the same problem.

Once inside, they lit the torches Adelrich pulled from his pack, and followed the scout as he led them down a twisting path. The marks along the floor were clear in the flickering torchlight – something large and heavy had scraped through here. They passed several branching passages, but kept to the marks, and finally emerged in an oblong cavern well below the ground.

The first thing Dietz noticed as he stepped in was the height. Along much of the tunnel he had been forced to crouch to keep from banging his head against the ceiling. Here, he could straighten up and even reach above him without touching rock. The second thing he noticed was the size of the cavern. It could fit all of them easily along one side, making it larger than Haas's command tent by a significant margin. The third thing he noticed was the protrusions. This cavern was the size of a large room, but it was not empty. It had its own furniture, rock spurs jutting out along the wall, springing up from the floor and hanging from the ceiling, as if someone had festooned the place with ribbons, garlands and drapes, and then transformed them all to stone.

The fourth thing he noticed was the statue.

It was right in front of them, perhaps forty feet away – and nearly ten feet up. The centre of the room was thick with those strange rock projections, jutting every which way, and somehow the statue had been placed in their midst. It was held well above the ground, supported by several loops of stone from both ceiling and floor, and only the faint reddish tint distinguished it from the grey stone around it. He could only see its base, besides – the head and shoulders had been inserted in a crack in the ceiling, wedging it firmly in place. Drops of blood dripped down it, raising oddly bright streaks along its surfaces. Clearly the centre of the depression was just above that crack.

'We've found it!' Alaric had eyes only for the statue, as did Kristoff. Fortunately, Adelrich was peering around the chamber, raising his torch high to see the other side. His quiet hiss alerted them, as did the sound of his sword sliding from its scabbard.

'Show yourself!' Kleiber shouted, raising his pistol, but the command proved unnecessary. They heard a barked order even as the witch hunter issued his demand. A moment later they all saw what Adelrich had seen, as a dozen orc warriors stomped into view on the far side of the cavern. They had their own weapons at the ready and hurled themselves at the party with harsh cries. Kleiber leaped to meet them, Kristoff and Dietz right behind him.

CHAPTER ELEVEN

'SIGMAR!' KLEIBER'S BATTLE-CRY rang out as he charged the orcs, his pistol levelled at the frontmost warrior. A loud crack resounded through the chamber as he fired, the orc collapsing in a spray of blood and bone, but the sound echoed on, shaking the rock all around and blinding them with rock dust.

'We have to get that statue!' Alaric tugged Fastred and Adelrich back as they moved to help their friends. 'Leave them! They'll handle the orcs. We have to deal with that!' He jabbed a finger towards the statue, and the other two reluctantly let themselves be dragged towards the room's centre and the statue embedded there.

'We can hack it to bits,' Adelrich suggested, sword raised, but Alaric shook his head.

'Too high up,' he pointed out. 'Even if we can climb up there, we'd be easy targets for those orcs.' All three of them glanced back towards the battle and then resolutely turned away.

'We could shoot it,' Fastred offered, raising his crossbow. Again Alaric disagreed.

'It's wedged in place,' he said, gesturing towards it. 'That crack is holding it together, and we can't get a clear shot anyway, not with all that rock in the way.'

'We have another problem,' Adelrich pointed out, brushing rock dust from his hair. 'Kleiber's shot was enough to create small cracks throughout this chamber. That's what caused the dust. If we fire again we could bring the roof crashing down.' He shook his head. 'It might destroy the statue, but it would certainly take us with it.'

Alaric frowned. 'We have to risk that – we can't leave it here, and the longer it sits the more blood it absorbs. We'd need a clean shot, or several shots close together.' He tapped his chin. 'We don't have time to waste.'

Alaric forced himself to think, ignoring the sounds of battle behind them. Blackpowder would definitely be more effective than steel, but the statue was well shielded by the rock, and held in place as well. They needed to hit it hard all at once and blow it apart: a concentrated strike. This reminded him of his early firearms instruction, and something his instructor had said about proper care and storage, and he slapped his thigh.

'Got it!' he announced, turning towards their embattled companions. 'Kleiber, I need your pistol and supplies!' The witch hunter was tugging his sword free of an orc corpse, parrying another's blow with his dagger, but he heard and nodded. A quick thrust killed the second orc, and then he stepped back to where he'd dropped the empty pistol. A quick kick sent it skittering towards Alaric, and Kleiber tossed his pouch of bullets and his powder horn after it. Adelrich caught the horn and Fastred fumbled, but managed to hold onto the pouch. Then Kleiber returned to the fray, parrying a blow that would have removed Dietz's arm, and carving off the offending orc's hand in return.

'We're shooting it?' Adelrich asked as Alaric quickly prepared the pistol. 'Despite the risk?'

'Shooting, yes,' Alaric replied, 'but not the statue itself.' He finished loading the pistol and then emptied the remaining bullets into his own belt pouch. Next he poured the powder horn's contents into the bullet pouch and tied it tight. Finally he turned back towards the fight. 'Dietz!'

Between them Kleiber, Dietz and Kristoff had finished off five of the orcs. At Alaric's shout Dietz hacked again at his current opponent, lopping off its right leg and then slashing its throat as it fell. Then he turned and trotted over to Alaric, sidestepping another orc who darted past him. 'What?'

'I need Glouste.'

The others stared at him, but Alaric ignored them, concentrating on Dietz whose face had set in a familiar stubborn glare. 'Don't, Dietz,' Alaric warned him. 'There isn't time.' He pointed up at the statue. 'We need to destroy that right away.' He showed Dietz the pistol he held in one hand and the pouch in the other. 'I need Glouste to climb up there and set this bag against the statue. Then I can shoot it. The bag has the rest of Kleiber's blackpowder. When it's hit it will explode, shattering the statue.'

'That's all you need from Glouste?' Dietz asked, still frowning. 'To climb up there and deposit that bag?'

'That's it.'

'All right.' He made a strange chittering sound and a furry head poked from his jacket. 'Come on, Glouste.' The tree-monkey – no, Alaric corrected himself, tree-fox – climbed from her warm nesting place up onto his shoulder, rubbing her forehead against his cheek. 'Yes, I know.' Dietz held out his hand and Alaric handed him the bag, which he then held towards his pet. 'See this bag, Glouste? I need you to take this bag up there.' He pointed up towards the statue, and the tree-fox chittered rapidly, tail puffing out. 'Yes, I know – it's ugly. I don't like it either, but I need you to take this bag up to the top and leave it there. Will you do that?' Glouste was still chirruping at him, practically vibrating with anger, excitement or fear, Alaric couldn't tell which.

'Glouste!' Dietz's tone sharpened, and his pet froze, watching him intently. He held the pouch right in front of her face. 'Take this up there. Please?' As if she'd been waiting for him to ask politely, the tree-fox finally leaned out and clamped her small, sharp teeth onto the bag. Then she bumped his chin once more and leaped from his shoulder to the nearest rock formation. She began scampering up, her claws finding ready footholds, and in a moment she was high above their heads.

'Sigmar! Sigmar!' Kleiber's battle-cry resounded again, and the others glanced towards him, surprised he and Kristoff had not finished off the remaining orcs yet. They quickly saw why.

Apparently the orc that had moved past Dietz a moment ago had not been charging; it had been fleeing, but not far. Now it returned with a dozen orcs behind it. They had already surrounded Kleiber, and Dietz, and Adelrich and Fastred quickly joined the fray, adding their blades and bolts to the fight. Alaric drew his rapier and skewered the nearest orc, but kept the pistol ready and turned so that he could keep an eye on Glouste's progress. The nimble tree-fox was negotiating a cluster of rock halfway between them and the statue. She needed more time.

'We need more time,' he shouted to the others, who nodded. Unfortunately, the orcs must have understood as well, because one towards the rear drew a large horn from his belt and blasted out a resounding note upon it. Almost immediately they heard a second horn blare in reply, and the distant sound of more footsteps growing rapidly closer.

'They've got another way in!' Adelrich called, narrowly avoiding an axe blow and slashing the orc across the chest in return. 'If that horn blast reached the valley we could have the entire warband down upon us!'

'I know!' Alaric stabbed at another orc, who wisely retreated. He glanced over his shoulder. 'She's almost there!' It was true – Glouste was mere feet from the statue. She had hesitated when the orc horn had sounded, frightened by the almost deafening noise in that small space, and by the vibrations it had created in the rock, but she quickly gathered herself and started moving again.

'She needs time to get clear!' Dietz hollered back, clubbing an orc with the side of his axe and then slicing its face as it reeled back from the blow.

'No time!' Fastred shouted, firing at an orc and narrowly missing Kristoff's arm. 'We need to end this now!'

Dietz paused and glanced at Alaric, their eyes locking. Finally he nodded. 'Do it.' He looked up to where Glouste had reached the statue, and then turned away, unable to watch.

'Run, Glouste,' Alaric whispered, knowing it wouldn't help. Either the tree-fox would escape or she wouldn't. The same was true for the rest of them. The statue was more important than any of their lives. Dietz knew that. Alaric suspected his pet did as well. That didn't make the pistol any less heavy as he raised it, took careful aim, and fired.

Glouste had done her job well. She had tucked the pouch into a nook halfway up the statue, what would have been a crooked arm on a man. Alaric had a clean shot at it through a stone loop, and he hit it perfectly. The pistol ball smashed into the statue, striking the pouch first, and the heat and impact ignited the rest of the blackpowder.

BOOM!

The crash was deafening. The entire chamber shook, throwing them from their feet, and rock fragments flew – Alaric saw one orc fall with a stone shard through its eye and felt a similar chunk soar past his head, narrowly missing his cheek.

'Get out!' he shouted at his friends, climbing to his feet and running back towards the tunnel that had led them down here. They couldn't hear him in the din, but they saw his motion or simply guessed the safest course for themselves, and all of them scrambled towards the exit. Several of the orcs proved smart enough to understand what was happening and they retreated as well, disappearing back down the passage they had used. Larger fragments fell, and then with a resounding crash the ceiling collapsed, filling the space with dust and rock.

Alaric had just reached the tunnel, having paused to help Fastred to his feet after the heavier man had tripped over a rock, when they were thrown forward by the impact behind them. Dietz helped Fastred back to his feet and they all stared back at the jumble of rocks blocking the exit, and completely filling the underground chamber.

'Is everyone all right?' Alaric asked, glancing around. Amazingly enough he and his friends had escaped with only bruises and battered bones.

'It collapsed the entire chamber,' Kleiber commented in what sounded almost like awe. Alaric nodded.

'The blast split the ceiling,' he explained, remembering what old Professor Haedilick had taught them about geology and fault lines. 'There was already a crack there and so the blast could reach much further into the rock and widen that gap.' He glanced back. 'I expect it's completely filled in.' He smiled. 'The statue is demolished, just more rubble mixed with the rest. The orcs won't be able to get back down here, either, I'm sure their passage must be choked up as well.'

Dietz stepped up to the exit and ran his hands over the rocks, as if checking to see if any could be pulled loose. They were wedged tight, though in some places he could stick his hand into the gap between two fragments. 'Glouste!' he called hoarsely, choking on the rock dust that had billowed out of the chamber. 'Glouste!'

'I'm sorry,' Fastred told him, stepping up and clasping his shoulder. 'I fear the clever little thing made the ultimate sacrifice.'

Dietz started to snarl a reply, and then stopped, his shoulders sagging. 'She knew,' he said softly, glancing up towards the spot where he had last seen her. 'She didn't want to do it. I made her do it.'

'She gave her life to destroy that monstrosity,' Kleiber pointed out, sheathing his blade and accepting his pistol back from Alaric. 'Many men have not shown such bravery or such devotion.'

Dietz only nodded and turned away.

It took several more minutes to gather themselves, but they were finally ready to depart. Dietz glanced back one last time at the cavern entrance.

'Goodbye, Glouste,' he said. He paused, sighed, and turned to go – and then turned back again.

'Glouste?'

'She's gone, Dietz,' Alaric told him gently, tugging at his arm, but Dietz pulled away.

'No, I'm sure I just heard something. Glouste?' He stepped back to the entrance, head cocked to one side. 'Answer me?'

The others followed him, loath to leave him alone, and it was Adelrich who nodded after a moment. 'I hear it too,' he assured Dietz. 'It's just a squeak, but it sounds like her.'

'It *is* her!' Dietz insisted, scrambling at the rocks. 'Glouste, where are you?' The others joined in, shoving and tugging at the rocks, trying to find a way back in. Finally Adelrich managed to shove a smaller rock aside and Kleiber tugged out the rock behind it, creating a space large enough to see through to the chamber.

Alaric had been right. The blast had collapsed the ceiling, filling the entire chamber with rock. They could barely see through the rock dust, but had an impression of large, jagged boulders piled everywhere. The statue was completely gone, as was the rock structure that had held it up.

Dietz stuck his head through the gap, and pulled it back out, coughing. Alaric handed him a handkerchief and Dietz took it without a word, tying it around his head and over his nose and mouth. Then he stuck his head back through. 'Glouste?' He could hear the squeaking more clearly now, and after a second he caught a glimpse of red-brown fur behind a rock. 'She's here!'

The others waited, hardly daring to breathe, as Dietz called again. He saw the fur again, a little closer now. Then it disappeared. After a moment it flashed past another boulder much closer, and suddenly Glouste was clinging to a rock right in front of him. Her sides were streaked with blood, but she was still very much alive. She leaped forward and Dietz stepped back just in time as she scrabbled into the hole. Then she wriggled through and leaped onto his shoulders, where she curled around his neck and nuzzled him fiercely.

'Yes yes, I'm happy to see you too,' he told her, reaching up to pet her gently. 'You did an excellent job. Good treefox.' She purred her thanks and head-butted him repeatedly.

'I don't think she's seriously injured,' Fastred said after studying her as well as he could from her perch. 'The wounds look minor. She must have leaped away from the statue and found shelter just before the explosion.'

'Smart,' Alaric admitted, eyeing the pet with surprise and a little wonder. 'Smarter than I thought.'

'Of course she's smart,' Dietz replied, scratching her under her chin. 'She's mine.' The others laughed, and they were all in a good mood as they made their way back up the winding tunnel and out into the valley above.

WHAT THEY SAW there only improved their mood. Neither side had expected the explosion or the resulting collapse, of course, but Haas had reacted quickly, pulling his men back to the valley edges and letting the unstable floor collapse beneath the orcs' combined weight. His archers had penned them in, keeping them atop the shattered stone, and his soldiers had killed any orc that broke free. Finally the tremors had subsided, the valley had settled to its new depth, and the orcs began to regroup. That was when Haas waded in, his men arrayed behind him, and made straight for the warband commander. It had been an impressive fight, Holst told them afterwards, the short Empire leader with his gleaming longsword and the hulking orc with its massive warhammer. Haas had triumphed, using a dagger to pin one of his foe's hands and thus the hammer, and then lopping off the creature's head. That had demoralised the remaining orcs and they had fled.

'They'll hide and regroup,' Haas admitted later, when they were all back in camp, 'but only in small bands. The warband died with its leader.' He studied Alaric. 'I take it you found your cargo?'

Alaric nodded. 'We did, and destroyed it.'

'And the explosion?'

'That was it.'

Haas hoisted his wineskin in salute. 'Then we owe you our victory.' He took a long pull and handed the skin to Alaric. 'My thanks.'

Alaric grinned. 'My pleasure.' He raised the skin in salute to Haas before drinking and passing it along. 'We'll be heading back tomorrow to report our success. Do you need us to carry any messages for you?'

Haas nodded. 'I'll pen a quick report to my superiors – if you could carry it to Nuln I'd be grateful.' He looked around at them, and frowned when his eyes reached Adelrich and Holst. 'I wonder if you would be willing to stay behind a short while. You,' he nodded to Adelrich, 'my scouts say could teach them much, and you,' he turned to Holst, 'have the respect of Sergeant Druber, a thing not easy to obtain. We'll be chasing down those bands and I could use another good scout and a second seasoned guard unit.'

Holst looked to Alaric, but Adelrich replied immediately. 'I will stay. Middenheim does not need me just now and here I can aid the Empire.'

Alaric shrugged in reply to Holst's unvoiced question. 'It's your choice, sergeant,' he said. 'You and your men have been the difference between life and death for us more times than I can count, and I thank you for that, but I cannot command you to stay or go. Our job is done. Do what you think best.'

Holst considered that, and looked at Kleiber. 'Will you be returning to Middenheim?'

The witch hunter nodded. 'I must report back on the success of our mission, and on the motives of our companions.' Surprisingly he smiled at Alaric and Dietz. 'Madmen you may be, and too cavalier with the gods, but you are no daemonspawn and I will slaughter any who say otherwise.'

'Thanks, I think,' Dietz replied dryly.

Holst smiled and nodded. 'Then I know you will see them safely back as well,' he told Kleiber, indicating Dietz and Alaric. He turned back to Haas. 'My men and I will assist you, sir,' he announced, saluting.

'Good man,' Haas told him, returning the salute and following it with the rapidly emptying wineskin. The conversation continued, but so did the drinking, and none of them was sure later exactly what was said.

THE NEXT MORNING Alaric, Dietz, Kristoff, Fastred and Kleiber readied their gear and prepared their horses. Haas, Adelrich and Holst saw them off, each handing Alaric sealed reports to deliver.

'Watch your back,' Dietz warned Adelrich, clasping the scout's hand.

'You too,' his friend replied. 'When I get back we'll share a drink.'

'Definitely.'

'Thank you, sergeant,' Alaric told Holst after mounting, looking down at the soldier.

'My pleasure, sir,' Holst replied, saluting him. Alaric didn't bother returning the salute, but smiled as he turned his horse and kicked her into motion.

'It seems strange to be done,' Fastred commented as they rode out of the pass and towards Grenzstadt. 'After all these months, the statues are destroyed and our mission complete.' He grinned. 'I cannot imagine what I'll do with myself.'

'I plan to drink, eat, and whore,' Kristoff replied, laughing. 'You're welcome to join me.'

'That may be a plan,' the explorer agreed, chuckling, 'and what of you two? Will you join us in our debauchery?'

Alaric shrugged. 'I don't know what we'll do next.' He frowned. 'Somehow this doesn't feel done. I can't say why, though.'

'Pessimism?' Dietz suggested, earning him a mock-kick that brought a chittering rebuke from the slumbering Glouste.

The four of them continued to banter as they rode into the village, Kleiber maintaining his usual dignified silence off to one side. It was going to be a long trip home.

CHAPTER TWELVE

'TRAVELLING WITH YOU does have its uses,' Alaric admitted to Kleiber as they rode into Middenheim through the same gate they had left through all those weeks ago. The witch hunter tapped his hat in mocking salute. The city guards had not dared search them this time and had waved the five men through with hasty salutes in Kleiber's general direction.

Their return to Middenheim had been far easier than their departure; at least they had not been searching for statues or fighting the creatures defending them. The four of them had taken the Old Dwarf Road down from the Black Fire Pass and across Averheim. That road had led them to the Old Forest Road, and they had followed that clear through the Great Forest, and up to Middenheim itself. They had been attacked by bandits twice, accosted by local soldiers once and harassed by desperate villagers three times. The travellers had fought their way through the first problem and talked their way past both the second and the third, finally arriving back at the City of the White Wolves only a little the

173

worse for wear. Even so, it was nice to know that soon they could dismount, stable their horses, sit down on chairs and perhaps even sleep on real beds, and eat food they did not have to hunt, kill and cook themselves.

'I must report to the witch hunter captain at once,' Kleiber informed his companions after they were past the city's defensive courtyard and had paused in one of the small squares nearby. He nodded to them each in turn. 'Gentlemen, I commend you for your assistance in ending this threat to our fair Empire. Rest assured my superiors will hear of your devotion.' And with that he was off.

'Assistance?' Dietz snorted, though he waited until the witch hunter was far enough away. 'As if he was responsible!'

'I don't care who gets the credit,' Alaric told him honestly, 'as long as they clear us of all charges.' He turned to face Kristoff and Fastred. 'What will you two do now we're back?'

'I am off to the guild offices,' Fastred replied, idly stroking his beard. 'I'll report on our particulars, of course, and sample the excellent brandy they keep there. You're all welcome to join me.' The others laughed – the explorer had depleted his meagre supply of wine two weeks back and had been lamenting the loss ever since.

'I must away to my own masters,' Kristoff said, 'though perhaps later I may avail myself of your kind offer.' He bowed to them all while still mounted, an impressive feat. 'Gentlemen, it has been an honour and a pleasure.' Then he tapped heels to his mount and was off, with Fastred not far behind him.

'So, here we are,' Alaric said with a sigh, glancing over at Dietz. 'Just the two – well, three – of us again. Seems strange now, doesn't it? Too quiet by half.'

'Strange, yes,' Dietz agreed, also missing their friends already, 'but I like the quiet.' He frowned. 'Should we report to someone as well?'

'I suppose so.' Alaric thought for a moment. 'What was that man's name, the one who worked for Todbringer? Stroder? Striner?'

'Struber.'

'That's the one. We should inform him of our success.'

Deitz fidgeted on his horse. 'Do you need me along? I'd hoped – I wanted–'

Alaric understood immediately. 'Go. See your family. I'll take care of it.' He searched his memory again. 'The Dancing Frog, isn't that where we stayed before?' His friend nodded. 'Let's return there, then – if nothing else it was serviceable and Kristoff and Fastred both know to look for us there. Meet me there after your visit.'

'Thanks.' Dietz turned his horse down a side street, and Alaric found himself alone for the first time in a very long while. Suddenly, he realised just how much he'd come to depend upon Dietz in the year since they'd begun travelling together.

'Well, not like I'm scaling a mountain,' he told himself softly as he kicked his own horse into a fast walk. 'Just a word with this Struber fellow and then off to the Dancing Frog.' His mind strayed back to their last visit, and he smiled. 'Oh yes, with one quick stop between.'

'Hello?'

The door was unlatched and Alaric pushed it open and slid past it into the half-darkness. He sneezed as he entered, yet the shop was less dusty than he remembered and lacked that ever-present sound of hammer and chisel on stone.

'Who's there?' A high-pitched voice rose from the back and Alaric followed the well-remembered path to the work table near the back wall. A woman stood there, tall and slender to the point of being gaunt, head covered in a black shawl. She was glancing through a thick ledger. Alaric recognised her from previous visits.

'Alaric von Jungfreud, fraulein,' he announced himself, bowing carefully to avoid his rapier bumping any of the carvings to his side. 'You must be Rolf's wife?'

'His widow, yes,' she replied, eyes narrowing, and Alaric straightened rapidly, trying to control his shock.

'Widow? What happened?'

'Executed for heresy and treason, he was,' the woman said flatly, though she could not look up as she spoke. Alaric graciously attributed her tears to the dust that still hung thick in the air.

'But he was innocent!'

'Well I know it,' she replied, sniffing, 'but the witch hunters chose to believe otherwise. They call a man heretic at the merest slight and attribute anything odd or defiant to witchcraft and Chaos worship.'

'Who is it, mother?' a voice called out from beyond the curtained door, and a moment later a young man stepped in from the stone yard beyond. He was as tall as Rolf had been and bore his father's eyes, but his frame and features were narrow like his mother's.

'An old friend and associate of your father's,' Alaric replied, bowing again. 'Alaric von Jungfreud is the name. I did business with your father on occasion, and knew him to be a fine and decent man.' He did not add that he had been present at Rolf's arrest, or that he and Dietz had been partially to blame for the incident. It seemed best not to mention such details right now.

Nonetheless the youth frowned. 'Alaric? I know that name. Ah, yes. I remember.' And he ducked back behind Rolf's worktable. After rummaging for a moment he produced a small wooden casket, handsomely carved of a dark polished wood. He handed it to Alaric.

'My father wanted you to have this,' the young man said. 'He mentioned it on my last visit to him before–' he trailed off.

'Thank you,' Alaric said quietly, accepting the casket. He lifted the lid and saw a familiar silk-wrapped object within: the mask. It was the reason he had returned, hoping to find Rolf out the back carving as usual. The stone carver's consideration, thinking of him in the shadow of his own certain death, brought tears to Alaric's eyes and it was a moment before he could speak.

Rolf's son and widow both noticed and relaxed slightly. 'Do not show that to anyone,' the youth cautioned, gesturing towards the casket. 'The witch hunters have eyes everywhere.'

Finally recovered, Alaric shook his head. 'The witch hunters? Why would they care about this?'

'They care about everything,' Rolf's widow replied. 'They are the real power in Middenheim now and their eyes are everywhere.' She shook her head and her hands tightened around the book held to her chest. 'Once they were cautious in their accusations, never attacking a man until they had proof of his wrongdoing. Not so now. Ever since the siege they've grown bolder, more aggressive, and more eager to feed the flames with human flesh.' She sniffed again to hold back tears. 'That's why they took my Rolf. He'd been tricked into carving those monstrosities, but the witch hunters refused to believe that. Said he'd been a willing participant. They'd no proof of that, none, but the elector count does as they say, and the White Wolves hide in their citadel and let those fanatics slaughter innocents by the dozen.' She shuddered. 'We withstood all the forces of Chaos before, but now our streets run red with blood and it's all let by men of the Empire.'

'It's not safe to talk of such things,' the youth cautioned with a quick glance to Alaric, who raised his hands.

'I'll not repeat it,' he assured them, earning a grateful glance from both. Inside he was trying to reconcile what they'd said with what he knew of the witch hunters, particularly Kleiber. The man was a fanatic, certainly, and eager to slaughter enemies of the Empire, but he had never struck Alaric as unjust. Was he merely the exception? Or was it only because they had come to know Kleiber as a person, and he them?

'Will you keep the shop?' he asked them, more as a way to bring the conversation to safer ground, but Rolf's son shook his head.

'I work in wood, not stone,' he said, not without a touch of pride. 'My shop is two streets over.' He glanced around them at the carvings everywhere. 'We'll sell what we can of the work, and then sell the shop itself. I know a man who offered to buy my father's tools as well.' He smiled a small, sad smile. 'If there's ought here you'd like for yourself, please take it. My father spoke highly of you, and tell Dietz I said hello – he and I knew each other as boys.'

'I will, thank you,' Alaric replied, 'and thank you for the offer, but I've no place to stand such fine pieces as these.' He paused for a moment. 'May I have a last look around, though?'

'Of course.'

He left them to their cleaning and sorting, and wandered the twisting paths through the shop, running his fingers along various statues and pedestals as he walked. It seemed impossible this could be the last time he would squeeze through these crowded aisles or sidle by looming stone figures. Even though Dietz had introduced him to Rolf only a year ago, they had been in this shop many times since. Alaric felt he knew its layout as well as any place in Middenheim, perhaps better than any place at all save only the family manse and the University of Altdorf's scholarly halls.

As he wandered, thinking back over his previous visits, Alaric found himself drifting towards the shop's far corner. Finally he stopped, unable to proceed any farther. He was facing the corner itself and on either side were statues of winged horses, armoured warriors and majestic wolves, all carved from the pale grey granite so common here. Directly before him was a gap through which he could see the heavy stone of the walls themselves and he nodded sadly. Even now he remembered quite clearly what had stood here before.

'I am glad to see that piece gone, at least,' he remarked after making his way back to the worktable. Rolf's widow and son were still there, the one still examining the ledger and the other wrapping a small figurine that had been sitting on a shelf just above.

'Which piece is that?' the youth asked, not even looking up from his task.

'The statue, of course,' Alaric said, and then continued when both of them glanced over at him as if expecting more. 'The corrupted statue, the one that started all this; I gather the witch hunters came for it?'

'Witch hunters! Feh!' Rolf's widow spat to one side, her face twisted in a grimace. 'They've not set foot in here since hauling my husband off to his death, and I'd not allow them entry if they tried!' Her son nodded, his own face hard and looking more like his father's as a result.

Alaric frowned as her words struck him. 'The witch hunters didn't take him,' he corrected softly. 'The city guard did that and then gave him to the witch hunters for trial. You're saying they've never been in here, the witch hunters?' The widow and her son both shook their heads, her vehemently. 'The city guard, then? They confiscated the statue?'

'They haven't dared show their face here,' Rolf's son contested. 'They knew my father would have no traffic with such things yet they left him to the witch hunters' lies.'

Now Alaric was puzzled and a bit alarmed. 'Where is the statue, then? If the guard didn't take it and the witch hunters didn't destroy it, what happened to it?'

STRUBER HAD SAID nothing about the statue, but then the count's aide had said very little at all. Alaric had found him without difficulty and had reported the success of their mission – it had taken Struber a moment and several reminders before he had remembered the matter at all.

'Ah yes,' was all he'd said after Alaric had described the particulars a third time, 'those dreadful statues. Didn't you have another man with you?'

'Several,' Alaric had replied with a sigh, 'including a witch hunter, an explorer, a trader, and a unit of the count's own guard.'

'Ah, that would be Sergeant Holst?' Struber had asked, showing real interest for the first time. 'Fine man, fine. Has he returned with you?'

'No, he is still in the Black Fire Pass, assisting the commander there in destroying the last of an orc warband.' Alaric had gestured towards the folded parchment Struber held absently. 'His report is there, in your hand.'

'Is it?' Struber had blinked at the paper as if surprised to see it there. 'Yes, yes, very good. And the mission went well? The statues were all recovered?'

'Destroyed.' Alaric had found it harder and harder to maintain a civil tone. 'They were destroyed, yes. It was a complete success.'

'Excellent, excellent.' Struber had looked past Alaric, his voice trailing off, hands still holding Holst's report, and for a moment Alaric had feared the aide had fallen asleep with his eyes open. After a full minute of silence he had coughed lightly and Struber had started and focused upon him again.

'Yes, was there anything else?'

'No, nothing else.' Alaric had left then, relieved that apparently it was over, but somehow feeling annoyed there had not been more resolution. Perhaps if Struber had at least remembered where they'd gone and why it might have helped. Thinking back on it now the aide clearly had no idea what he'd been talking about. He hadn't mentioned the first statue or its later destruction, but that was hardly surprising – even if it had been destroyed Struber either wouldn't have known or would have known at one time, but forgotten about it shortly after.

ROLF'S WIDOW WAS frowning now as well. 'I'd thought they'd taken it when they took my husband,' she admitted.

Alaric shook his head. 'No, they arrested him and said they would confiscate and destroy the statue.' He shrugged. 'Perhaps they did come back for it that night. I was otherwise occupied.'

'No one came that night,' Rolf's son contributed. 'I closed up the shop after I heard about the arrest.' He stopped to think. 'There was a man the next day, however, said he was here to claim a piece my father had done for him.' He shrugged. 'The man had his receipt in my father's hand so I saw no reason not to complete the sale.' He smiled. 'My father would have approved of that – he hated loose ends.'

'Did he arrive alone?' Alaric asked.

'No, he brought several men with him and had a sturdy wagon just outside. He needed it, too – the piece was taller than me and solid.' Now his frown deepened into a scowl. 'I thought the piece unfinished at first, since it had no clear features, but as I looked I could make out more detail. They covered it with a cloth, to protect it, I suppose.'

Alaric had gone past puzzled and into worried. 'Do you know the man's name?' he asked, trying to shake the chill that had gripped him.

'I cannot remember it,' Rolf's son admitted, 'but I put the receipt there.' He pointed to the ledger his mother held, and she handed the book to him. He turned to the last page and pulled out a folded paper stuck between the binding and the endpapers. 'Here it is.' He handed the sheet to Alaric, who carefully unfolded it.

'One statue, part of a matched set of four,' he read softly. 'Commissioned by–' he paused, and then read it again. 'Wilfen von Glaucht.'

'Taal's teeth,' he muttered, and then glanced up at Rolf's son, who was watching him closely. 'When was this?'

'The next day, as I said,' the youth replied. 'Right at dawn, why?'

Alaric shook his head, turned to go, and then stopped. 'Can I keep this?' he asked, waving the receipt.

'If you like,' Rolf's widow told him. 'We've no need of it.'

'Thank you, and I am truly sorry for your loss,' Alaric told them. Then, clutching the casket under one arm, and still holding the receipt in his other hand, he headed for the door. He barely glanced about him as he walked.

Wilfen von Glaucht! That was the name used by the man who had commissioned the statues! And he had

claimed the first one – really the fourth and final one –
the day after they had seen it. The day after Rolf had been
arrested. The same day they had spent locked in a jail cell.

That meant that one of the four statues had not yet been
destroyed, and its creator, the man behind all this, had
retrieved it even before he, Dietz and the others had left to
find and destroy its counterparts.

All this time they had thought they had only three statues to find and dispatch. In fact they'd had four, and the
fourth one was now loose somewhere in Middenheim,
assuming it had not been carried beyond the city already.
Wherever it was, it had been there for months while they
traipsed around the Empire, probably drawing power the
entire time.

He had to find Dietz.

CHAPTER THIRTEEN

Dietz walked slowly through Middenheim's streets, in no hurry to be anywhere. The afternoon and evening had gone as well as could be expected.

He had called on Dracht first, thinking to get the worst part out of the way. His brother had been at the shop that had been their father's and it still looked the same: neat and tidy, and prosperous. Dracht himself looked much the same as well, though his hair was thinner and more grey than black, and his face was more lined – Dietz had pretended not to notice his older brother's right leg, which ended just above the knee. They had never been close and the visit was more a formality than anything else.

Next Dietz had gone to see Dagmar and their father, which was far more pleasant. They still lived in the small, tidy house his father had purchased when first starting the family. His father was blind, as he had been since Dietz had first reached manhood, and Dagmar cared for him – lovely, sweet Dagmar who could have had men waiting on her instead of the other way around. She had been thrilled to see him, as she always was, and over dinner he had regaled them all with stories of his adventures. His father had listened and nodded. Dracht had clearly not cared, but Dagmar had hung on every word. Before Dietz left he begged her to come with him, as he always did, but she refused. It was Dracht's responsibility to care for their father, but he claimed his house was barely large enough for his own family, with no room for the old man, and Dagmar was too dutiful to leave their father alone. Dietz sent money when he could, but he wished there was more he could do.

As he pondered the problem Dietz noticed a man turning the corner a few blocks away, a large heavy-set fellow in a long cloak and a velvet cap. For an instant he wondered why it seemed so familiar and then his mind snapped from the past back to the present and he remembered.

'Fastred!' The man was already around the corner and Dietz ran to catch up. 'Fastred, wait! It's me, Dietz!'

As he barrelled down the street Dietz passed a large building with a worn wooden plaque on the door and realised it was the Middenheim office for the Guild of Explorers. He had come here once with Alaric and was surprised to see just how far his wanderings had taken him. Fastred had said earlier that he planned to enjoy the guild office's comforts – why then was he leaving?

Still running, Dietz reached the corner and skidded around it, catching a glimpse of the man up ahead. 'Fastred!' he called again, but the distance was too great. Even as he watched, the man pulled off his cap and tugged up a hood attached to the cloak, covering his head completely.

This was getting stranger and stranger, Dietz thought, slowing slightly. Why would Fastred be wearing a hood, unless he didn't want to be recognised?

Dietz was only two lengths behind the man and was certain it was Fastred Albers he pursued, but he did not call out again. Instead he slowed to extend the distance between them and caught his breath, calming his heart and forcing his footsteps to match the same beat. The more he watched, the stranger this seemed. Fastred was a wise man who valued his own skin, sometimes a little too much. What would he be doing out here at night, walking alone and hiding his face? If he had somewhere to go, why not go in the company of friends, or send someone else instead? The portly explorer was also something of a show-off and loved attracting attention, which made it even harder to imagine him skulking along in a hooded cloak. Something was not right.

Dietz followed Fastred, careful to keep his footsteps light and his shadow behind them or hidden within Fastred's own. They were in a residential district, not the nicest in the city, but certainly not the poorest. As he watched, Fastred crossed the street and walked right up to the front door of one of the buildings. It was a handsome house, built of rough stone bricks, but it was not large and like its neighbours it had seen better days. Fastred raised his hand to the front door, first glancing around and tugging his hood down farther, and Dietz shrank back against another building to avoid the explorer's notice. At last Fastred rapped on the door, three quick sharp knocks. After a moment it opened and he stepped inside.

'Definitely odd,' Dietz muttered to himself, staring at the closed door. Why would Fastred come here and take such trouble to conceal his identity? Could he be romantically involved and hiding the fact to protect the woman? Perhaps – Fastred had regaled them with tales of his romantic encounters during their trip and clearly the large man had more than one powerful appetite. But why do this in such sly fashion? The Fastred he knew would have marched boldly to the front door, loudly demanded entry, and then trumpeted his presence to anyone within hearing range and a great many without.

'Why else would he be skulking about?' Dietz asked himself, and suddenly an answer came to him, and with it, something else.

'I need Alaric,' he decided.

* * *

'THERE YOU ARE!'

Both men said it simultaneously as they entered the Dancing Frog's taproom and spotted each other in the light of the guttering torches. Alaric commandeered a small, rickety table off in one corner while Dietz ordered two ales from the barman and carried them over. They each drank half their tankard's contents in a single gulp, and both started talking at once.

'I found a–'

'I think that–'

'It looks like–'

'I just saw–'

They both laughed. Finally Dietz said. 'Right, go ahead.'

Alaric related the events of the day, from reporting to Struber to his visit to Rolf's former shop and the disquieting conversation he'd had with the stonemason's son and his widow. He talked as quietly as he could and still have Dietz hear him over the noise of the other patrons. Fortunately the other men were more intent on drinking, singing and fighting than eavesdropping, but he still thought it best to exercise some caution.

'It's supposed to have been destroyed,' he pointed out to Dietz, 'the statue. It was taken away instead.'

'Taken away?'

Alaric nodded and pulled out the receipt, squinting to read it by the dim light from the torch mounted on the wall above them. 'By Wilfen von Glaucht, the same man who commissioned them.' He leaned forward. 'And this is convenient, he claimed it the morning after Rolf's arrest. The same morning we spent locked in that miserable jail cell.' He smiled, though the expression was more determined than pleased.

'He knew we were going,' Dietz pointed out, tapping the receipt. 'And knew exactly where and when, and took advantage of our imprisonment to hide the last statue somewhere safe.'

'Exactly.' Alaric banged his hand flat on the table, causing their ale mugs to jump. 'Sorry, but that means whoever it was knew our plans.'

Dietz's mind slid back to another man they had known, a short, slight man with narrow features and a deft quill; a man who would never ride with them or scold them or cook for them again.

'Renke was killed by a knife in the back,' he reminded Alaric, which sobered them both immediately. 'Who's to say it is not the same man?'

'It could be,' Alaric agreed. He stroked his chin. 'Each of our companions arrived here that night or the next morning. Their respective superiors sent them to keep an eye on us. That means their superiors had either been in the courtroom or had heard the results. How much else did they hear? Were they really all sent, or did someone claim that to blend in with everyone else? If he knew we had found the first statue, and had moved it to safety, he might want to keep an eye on us and hopefully prevent us from destroying the other three. Plus it gave this one a chance to receive sacrifices, and power.'

Dietz pushed that image away. 'So one of our friends, the same ones who mourned Renke not long ago, may be not only Renke's killer but the statues' creator?'

'Could be.'

That was when Dietz told the story of his own recent encounter. He was also careful to pitch his voice so only Alaric could hear him. 'Fastred was definitely acting suspicious,' he finished. 'I wonder why. What could he be doing that's so secretive he needs to sneak into it rather than marching in openly? What could be in that house that's worth making such a dangerous trek so late at night?'

'Something the witch hunters would kill for,' Alaric replied, thinking. Finally he drained his ale cup and stood. 'I think we should pay a visit to this house you found. Let's ask Fastred, or whoever answers the door, what they are doing up so very late, especially when there's a military curfew.'

'You think he'll answer?' Dietz asked, standing as well and lengthening his stride to keep up with Alaric, who had navigated past several other patrons and was already at the inn's front door.

'He might,' Alaric answered. 'He might feel it's too late for anyone to stop him. Or he might have an overwhelming urge to tell someone, anyone, what he's done.' He grinned at Dietz. 'Much as you said to me some time back – I'd wind up lecturing about anything before too long, just because I hate the quiet.'

'He'd be a fool to admit to anything,' Dietz said quietly, quiet enough that only he and Alaric heard it, 'but that doesn't mean he won't.'

THE STREET WAS silent and empty when Dietz finally led Alaric to the correct row – houses, he'd discovered on the way here, look a lot more alike in the dark, but at last they were standing across from the door Fastred had entered.

'That's it,' he confirmed. 'I remember this stone on this building here, the one shaped like a foot.' They both glanced up at the house beside them, at the footprint-like stone nestled among the other stones of the wall. 'I watched from here as he walked up – crept up, more like – and knocked. Then the door opened and he stepped inside.'

'Shall we?' Alaric asked with a bow, and once again Dietz followed his employer as they crossed the street and walked right up to the battered wooden door.

Alaric raised his hand to knock, but Dietz caught it before his knuckles made contact with the wood. 'Listen,' he hissed, and they both froze.

Someone inside the house was awake. Not just awake, but shouting. They heard arguing, though they could not make out the words through the heavy stone and thick wood.

'Trouble among thieves?' Alaric suggested lightly, one hand coming to rest on his rapier hilt. Dietz nodded, drawing a long knife with one hand while the other tugged open his jacket. Glouste took the hint and leaped inside.

'What now?' Dietz asked his employer after his pet was safely stowed. 'Fetch the city guards? Summon the witch hunters?'

Alaric frowned. 'The guard will take too long,' he pointed out, 'and the witch hunters will arrest us along with whoever's within. Besides, we've no certainty one or both are not involved already. No, let's confront whoever's inside ourselves and see what we shall see. We can send for help later if necessary.' He tried the door, but shook his head. 'Locked.' Then he stepped aside and gestured towards it with a mocking bow. 'Will you do the honours?'

Dietz growled at him and stepped forward, knife in hand. The door was solid and the lock secure, but his brothers had taught him many tricks over the years and entering without a key had been one of them. Inserting the knife's tip into the keyhole, Dietz felt around, feeling the tumblers pressing against his blade. When he was sure the knife was in position he jiggled it slightly, feeling as much as hearing the faint click of the tumblers falling into place. Withdrawing the knife he turned the knob and pushed gently. Despite its battered exterior the door was well-oiled and it slid open without a sound, revealing a short entryway with a polished stone floor and handsome candle sconces on either side.

The voices had not stopped, and with the door open Dietz and Alaric could hear them clearly. They listened as they picked their way past the swaying door and into the polished entryway, towards another door that stood partly ajar.

'–won't let you do this!'

'You can't stop me!'

'Oh, I can and I will!'

'How? Run to the guards? Summon Kleiber? They'll turn on you as well!'

'I don't care. As long as you're done for that's enough!'

Dietz wanted to wait and listen, but Alaric charged forwards as usual, shoving the door wide and drawing his rapier as he strode into a room.

'Hello,' he called out merrily. 'Is it a party?'

Dietz, glancing over his friend's shoulder, froze, the knife still in his hand. The door had opened onto a large room whose stone walls had been panelled in polished wood, creating a cosy space around the fire that burned merrily in the large fireplace against the side wall. Several large, comfortable-looking chairs sat here and there, though from their positions he guessed they'd been arrayed around the fire and had since been shoved aside to create the empty space near the centre of the room. He spied a crystal decanter and several glasses on a writing desk off to one side. All in all it was a handsome room and far nicer than the exterior had suggested.

Fastred stood in the room, his hood thrown back. Kristoff was there as well, and the lack of a cloak, cape or jacket suggested that this was his residence. Both men stared at them for an instant, and then returned to glaring at one another across the room.

'Let's talk about this,' Dietz urged quietly, stepping around Alaric and sheathing his knife as he did so. He held both hands up, palms out, to show he was unarmed. 'We can discuss it.'

All the while he was careful to stay back behind the furthest chair, well beyond the reach of his two friends, and, more importantly, beyond the range of the swords they were pointing at one another.

CHAPTER FOURTEEN

'HE'S THE ONE!' Fastred shouted, keeping his eyes on Kristoff and his short sword – once Renke's short sword – raised. 'He commissioned those statues!'

'It's not true!' Kristoff protested, glancing at Dietz and Alaric for an instant before returning his focus to the man and blade before him. 'I wouldn't do something like that! You know I wouldn't!'

'Liar!' Fastred shouted, swinging wildly. Kristoff blocked the attack easily and lashed out in return, causing the larger man to leap back out of the way.

'Hey!' Dietz said. 'Let's put the swords down, all right?' Neither man appeared inclined to listen, however.

'Fastred,' Alaric said calmly. 'Dietz tells me he followed you here earlier. What were you doing here?' His rapier was still drawn, though now he had his sword arm draped casually over a chair, the blade dangling idly from his hand.

'I came to see Kristoff,' Fastred said, frowning, his sword point wavering slightly. 'I knew he was up to something and I begged him to stop whatever it was. He wouldn't listen.'

'Lies,' Kristoff countered, his own sword still weaving like a drunken man, drawing Fastred's eyes. 'He came here to threaten me!'

'Why would he threaten you?' Alaric asked, and Dietz had to admire his calm. He sounded as if they were sitting and discussing something over dinner, not watching two of their friends face each other over drawn blades.

'He's the one behind all this,' Kristoff replied. 'He used me to arrange transportation for the statues. I had no idea what they were, of course, but he had certain… information on me. I couldn't refuse. When we returned I told him I'd have no part in it any more, not now I knew the statues' true purpose. He threatened me, said he'd kill me if I said anything.'

'That's not true!' Fastred yelled, sword shaking with his anger. 'He's twisting everything. I didn't use him – he used me!'

'Who hired the wagons?' Alaric asked softly, watching both men.

'I did,' Kristoff admitted. 'I have access to all the necessary documents through my employers. That's why Fastred wanted – demanded – my help.'

The explorer shook his head. 'I didn't need anything because I didn't do anything!' He jabbed his blade at Kristoff. 'He came to me, asking for aid in selecting locations. Said his employers wanted to establish trading posts at the corners of the Empire. Asked for suggestions, spots on the map, both the actual compass points and the nearest accessible areas.'

'Then you knew where we were going?' Dietz asked, earning a surprised look followed by an approving nod from Alaric. 'When we were searching the Howling Hills, when we were combing the riverbank, you knew where the statues were?'

Fastred shook his head again. 'No. Not precisely, anyway. I knew we were going to the Hills, and roughly which part of them we'd need. I knew the second one would be near the river and roughly centred in von Drasche's lands. I didn't know anything beyond that. I wasn't the one who made the actual travel plans. I just pointed out some areas on the map.' His face was red and dripped with sweat as he glanced at Alaric. 'I didn't know what he wanted, Alaric! You have to believe me! Dietz, you believe me, don't you? I thought it was just for trade routes! I never would have helped him if I'd known about the statues!'

'He told me where to send them,' Kristoff argued, glaring at the larger man. 'He told me where to get the statues and where to take them, but nothing about what they were or what they could do. When I asked he said I didn't need to know.' He looked embarrassed. 'I couldn't argue. He'd have destroyed my career, my reputation, everything. I couldn't risk it.'

'More lies!' Fastred attacked again, just as wildly as before, and Kristoff blocked again. He didn't counterattack, however. Alaric and Dietz looked on, both wanting to stop the fight, but both realising that to intervene physically would only put them in danger as well.

'So you ordered the wagons,' Alaric said to Kristoff. 'You both agree upon that, but who commissioned the statues themselves?'

'He did!' both men shouted, pointing their swords at one another.

'Of course,' Alaric agreed, 'and we can't ask Rolf to describe his client any more, can we? That was a clever move on someone's part.' His face hardened. 'And all it cost was the life of an innocent man.'

'I didn't even know the stone carver!' Fastred called out, wiping sweat from his forehead. 'I never met him!'

'I'd never heard the name Rolf until just now,' Kristoff claimed. 'I deal with merchants and traders, not craftsmen.'

'One of you knew him,' Dietz said softly, 'hired him, and killed him.'

'I didn't kill anyone,' Fastred said almost in a whimper, 'but he did!' he jabbed his sword at Kristoff. 'He killed Renke!'

'I? I didn't kill him,' Kristoff replied, shouting. 'You did!' He glanced at Alaric. 'During the fight with the baron,' he explained, his sword steady even while he looked away from his opponent. 'I saw it – he moved behind Renke, drew his dagger, and–' he trailed off, apparently unable to continue.

'I was nowhere near Renke during that fight,' Fastred bellowed. 'You were alone with him before that, while we were destroying the statue. You stabbed him then. What had he learned?' he sneered. 'Had he figured out your plans and threatened to expose you?'

'The two of you had been talking a great deal up until then,' Kristoff snapped back. 'He must have found out about your crazed schemes and denounced you. You killed him before he could tell anyone!'

Alaric had gone silent, his eyes no longer seeing the scene before him, and Dietz knew his mind was elsewhere. His employer was remembering the conversation he'd had with Renke right before the battle. Renke had wanted to speak with him privately. The little geographer had looked awful, pale and sweating, but Alaric had thought it was concern about the baron. What if he had already been stabbed at that point and his appearance had been caused by pain and blood loss?

'One of you is a killer,' Dietz confirmed, eyeing them both, 'but both of you were involved in this somehow. I say we summon the city guard, or perhaps the witch hunters, and let them sort this out. I'm sure Kleiber could find out the truth quickly enough.'

'That ham-handed fanatic!' Kristoff snarled. 'I wouldn't trust him to find his own boots in the morning! He's a witch hunter – they're not interested in truth or justice, just blood and death. He'd try us all for heresy, you two as well, and tighten the ropes himself at the gallows.'

'Aye, he might,' Fastred replied. 'Not that you don't deserve it, but that wouldn't solve anything.' He glanced at Alaric again. 'There must be some way to prove my innocence.' Seeing Dietz's glare, he amended his statement. 'To prove I was not the one who commissioned those hideous statues.'

Alaric started to reply, but Dietz beat him to it.

'There is one thing,' he said, and all three men stared at him.

'There is?' Kristoff asked, parroted by both Fastred and Alaric.

'Oh yes,' Dietz said, shooting his employer a glance. Fortunately they had travelled together for over a year, and Alaric had learned to read many of Dietz's subtle cues.

'Oh, that,' he replied, nodding wisely. 'Yes, we could use that, I suppose. I'd hoped to avoid it, but I see there's no other way.'

'None,' Dietz agreed. 'At least we'll know for certain.'

'Yes, of course,' Alaric said, but whatever he'd meant to say after that was cut off. Kristoff said something to Fastred, too softly for them to hear, and Fastred snarled a curse in reply. Then blades clashed and the time for talk was past as the two men circled, each seeking an opening for his sword.

Dietz looked at Alaric, who shrugged. There was nothing they could do now other than watch and wait.

Fastred had a clear advantage in height, weight, and possibly strength, and he used it eagerly, lashing out with strong blows and dancing back from Kristoff's parries. Kristoff, on the other hand, was considerably faster than his opponent. He also used a longsword while Fastred had a short sword, the weapons' size difference reducing Fastred's height advantage.

The two men paced and charged and back-pedalled, blades weaving about. Fastred lunged again, his blade narrowly missing Kristoff's arm and scraping along his side instead. Then Fastred overextended and had to slash downward, blocking what could have been a disembowelling blow if it had landed. Kristoff swivelled his sword out of the block and looped around, slicing down and across, and leaving a bloody trail across Fastred's chest.

'What can we do?' Dietz asked Alaric softly as they watched, but his employer only shrugged.

'There's nothing we can do,' he said finally. 'We wait for them to finish, one way or another.'

The end did not take that long. Kristoff swept his blade across, but the blow was surprisingly clumsy and slow. Fastred laughed, his short sword descending to block the blow and then arcing up again to pierce the trader's chest or stomach. Then suddenly Kristoff's sword spun in his hand and reversed course as if Fastred's own blade had caused his return. The longsword slashed across and back again, and suddenly Fastred's blade was falling to the floor. The big man staggered, hands moving to his chest as blood fountained forth, and Kristoff stepped back, his own sword tip tapping the floor.

'Damn!' Alaric dropped his rapier at once and leaped past the assembled chairs. He was too slow to catch Fastred, but by the time the explorer's head reached the floor Alaric was there to cradle it and to check his wounds. 'Fastred!'

The portly traveller peered up at him, his face chalk-white. 'I'm… sorry… Alaric,' he whispered, blood already bubbling up with each breath. 'Tell… Waldemar… to start class… without me.'

The big man's eyes glazed over, a rattling cough emerged from his slackening lips, and he shuddered and went limp.

'Damn!' Alaric said again, still bent over Fastred's body. 'He's gone.'

So wrapped up in mourning his friend, Alaric never even saw the longsword that flashed towards his neck – or the heavy candlestick that slammed into it, knocking the blade aside. Turning at the sound of metal upon metal, Alaric stared up at Kristoff behind him, the trader's lips pulled back in a rictus of either hate or fear. His sword was down at his side, still vibrating from the force of the blow, and glancing around Alaric saw Dietz beyond, climbing over the nearest chair.

'It was you,' Dietz snarled as he tried to reach his friend and their treacherous former companion.

'Yes,' Kristoff admitted, grinning at them both even as he backed away. 'It was me. That bloated fool,' he gestured towards Fastred, 'had it right all along!' Now that the pretence was gone, the trader seemed delighted to take credit for his villainy. 'I commissioned the statues. I hired the wagons. I blackmailed Albers into helping me select locations. I killed Renke.'

'Why?' Dietz demanded, now past the chair and standing between Alaric and Kristoff. 'Why kill Renke?'

The trader laughed. 'He found out, that pathetic little fool! He realised I'd deliberately caused a scene with the gypsies, hoping they would kill us.'

'You wanted to die?' Alaric asked, laying Fastred's head gently on the ground and rising to his feet.

Kristoff shrugged. 'Death has no fear for me,' he replied proudly. 'My master will raise me again in his service, and with our deaths the statues would have remained safe.' He shrugged. 'But you talked your way out yet again, and Renke noticed my frustration. He figured out my real motives and I couldn't let him tell you. So I stabbed him while the rest of you were off playing hero, just as Albers claimed.'

'Why are you telling us all this?' Dietz demanded, keeping himself in front of his employer. This was no time for Alaric's famous tendency to leap in blindly. 'We will tell Kleiber everything and he will bring the witch hunters down upon you.'

Kristoff laughed. 'Do you think I fear those arrogant, power-mad fanatics? They do my bidding without even knowing it!' He smiled a cold, unpleasant smile. 'Besides, you may tell Kleiber anything you like. It will do you no good.'

'Why, because he won't believe us?' Alaric asked.

'Because I won't be here for him to accuse,' Kristoff replied. He lashed out with his sword, causing Dietz to step back and shove Alaric behind him. The blow never landed – Kristoff pulled his blade back even as it darted forward, and then turned. 'K'ra'tick will be exalted! The Blood God will claim this land!' he shouted. His free hand grasped the arm of the nearest chair and he heaved it at them, striking Dietz in the chest and knocking him back. He slammed into Alaric, whose feet became tangled in Fastred's cloak on the floor, and they collapsed in a heap, the chair sliding down to partially pin Dietz's legs. Kristoff was running from the room before Dietz's feet had left the ground.

'GET OFF ME!'

'I am trying,' Dietz snapped. 'Stop wriggling!'

'I'm wriggling because you're crushing me,' Alaric gasped, 'and because I'm lying on a dead man.'

'Just sit still a moment,' Dietz said sharply. He groped about him with both hands, feeling fabric and wood. Finally his fingers found a corner, and he traced that to another corner with his other hand. Gripping both corners firmly, he shoved up and forward and the chair flew off him, striking the table beyond and sending crystal and wine to the floor. Dietz didn't waste any time mourning the loss of good liquor, however. As soon as the chair's weight was off him he levered himself to his feet and turned to give Alaric a hand up as well.

'Thanks.' Alaric brushed himself off, grimacing at the dark stains on his back and side where he had brushed against Fastred's corpse.

'Are you all right?' Dietz asked him, retrieving his knife and, after a moment's thought, the short sword that had been first Renke's and then Fastred's. When Alaric nodded he turned and glanced around the room. 'Where did he go?'

'Not out the front,' Alaric replied, looking as well. 'We'd have seen that.' The room had two other doors, one on either side. The one to the right stood slightly ajar. 'That way.'

Dietz collected Alaric's rapier from where he'd dropped it and handed it over. Then, sword in hand, Alaric pushed the door open and stepped beyond.

It had to be the dining room, they both realised at once. The room was smaller than the one where Fastred's body lay, but equally sumptuous. The walls were handsomely panelled and another fireplace filled the far wall, though this one was cold and dark. A long table of polished wood dominated the room, high-backed chairs arrayed around it, and a handsomely carved sideboard occupied one wall, several decanters sitting atop its polished surface. Another door stood in the opposite wall and they skirted the table to reach it.

'Kitchen,' Dietz said when they entered, and Alaric nodded. The fireplace was larger and wider, with spits for roasting meat and hooks for heating kettles and pots. A table against the far wall held knives, forks and platters, while a wide basin beside it was for washing and preparing food. This room had only one other door, a smaller one of unpolished wood fitted more loosely together, and they could feel a cool draft from between the boards even as they hauled it open. Beyond the door was a narrow staircase leading down.

Thinking privately that, despite everything else, he envied Kristoff his house, Dietz led the way down the stairs. The basement was a single large room with crates and barrels strewn about, and sacks and small casks piled off to the sides. Salted meat hung from hooks above and various household implements hung from the walls or leaned against them. Torches sat in black iron sconces nailed to the wall in several spots, and one of them had been lit, providing a dim, guttering light. The floor was straw and earth strewn over rough stone, and the room had no other entrance. Nor was there any sign of Kristoff.

'He can't have vanished,' Alaric protested, spinning about and squinting to see better. 'Did he go the other way instead?'

Dietz shook his head. 'That door was closed tight,' he pointed out, 'and we'd have heard him open it. He came this way.'

'Where is he, then?' Alaric demanded, gesturing around them. 'Hiding in one of these barrels? Perhaps curled up inside a flour sack? Maybe he's hanging from the ceiling, playing at being salted pork!' When Dietz stared at him he shook his head. 'Sorry, I'm sorry,' he muttered. 'It's just – I'm–' he stared at his own bloodstained hands. 'Fastred is dead, Dietz. Kristoff killed him. All those weeks and months we travelled with them, they were both our friends. Now one's dead and the other's a heretic.'

Dietz sighed. 'I know. I hate it too. I wish none of this had happened, but it did, and now we have to finish it. We cannot let Kristoff get away. We owe Fastred that, and Renke.'

Alaric rubbed his cleaner hand across his face. 'You're right. We have to find him. So where is he?'

They looked around the room again, but could barely see their own feet, let alone any signs of the missing trader. Dietz grabbed the torch from the wall, waving it around to help. It did brighten the space right around him, but it darkened the rest of the room as a result.

'Here, light this one,' Alaric suggested, grabbing a second torch from its wall sconce. 'Then we can – Taal's teeth!' That last part came out as a yelp as he leaped backward. When he had removed the second torch its wall sconce had swivelled down. A click had echoed through the basement, much like the sound Dietz had gotten from the front door, but louder. Then a stack of crates shifted towards them.

Dietz's first thought was that Kristoff was in the crates after all and was attacking them. Then he realised the crates had stopped moving. Beside them, where they had rested a moment before, was a hole in the floor – a large, rectangular hole.

'The tunnels,' he muttered, more to himself than to Alaric. 'Of course. Where else could he hide a statue that size without it being noticed?'

Alaric was glaring at the hole with distaste and even a little fear. 'Does this mean we have to go down there?' he asked plaintively.

CHAPTER FIFTEEN

'How can you stand this?' Alaric asked. They had lowered themselves through the hole and were now walking as quickly as they dared through a narrow tunnel carved from the black rock on which the city had been built.

The tunnels; Dietz had heard stories about them all his life and had even ventured into them once or twice, usually as a dare from other kids. Middenheim had been carved atop a single spire of black granite, but some said the rock had already been riddled with holes, created by some unknown race that had dwelt there before and fled at the coming of men. Others said the city's founders had created these passages as a way to move through the city undetected and as an escape route if the city was ever taken. No one knew for certain.

Dietz had never heard of a map of the tunnels, though he had heard men claiming to know their way through the narrow, winding passages. Most of those men had been drunk at the time and probably bragging about nothing, but a few might have had some truth to their claims. The

city's sewers ran through here, and someone had to clean
them out from time to time – it was not a pleasant job, but
it was a necessary one, just like being a rat catcher. Such
men would know their way around, at least through their
portion of these catacombs. He doubted anyone knew the
entire system, however.

It had been years since he had been down here, but the
tunnels had not changed. They were still narrow, still tight,
and still rough, but far too smooth to be completely natural. The passage they were in now, the one they had
found upon using Kristoff's bolthole, had an almost flat
floor and ceiling with almost vertical walls, all carved from
the same glossy black rock of the mountain. The walls
reflected his torchlight back as a dim glow, and flecks
within the stone glittered like eyes. Dietz had to hunch
over and keep his arms close to avoid catching on the
rough walls, but it was Alaric who looked pale and kept
starting at every sound.

'Stand what?' Dietz replied, holding the torch carefully
before them. He wasn't thrilled about bringing an open
flame down here – too many stories about strange gases
and liquids underground, and people catching fire by
breathing them or stepping in them – but they had little
choice. Even with the torch they could barely see twenty
paces, and the water sloshing around his boots was nothing but a single dark, roiling plane. It was probably better
that way. One man had claimed that if you stared at the
walls of the tunnels for too long you began to see faces in
them, faces of people who had died long ago – faces that
moved and spoke to you and called you to join them. He
thought the man had been deranged, but was not interested in discovering he had been right.

'This!' Alaric gestured around them. He had sheathed his
rapier and had only a dagger in his hand, which he
clutched tightly. He winced when the tip scraped against a
wall. 'Being surrounded by so much rock. We're beneath
the city! This tunnel could collapse any second, and we'd
be crushed. There's no way to escape!'

'These tunnels have been here longer than we've been alive,' Dietz pointed out. 'They were here when the city began. They haven't collapsed yet.'

'But they could. They may have been getting weaker all this time!' Alaric was sounding dangerously close to panic.

Dietz shrugged. 'Why worry about it?'

'I can't help it,' the younger man admitted. 'It weighs upon me – I can feel it pressing down.'

Dietz glanced back at him. 'You explore ruins for a living,' he pointed out.

'Yes, but I have you to crawl through them for me.'

Dietz started to respond to that and decided against it. 'What did Kristoff say before?'

'When?'

'Right before he threw the chair at us. He said something.'

'Oh, that.' Alaric thought about it. 'He said, "K'ra'tick will be exalted! The Blood God will claim this land!"'

'Right. What does it mean?'

Alaric shrugged, though his friend wasn't looking back and missed the gesture. 'He's a Chaos cultist, obviously. Khorne is their god – chaos and war and bloodshed. The Blood God is one of his titles, as is the Lord of Skulls.' He frowned, forgetting the walls and the tons of rock for a moment. 'The other part – K'ra-tick – I don't recognize. From what he said I'd guess it was his cult, or the creature they worship. The name must be in the foul language of the Dark Gods.'

'The followers of Chaos have their own language?' Dietz asked.

His friend nodded. Yes, they do. Its real name is undoubtedly much longer and unbelievably complicated...' His eyes unfocussed as he pondered the problem. 'K'ra-tick... Hm. "K'ra" would be "meat" – no, that's "h'n'eyir" – something like meat. The initial K means "aged" I think–' his voice trailed off, but Dietz was not listening anyway. He was glad Alaric had found something to distract from his fear, but it wasn't something that interested Dietz himself. He knew Alaric would tell him if he figured out the name's meaning. In the meantime Dietz concentrated on the tunnel ahead of them. Already he had encountered two branchings and had simply chosen the leftmost path each time. He suspected Alaric hadn't noticed at all. He wished he'd thought to bring along chalk to mark their route, but then he hadn't been expecting to go exploring this evening.

They walked on for several more minutes, Dietz selecting the left path every time he had a choice, and Alaric mumbling occasionally about linguistic intricacies. The only sounds were the drip of water, the splash of their feet, the occasional scrape of Alaric's dagger or Dietz's elbow against the wall, and the hiss of the torch. They'd seen no sign of Kristoff, and the farther they went the less likely it became that they would find him. Dietz figured the trader knew these tunnels well enough to navigate them in the dark – he was probably miles away by now.

'I've got it!' Alaric said at last, his raised voice echoing around them and vanishing down both of the branches Dietz saw before them. 'The K does mean "aged" but in the sense of "aged past its prime". In this case, it would mean rotted. "K'ra" means, "Rotted flesh!"'

'It means "carrion," actually.'

'Yes, well, carrion is rotted flesh, isn't it?' Alaric replied testily, and then glanced up. The voice had not belonged to Dietz.

Suddenly, from tunnels off to the side that Dietz had missed in the dim light, several figures emerged. They rapidly surrounded the two travellers and Dietz noticed they had no torches, but held nasty looking short swords, axes, hammers and clubs. They looked like men, though he had a hard time seeing detail, and they all wore long robes of a red-brown cloth, the colour of dried blood. They all had hoods, but the one nearest Alaric pushed his back to reveal a young face fringed with black hair and dominated by blue eyes lit with the gleam of a fanatic.

'K'ra-tick means "the Hounds of Carrion,"' the black-haired youth supplied, 'or "Carrion Beasts".'

'I would have gotten that,' Alaric snapped, and only then seemed to notice that they were surrounded and outnumbered. 'Thanks.'

'Certainly,' the cultist bowed mockingly. 'One should always know one's killers.'

'Why kill us?' Dietz asked, shifting the torch in his grip. He'd never have time to draw a knife, but he could thrust the torch at someone's face. Perhaps their robes were flammable. As if reading his thoughts one of the cultists reached out and tugged the torch from his hand, grinning at his obvious disappointment.

'Why not?' the first cultist replied, shrugging. Then he grinned. 'We've been ordered to, actually. Our high priest set us upon you.'

'Kristoff?' Alaric asked, and the youth nodded. 'He wants us dead? Why? We're no threat to him, not lost down here.'

'Your blood will feed the Lord of Skulls,' the cultist explained. 'He will reward us for this offering when the gates are opened.'

'The gates? You mean the statues?' Alaric actually looked more relaxed now than he had upon entering the tunnels, though Dietz knew it was a pose. His friend was tense, but hid it well. His casual attitude and barrage of questions were confusing the cultists, who had no doubt expected pleas, cries, and a quick kill. He doubted Alaric had a plan beyond delaying the inevitable, but that was fine. The longer they avoided combat the longer they had to think of something… anything.

'The others are gone, you know,' Alaric was explaining to the youth, who seemed to be the cultists' leader. 'We destroyed them. Kristoff was there.'

'Destroyed? No!' One of the other cultists wailed, but the youth seemed unfazed.

'He did not mention that,' he admitted, 'but he was rushed.' He shrugged. 'It matters not. The four together formed a powerful ward that amplified every sacrifice, but each statue is a complete gate, and we have fed the one here, regularly.' He grinned. 'Soon, very soon, the gate will open and the Blood God's champion will emerge. Then we will be exalted above all, placed at our master's side to rule this ravaged world!' His eyes grew even wilder as he ranted, and flecks of spittle appeared at his mouth. The grin he gave Alaric was little more than the wide, hungry look of a rabid dog. 'Perhaps your deaths will be the final sacrifice,' he whispered gleefully. 'Your blood will tear open the veil and allow him entrance!'

'I like my blood where it is, thank you,' Alaric replied, though he did back away slightly. The youth noticed, and his grin widened. The other cultists began closing in, weapons raised, and Dietz abandoned all thoughts of escape. His only hope was to knock out a cultist, take his weapon, and fight his way clear. Perhaps he could run for help, or at least lose himself in the tunnels, though he suspected these cultists knew the passages by heart.

His planning was interrupted by a strange sound. It came down one of the forward passages, a grunting, groaning, slobbering noise. The sound of feet splashing through muck accompanied it, and both were growing louder. It did not sound like cultists and Dietz hoped it would at least provide a necessary distraction. Perhaps it was an animal that had slipped into the sewers and survived upon the rats and other vermin that infested the underground?

Dietz's hopes sank as the sounds grew closer and their source came into view. It stood as tall as him and slightly wider, and at first he thought it was a man. Then he noticed its arms, which were rubbery like an octopus's and tapered to dull points instead of bearing hands. It wore only rags, and even in this light he could see strange sores covering its skin, which had a dull sheen. Its eyes were bright yellow, however, and almost perfectly round, with strange slit pupils.

Mutant. It was a mutant, one of the poor human-born monsters rumoured to appear in Middenheim from time to time. More had been born over the past two decades, which some said had been the first warning of Chaos's renewed efforts. Many killed such deformed infants, but others, whether from shame or from some twisted mercy, dropped them through the sewer grates instead. Dietz had heard stories of mutants forming enclaves in the tunnels, establishing their own twisted society beneath the city that had spurned them, but he had thought them just tales to frighten children into staying clear of the sewer grates. Now he knew better, as he watched a second and then a third figure appear behind the first, and several more shuffling into sight behind them.

'Amazing!' Alaric, as usual, forgot their immediate danger and stared, fascinated, as the mutants approached. 'Sub-surface dwellers! And clearly mutated! Did you know about this?' The look he shot Dietz was almost laughable, the expression of a little boy just discovering he'd been denied a treat.

'I'd heard of them,' Dietz admitted to him, trying not to panic as the mutants shambled closer. The cultists were now glancing around, clearly debating whether to run or fight, and who to target if they stayed. At least these creatures were a distraction, Dietz thought. Yet he couldn't help but feel their own situation had worsened with the monsters' arrival.

'Can they talk?' Alaric asked eagerly, and even the cult leader stared at him.

'I don't know,' Dietz said softly. 'I never met one before.'

The mutants were within arm's reach of the cultists, forming an outer layer along the side, and several of the Chaos followers looked less than thrilled. Dietz almost laughed at that – here were living embodiments of Chaos! The cultists should be thrilled to encounter them. Perhaps they should be worshipping the mutants, who clearly had a closer tie to Chaos than any normal human and thus could act as an intermediary.

While he was enjoying the cultists' discomfort, Alaric stepped forward, past the cult leader and towards the tentacled mutant. 'Hello,' he said, keeping both hands at his sides. 'Can you understand me?'

The creature nodded slowly, swaying as if it wanted to respond, and for the first time Dietz realised its mouth was tiny and beaked, not like a bird, but like the squid he had seen in markets once or twice. It might be able to understand Alaric's words, but it could not respond in kind.

'These are your tunnels?' Alaric asked, but the mutant uttered a strange whistling sound. 'Do you live here?' Alaric tried again. Still the mutant replied only in whistles and clicks. 'You... live... here?' Alaric asked a second time, this time using hand gestures to indicate the mutant, include the area, and make a strange clasping motion that somehow suggested belonging. This time the mutant nodded.

'Ah, good,' Alaric said softly, more to himself than anyone else. 'A combination of Reikspiel and gestures, then. Simple, really – just keep it basic.' He turned back to the mutants.

What was he thinking, Dietz wondered? He felt like cursing, but kept himself quiet and still, avoiding anything that might draw attention from either the cultists or the mutants. Still, he was amazed. He had known Alaric to be easily distracted, easily excited and easily enthralled – much like any child, but even he would not have believed his friend was capable of this. Here they were, surrounded by bloodthirsty cultists determined to use them as sacrifices, facing mutants who might intend exactly the same thing, and Alaric was completely focusing on how to talk to the creatures! Dietz felt his hands clench into fists despite himself, and wondered how the others would react if he started beating up Alaric himself. Just as he thought this, however, his friend glanced over at him – and smiled.

He's up to something, Dietz realised. Alaric was smart, extremely smart, and he was definitely up to something – that smile had been his 'watch this next bit' expression rather than his 'isn't this fun?' look. Suddenly Dietz felt worlds better. Whatever he had planned, Alaric was only pretending to be a fool. Dietz had to trust him, and he'd have to be ready for whatever occurred next.

'These… people,' Alaric was gesturing to the cultists now, talking slowly so the mutant would understand. 'Live… here.' His hands indicated the tunnels again.

The mutant responded with clicks and what sounded almost like short barks. The other creatures behind him stirred as well. Dietz could see one that had an impossibly wide mouth and skin scaled like a fish, and another with eyes ringed around his forehead, and arms and legs with too many joints, and a third covered in thick fur whose arms were so long its clawed hands brushed the water. All of them were watching Alaric or the tentacled mutant, and judging by the strange groans and clacks and muted roars none of them were happy.

'Their… tunnels,' Alaric continued, gesturing to the cultists and then the tunnel, and using that strange clasping motion again. The mutants' barks grew louder and more agitated. 'Not… yours.' He pointed at the mutants, slashing his hand in negation, and the creature hooted, its tentacles lashing about.

'Hey!' the cultist leader had been watching, as fascinated by this exchange as everyone else, and only now seemed to realise what Alaric had said. 'Stop that!'

'Why?' Alaric glanced over at the youth. 'It's true, isn't it? This is your home? You control these tunnels?' Unnoticed by the cultist, he was still making hand gestures as he talked, and Dietz was amazed to realise his employer was carrying on two conversations at once.

'Well, yes,' the youth was caught by his own bravado. Then common sense intruded. 'But don't get them riled.'

'What will you do if they get upset?' Alaric asked him, his hands indicating the cultists and making punching motions. 'Kill them?' He mimed hacking someone to pieces. 'Burn them out?' He gestured towards the torch Dietz had brought down, still held by the cultist near him. 'Destroy them?' He made another negation gesture and then swept his hands to encompass all the mutants massed before them.

The mutants, who had been following Alaric's nonverbal comments, went berserk.

'Wha–?' Before the cult leader could react the first mutant had grabbed him with its tentacled arms. It shuddered and raised the youth high above its head, and he gasped in pain and surprise as his flesh tore against the rough ceiling. Then the mutant's limbs tightened, crushing the air from him, and spasmed, sending him crashing into the far wall. Dietz heard a clear snap as the youth hit rock, and he watched the body slide to the ground, and all but disappear beneath the standing water. The youth did not move again.

Nor had the other mutants been idle. They had charged past their leader, ignoring Alaric and snatching up cultists left and right. Dietz, staying motionless, watched the ape-like mutant tear the torch-bearing cultist to shreds, flesh and blood spattering them both. The eye-browed one lashed out with its arms and speared a cultist with barbs on the back of its hands. The fish-scaled one leaped forward and, stretching that impossibly mouth wide open, revealed row upon row of tiny triangular teeth, took a cultist's entire head between its jaws. Dietz turned away, but not soon enough to avoid hearing a chomping sound and a muffled shriek, and seeing, just for an instant, the mutant moving away from the headless body toppling to the ground.

After the initial shock, the cultists reacted, shouting and cursing, and raising their weapons to fight off the creatures. The tunnel was suddenly filled with the sounds of battle: the dull thud of metal, stone and wood striking flesh and bone, the shouts and grunts and sobs of people trying to kill, and of people being killed, the stomach-churning squirt of blood spraying from an open wound, and the dull crack of bones breaking. The cultist next to Dietz had dropped the torch, which had fizzled as it struck and sank beneath the water. Without that light Dietz found he could make out only dim shapes churning about him, the cultists faint hazes of bloody brown and the mutants lighter and darker patches that moved in strange ways. He held himself as still as possible and prayed that Morr was too distracted by the carnage to notice him in its midst.

That was when Alaric gestured to Dietz, just a little nod and then a head toss to the side, and began backing away. Dietz followed his lead, moving slowly, step by step, barely breathing as almost-seen figures clawed and bit, and leaped and struck all around him. He paused at one point, ears and skin registering something large just past him, and felt water splashing his feet as something man-sized struck the ground just beyond his toes. Whatever it was did not get up, and after a moment he took another step back, then another, easing away until it was just another faint impression in the darkness.

'Stop.' Alaric's voice was close by and Dietz felt a hand against his back. He stopped and set his right foot, which had risen to retreat another step, back on the ground.

'Can you see anything?' he whispered.

'A little,' his friend replied. 'I was further from the light than you were. Close your eyes a second and let them adjust.'

Though he hated the idea of standing on the edge of a battle with his eyes shut, Dietz hated the idea of stumbling around blind even more. He did as Alaric instructed, and a moment later opened his eyes to discover that he could make out his surroundings, though everything was still dim.

The cultists were still battling the mutants, though there were fewer brown robes than before. The creatures clearly had the upper hand. Alaric had angled to the left as he'd retreated, and Dietz found they were now standing in front of another tunnel, one of the two from which the cultists had ambushed them.

'I don't think we should wait to see who wins,' Alaric pointed out, backing up again until he was in the new tunnel and could no longer see the fight. Dietz agreed wholeheartedly and followed him, waiting until they were a good twenty paces away before turning around and walking more quickly from the fading sounds of carnage.

'Carrion Hounds,' he muttered as he followed Alaric, who seemed to have forgotten his fear of being underground. 'Well, the name certainly fits now.'

CHAPTER SIXTEEN

THEY WALKED FOR what felt like hours, their eyes adjusting enough to the darkness so that they could make out the tunnel walls. Some light did filter down from various grates here and there, the dim light of the moon and stars providing at least some illumination. In other places the tunnels' walls were coated with a strange ooze that glowed faintly. Some sort of fungus, Alaric decided, and would have taken a sample if Dietz had not stopped him, pointing out that the substance could be poisonous. Between the two light sources, they found they could manoeuvre without too much stumbling into things. More than once they detoured around large, still shapes that rose from the standing water, unsure whether they were rocks or refuse, or corpses, and unwilling to find out. Water dripped down on them, slicking their hair and fouling their clothes – at least, most of it was water.

'This is disgusting,' Alaric offered after a particularly thick, smelly glop of something struck his shoulder, leaving a dark splotch and a wet trail down his back. 'I'll never be clean again.'

'It's just water and refuse,' Dietz commented, though not without a shudder at the thought of how much offal was now caked into his hair and clothes. 'City waste.'

'How is trudging through this helping us?' Alaric asked, wiping at his shoulder and doing little more than smearing the filth about. 'Why are we still down here?'

Twice they had passed rungs hammered into the rock walls, the first time finding them only when Dietz skinned his elbow against one. The rungs rose to the ceiling, where thin beams of light marked a grating overhead. These were the sewer entrances, set so that workers could clean them if necessary. They had considered leaving each time they'd found more rungs, but had decided against it.

'We still need to find Kristoff,' Dietz reminded his employer, 'and quickly.'

'And wandering lost down here is helping with that?' Alaric retorted. 'We don't even know where he is! Taal's teeth, I'm not even sure where we are!'

'Below the crafters,' Dietz replied. He pointed towards a tunnel ahead. 'That leads to Canal Street, where we found that livery.'

'How can you be sure?'

Dietz shrugged. 'The first set of rungs. They led up near the marketplace. I know my way from there.'

'Oh.' Alaric brightened. 'If we know where we are, then, we can find any place else in Middenheim, correct?' Dietz nodded. 'Then we just need to determine where Kristoff would go and find our way there.' He frowned. 'Where would he take that statue?'

'Someplace he could feed it,' Dietz said, still intent upon their path. 'The cultists said they fed it regularly.'

'So some place they could bring victims?' Alaric asked, but shook his head immediately. 'No, that makes no sense. Why drag victims down here and then kill them? It'd be far quicker to kill them above and just bring the blood down in buckets.'

They passed below another drip of something and a drizzle struck Dietz's cheek. He wiped it away quickly before his nose could register the smell. Then he paused and turned back towards his friend.

'Why carry it at all?' he asked. He gestured towards the walls around them and the small holes near the top. 'Those are drainpipes,' he pointed out. 'They carry the waste down here.'

'So all they'd need is a place that has a lot of blood,' Alaric finished, catching on immediately, 'and they could feed the statue with no effort and without anyone noticing! Brilliant!' He looked around. 'Where would you go in Middenheim to find a lot of blood?'

Dietz thought about it. 'The hospital,' he said finally. 'Marketplace, maybe, but it might be spread too thin there, Morr's central chamber.' He shuddered a little, as if mentioning the place of death might invoke its patron god. 'The witch hunters' headquarters – that's always awash in blood.'

Alaric frowned. 'But they haven't been killing people there lately, have they?' he asked, trying to remember what Rolf's widow had said. 'They've been performing public executions instead; in great numbers.'

'The execution square, then.' Dietz nodded, glancing around. 'This way.' He led them off to the right, down another tunnel, which branched off into three more corridors. At each branching Dietz stopped to glance around and mentally compare their location to the city above, and then led them on. After some time they rounded a corner and saw a light flickering up ahead.

'The execution square is right above that,' Dietz confirmed, gesturing towards the glow.

'And the statue will be there as well,' Alaric agreed. He straightened and made one last futile attempt to clean his clothes, face, and hair, before finally giving up with a grimace. 'Well, let's not keep Kristoff waiting, shall we?' And he strode towards the light.

THE TUNNEL EMPTIED into a larger chamber, one of the few they had seen underground. Several more tunnels branched off from the other sides, but the chamber itself was the size of a large room, almost as big as the cavern beneath the Black Fire Pass. This chamber was much smoother, however, its walls chiselled and its ceiling domed, and the floor had been cleared of protrusions as well. Fortunately several large, rough columns had been carved on either side of the tunnel entrance. Alaric and Dietz quickly moved to one side and pressed themselves into the shadows of a column, hoping it would be enough to conceal them. From their new vantage they studied their surroundings more carefully.

Torches hung in sconces mounted around the space and in their light Alaric and Dietz could see several figures swaying around the centre of the room. The figures all wore the red-brown robes of the Carrion Hounds. Before them stood Kristoff, his own robe offset by scarlet gloves and a matching cape, and his hood thrown back. Just beyond him sat the statue.

Alaric glanced at the statue and then quickly looked away, shuddering. Each of the hideous carvings had repulsed him, but this one was worse than the others had been, far worse than it had been in Rolf's shop. A reddish sheen coated it and he knew it was blood dripping from the large circular grating directly above it.

This statue had indeed been fed regularly. It looked bloated, if stone could manage that feat, and he realised with a jolt that it was in fact larger than he remembered. As if it had swelled from its offerings. The stone possessed an odd lustre, resembling well-polished old brass, and its edges seemed softer, almost hazy. The details were sharper and more hidden – harder to make out right away, but then suddenly a tentacle or claw would spring into focus. The entire statue throbbed, stabbing at his eyes even after he had averted them, and it was not the torchlight creating that impression. The statue was beating, expanding and contracting like a massive misshapen heart.

'It's almost open,' he whispered, realising the truth even as he said it. 'The sacrifices are opening the gate.' He turned to Dietz and grabbed his arm. 'We have to stop it!'

Dietz nodded and pointed towards the grating. 'Almost dawn,' he said. Alaric followed his gesture and saw that the grating was providing a faint rosy light of its own, heralding the moment when night would give way and the sun would reveal itself once more. 'Executions are at dawn.'

'They're waiting,' Alaric said, glancing at the cultists who all stood and swayed, but did not otherwise move. 'Waiting for the witch hunters to kill their latest victims and for the blood to pour down. It will open the gate!'

'Not if we shatter that thing first,' Dietz said grimly. He drew his knives and strode forward, forcing Alaric to follow.

The cultists were so wrapped in ecstatic worship they did not notice the pair approaching. Dietz reached one of them, a middle-aged man standing at the rear of the group, and quickly yanked the man back, one arm wrapping around the cultist's throat. His other arm jerked across, slicing his knife along the man's throat, and then he hurled the spasming cultist aside to lie bleeding upon the ground. It was only then Alaric realised the stone floor was bone dry, unlike the slimy water-coated floors of the various tunnels. He also noticed a slight slope. This room had been carved so the refuse that fell through the ceiling grate would strike the centre of the floor and then spill down on every side, eventually washing into the tunnels beyond.

Then one of the cultists had turned, hearing his brother's choking gasps, and saw Alaric.

'Intruders!' the man shouted, raising his short sword. Alaric had his dagger still in hand and stabbed the man in the stomach, pulling the sword from his grasp and shoving him to one side just in time to block an axe from another cultist.

'Kill them!' Kristoff shrieked, raising both arms high. 'Kill them, my Carrion Hounds! Offer their blood to the

Lord of Skulls and he will praise your devotion! Give their bodily fluids that we might open the gate and usher forth his champion!'

All the cultists turned towards them and Alaric realised that the group they'd encountered before had only been half of the whole, perhaps less. Nor did they have any mutants to aid them this time. He slashed with his stolen short sword, cursing the weapon's short reach and awkward weight, but nonetheless carving a long gash into a man charging him with a club. Even before the man stumbled back two more had taken his place, and Alaric quickly forgot all sense as he slashed and blocked, and kicked.

'Kristoff!' he shouted, trying to distract both the cult leader and his followers. 'Is this the best you can do, sending your minions against us? Afraid to face us yourself?' he taunted. 'What would Khorne say about that?'

For an instant, everyone fell silent, shocked at such casual blasphemy. Then Kristoff tilted back his head and howled in rage, more like a beast than a man.

'Release him!' he shouted, pointing at Alaric, and the cultists around him fell back. Unfortunately that left more of them to swarm Dietz, who all but disappeared beneath a barrage of arms, fists, clubs, and blades. 'Do not kill him!' Kristoff added, this time gesturing towards Dietz, and the cultists obediently stepped back, raising their weapons, several of them hauling a bleeding, stunned Dietz back to his feet. His knives were knocked from his hands and his arms secured on either side. 'Let him watch as his friend dies,' Kristoff commanded, 'and as the Blood God steps forth to destroy this city!'

'Impressive,' Alaric commented, turning towards Kristoff and advancing a step, but only one step, which forced the cult leader to take several towards him instead. 'You command them well, Kristoff. Like well-trained dogs, they are. I suppose that suits you.'

The trader smiled, a far less pleasant expression than the one he had worn so often on their travels. 'The Carrion Hounds are loyal,' he replied. 'They know I serve the Lord of Skulls, as do they. Together we will summon forth his champion to rend this city from within. Then the Empire will fall around us, feeding our master with its demise!'

'Interesting notion,' Alaric replied, taking another small step and watching as Kristoff took two more in return. That's it, he thought, away from the statue. He wasn't sure how that would help prevent it from receiving the blood from above, but at least the cult leader would not be able to aid the process. 'Yet you helped us destroy the other three statues. Why?' Out of the corner of his eye he saw several cultists stiffen and remembered what the youth in the tunnels had said. Kristoff had not told them about the statues' destruction, or his part in it.

Kristoff only grimaced at him and took another step, his hand going to the sword at his side. 'I knew you would accomplish your mission,' he replied. 'There was no way to stop you altogether. I delayed you as much as possible, though.' Alaric suddenly remembered how Kristoff had often been the voice of caution, even of negativity, pointing out ways they might fail and things to worry about. 'And with every delay the statues received more blood and the gates came closer to opening.'

'You had moved this one before we even left,' Alaric stated more than asked, though the cult leader nodded anyway, 'before even meeting us.' Another nod and another step forward. Only ten feet separated them now and Alaric knew he could not stall much longer. 'This was always the one you wanted open.'

'I wanted them all open,' Kristoff corrected, grinning, 'but this was the most important one, yes. It was the key, both to summoning the Blood God's champion and to atoning for our previous failure.' His face showed that the last comment had slipped out unintended, and Alaric pounced upon it.

'Failure? What happened?' he asked, taking a small step back as the cult leader took several forward. 'You tried this once before?'

Kristoff eyed him carefully, clearly weighing how much to reveal, and then shrugged. 'Aye, during the siege,' he admitted finally. 'We hoped to summon the Blood God through battle, through our own sacrifices and the blood of our enemies. His champion would come forth and slaughter all the city's defenders, and then lay waste its walls.'

'Not enough blood?' Alaric asked. 'You and your friends not as skilled as you'd thought?' He gestured towards the other cultists, who still held Dietz captive off to one side, watching the exchange.

'Them?' Kristoff's face twisted into a snarl. 'They are nothing, replacements only, filling in the space my true brethren left behind!' If he heard the gasps from his followers he paid them no heed. 'We were warriors, my brothers and I! The Warmongers' elite! We slaughtered men by the dozens, the hundreds!' His eyes blazed. 'Many of my brethren are called hero now, for their deeds upon the battlefield!'

'Yet you failed,' Alaric reminded him, pleased to see the trader losing control, 'and where are they now?'

'Dead!' Kristoff howled at him. 'All dead, all but myself and one other! Too many of them, even for us – the swarms overwhelmed us! We could not kill enough to open the gate!' He drew a great, shuddering breath and for a moment Alaric thought the trader would charge at him. Much to his disappointment, Kristoff took several more rapid breaths, and then several deep ones, visibly forcing himself to remain calm. 'But I survived,' he admitted, and there was an odd mixture of shame and pride in his voice. 'I kept the cult from being discovered. My brethren were treated as fallen heroes and buried with all honours, their souls laughing at the irony. We rebuilt the cult, brought in new members, and continued with our ultimate goal.' He grinned, in full control of himself again. 'And I realised the truth. We did not need to perform the kills ourselves. Any deaths would do. The gates require blood, blood spilled by violence, but they care not about the source.' He took another step towards Alaric, who realised that he was almost to the wall behind him. 'As long as the statues were dedicated to the Blood God every drop of blood that struck them became an offering,' the trader said, clearly pleased with his own cleverness. 'And now,' he added, grinning, 'now your blood will join the rest.' He yanked his sword from its sheath, his grin showing that he knew Alaric had nowhere to run.

'We'll see about that,' Alaric replied finally. He raised the short sword, and then studied it with distaste. Finally he threw it aside. 'Shoddy blade, that,' he commented, enjoying the look of surprise on Kristoff's face. 'No balance, poor edge – really, you should be providing better.' He drew his rapier instead, holding it out so the point was aimed at the trader's right eye and the blade caught the light. 'This is far more to my liking.'

'Use any weapon you like,' Kristoff told him, lips drawing back in a snarl. 'I'll still spill your blood and take your life! For Khorne!'

He leaped forward, his wave-edged longsword slashing through the air, its razor-sharp edge aimed at Alaric's throat.

CHAPTER SEVENTEEN

Dietz struggled against his captors, twisting this way and that, trying to pull free of their grasp. It was no use – a man on either side had hold of him and several more hemmed him in so his every motion tangled him in their robes. He had to get free! He had to help Alaric!

He watched, horrified, as Alaric and Kristoff moved towards one another, and gasped despite himself as the trader lunged forward, the wicked-looking longsword slashing towards Alaric. His concern drew nasty chuckles from several of the cultists, who leaned eagerly forward, excited by the sight of their leader's vicious attack against the bedraggled, weak-looking noble before him.

Their laughter turned to outcries and groans, and even gasps as Alaric's rapier danced up and across, blocking Kristoff's sweeping attack. A quick twist of his wrist and Alaric had spun the trader's sword in a short circle, forcing it away from him and almost removing it from Kristoff's grasp.

'Oh, surely you can do better than that?' Alaric asked in his best 'arrogant nobleman' voice, and received a howl of rage in return. Even from where he stood, Dietz could see the gleam of rage in Kristoff's eyes as he leaped in again, his blade flashing in the dim light.

Only to have his attack blocked a second time, and a third.

With a growing respect that bordered upon awe Dietz watched the fight unfolding before him. He knew that Alaric had received weapons training and had even seen his employer fight. He had known that Alaric could handle himself. Those had been battles with ruffians or soldiers, beastmen or orcs, however, several on each of them at once. Now, for the first time, he saw Alaric in a proper duel, and he finally understood his employer's true skill with the blade.

After the first few foiled attacks Kristoff forced himself to calm down, and his attacks became less wild, more studied. The two men moved back and forth, advancing and retreating with each blow, and the clang of their blades filled the chamber, creating a series of overlapping echoes that threatened to deafen them all. Kristoff was shorter but broader, with thick arms and chest, and his technique put that strength to good use. His attacks were powerful, intended to cave in the opposition, and his longsword flicked back and forth, its strange waved edge throwing odd glints of light that could easily confuse and distract a lesser foe.

Fortunately Alaric was hardly lesser. Though thinner than Kristoff he was also taller and used his added reach to stay well clear of most attacks. He held his rapier loosely but firmly, and could pivot the blade in an instant. Every attack was met with a quick parry, the weight of Kristoff's sword against the hilt of the rapier where it was strongest. Alaric's ripostes and attacks were lightning-fast: mere flicks of the wrist, and small tears appeared in the trader's robes, matched by tiny cuts along his arms, hands, and even face. That, along with the mocking smile Alaric wore, threatened to overwhelm the cult leader's self-control and send him into a mad frenzy…

...Which was exactly what Alaric wanteds, Dietz realised. He wanted Kristoff to lose control and charge him.

Why wait, though, he wondered? Alaric was clearly the better swordsman – not one of Kristoff's attacks had landed and the trader was bleeding from half a dozen small wounds already. Alaric could finish him easily. He probably could have done so with that first attack, when Kristoff had left himself wide open. Why was he drawing this out?

Alaric glanced towards Dietz. Their eyes met for just an instant, and then Alaric's gaze dipped towards Dietz's chest. Then the young noble was all focus once more as Kristoff attacked him yet again, this time with a clever feint that almost got past Alaric's guard.

My chest, Dietz thought. His employer was telling him something, but what? What about my chest? His arms were still held tightly, but he shifted, twisting his torso, trying to figure out what the glance had meant. Then something moved within his jacket and he understood. Glouste! He had tucked the tree-fox inside when they had entered the tunnels, what felt like hours ago, and his pet had curled up and gone to sleep in her warm little nest. In all the confusion he had completely forgotten about her. Now she stirred slightly, awakened by his movements, and began to poke her head out of his jacket.

'Stay,' Dietz whispered to her, meeting her bright-eyed gaze. 'Stay, Glouste. Wait. Be ready.' She twitched her whiskers at him, and then retreated so only the tip of her nose was visible. A quick glance around assured Dietz that none of the cultists had noticed. They were too busy watching the fight.

I have a weapon, Dietz thought, his eyes still following the back-and-forth of longsword and rapier. I may be able to break free, but what then? And when?

Even as he watched, Dietz heard muttering around him. Several of the cultists whispered together off to one side, and then slid away from him. They skirted the chamber, moving quietly along the wall towards the duel – three of them, each holding a short, heavy club.

They're going to attack Alaric, Dietz realised. They're tired of watching and worried that Kristoff might lose, so they're going to even the odds. He started to shout a warning, but just then Alaric, who had just tagged Kristoff again along the cheek, disengaged for an instant and looked right at him. He knows, Dietz realised suddenly as his friend and employer resumed the duel. It's what he's been waiting for.

Ten cultists had been here when Dietz and Alaric arrived, not counting Kristoff. Four had died during their initial attack. Three had just moved to flank Alaric. That left only three on Dietz – one holding each arm and another in front of him. Alaric had been slowing his duel until the cultists came for him, knowing it was the only way Dietz would have a chance to break free.

Dietz wanted to shout anyway, to tell Alaric not to sacrifice himself like this, but he couldn't. He understood. This wasn't just about Dietz – Alaric was no more eager to meet Morr than he was and knew they had both understood and accepted the risks when they entered the tunnels, but they had the statue to consider. One of them had to live long enough to destroy it and dawn was upon them now. Any moment the witch hunters would give the order and men would die above, their blood sluicing down the gutters and through the grating overhead. If the statue was there to receive that offering, the gate would open and Chaos itself would pour forth beneath the unsuspecting city. They could not allow that to happen. Alaric thought Dietz would stand a better chance of stopping that, apparently, and Dietz knew he had to respect that decision.

The three cultists were only a little way from Alaric, and judging from his stance the young nobleman knew it. So did Kristoff, whose desperation had shifted back to confidence at the sight of his followers.

'Glouste,' Dietz called softly, and the nose protruding from his jacket twitched in reply. 'Attack when I give the word. Understood?' The nose bobbed slightly in what he thought was affirmation, though he could never be sure how much she really comprehended. Then he glanced back up at the duel.

'You die now!' the trader snarled, advancing again, his sword held high.

'Not by your hand,' Alaric replied, laughing. 'Or will you ask Khorne to handle it for you?'

As planned, the insult and the casual use of his god's true name goaded Kristoff into action and he stepped forward, longsword slashing across and down, its point twitching suddenly to one side in an attempt to dart past Alaric's defences.

For an instant it looked as if the ploy had succeeded. The longsword was met by Alaric's rapier, catching it full on, and then Kristoff shifted his weight and his sword angled inward, gliding along Alaric's as its point thrust at his chest.

Alaric altered his stance in response, his elbow lifting and pointing his own sword downward, knocking Kristoff's longsword back away from him. Alaric leaned in, his forearm striking the trader's sword at its guard and shoving it farther out of the way, and then Alaric leaned back, arm cocked back as well, and jabbed forward suddenly. The rapier pulled back across Kristoff's body, leaving a neat cut across his robes. It suddenly moved forward and its tip pierced the trader's chest, half the sword's length following it into his body.

With a gasp and a gurgle, Kristoff collapsed, pulling his body off the sword as he fell.

'No!' One of the cultists next to Alaric shouted in disbelief as he saw his leader fall, and he stepped forward, weapon raised. One of his companions moved as well, and two clubs fell upon Alaric's head and shoulders, striking bone and flesh with a meaty thunk. Without a sound Alaric crumpled to the ground, the rapier falling from limp fingers.

'Now!' Dietz hissed to Glouste. 'Attack!' His pet darted forwards, out of his jacket in an instant. As he'd hoped she made for the nearest target, the cultist to his right, and her sharp teeth lanced into the hand on his right arm.

'Aargh!' The cultist screamed and jerked back, colliding with the one beyond, clutching his torn hand.

'Get off!' Dietz snarled at the remaining cultist, twisting and grabbing the man's hand with his now-freed right hand. He squeezed, feeling the cultist's bones grinding together, and yanked the man in front of him. A quick kick struck the first cultist in the groin, doubling him over, and another took the second cultist in the head as he struggled to regain his feet, felling him for a second time. The three around Alaric were too far away to interfere, torn between beating up Alaric, aiding Kristoff, and running to apprehend Dietz. He was free, at least for the moment. Even as he realised that, however, Dietz heard a pattering sound and knew it was almost too late. The executions were done and the blood was starting to pour down.

'You failed,' the cultist in his grasp said, his face still twisted in pain, but bearing a mocking smile nonetheless. 'When the blood strikes the statue the gate will open and the Blood God's champion will step forth!'

Dietz thought quickly. He was too far from the statue to reach it in time. He had no weapons except the ones the cultists had dropped, Glouste – and the man trapped in his grip. He grinned back and was pleased to see the doubt and fear blossom in the other man's face. 'Not yet,' he said, and his other hand grabbed the man's waist while his right hand shifted from hand to shoulder. He bent as his hands moved, shifting his feet to get better leverage. Then, with a grunt, Dietz straightened, lifted the stunned cultist from his feet – and hurled him across the room.

It was not as prodigious a toss as the tentacled mutant had managed back in the tunnels, but Dietz was tall and his muscles had been hardened by years of labour. He also had fear and rage on his side, powering his desperate attempt. The cultist flew backward, sailing across the floor – and struck the statue full-force.

'Oof!' The man's shoulders and back collided with the heavy stone carving, doing him only a little damage and knocking the wind from him, but the impact rocked the statue on its base, unsettling it where it rested on the uneven stone floor. It teetered, causing Dietz's heart to skip – and then it fell.

Wham! The statue slammed to the ground, causing a small cloud of dust and tiny rock fragments. Cracks spider-webbed its surface, visible through the bloody coating, but it remained intact. It was no longer directly beneath the grating, however.

And just in time, as blood began to spill down from above, so much that it formed a thin curtain across the centre of the room. Droplets sprayed everywhere, some striking Dietz where he stood, others hitting Alaric as he lay upon the ground. Most of them, however, flowed straight down, pooling in the room's centre where the statue had been instants before, drenching the cultist, and all but drowning him–

–and then flowing down from that high point, a thin layer of blood creeping across the floor in every direction.

'No!' Even as Dietz watched, some of the blood touched the statue where it lay – and was sucked into the stone. A strange light appeared within the statue, a blood-red glow that soon filled the room and dwarfed the torches and the sunlight visible above. The glow rose, breaking free of its carved prison, compressing and elongating until it towered above the statue, and where it touched the carving the stone seemed to melt. The air around the glow shimmered, and everything in the chamber seemed to shudder and swell, and shrink, as if the light itself was causing the room to alter.

Then the glow deepened, turning darker. The light shifted to darkness, shadows roiling across it, and the mere sight of that swirling caused Dietz's stomach to heave and his eyes to burn. He tried to look away, but could not. Neither could anyone else. Everyone in the room stared, barely breathing, as the shadowy disk widened, its colours dimming until it resembled blood and ash, and blackened sludge all teeming about one another in mid-air.

Then, through that strange swirling mass, a shape advanced. A limb pierced the curtain: a great scaled foot settling onto the stone floor, its claws digging into the rock.

The gate was open. Khorne's champion, a daemon of Chaos, was loosed upon Middenheim, and the world.

CHAPTER EIGHTEEN

'Aaah!'

The cultist Dietz had thrown had rolled over onto his hands and knees, and shaken the blood from his face. Unfortunately that meant he saw the daemon standing before him. His scream was high, almost girlish, and quickly faded away, leaving nothing but an odd tittering sound to issue from his slack lips. The cultist's eyes were wide but unfocused and blood dripped from his ears and nostrils as he turned in a circle, around and around, never stopping, still tittering. The sight had driven him mad.

Alaric, lifting his head as he struggled to regain his senses, could hardly blame the man. He could feel his own sanity fighting to break free, desperate to run screaming from the sight before him. The daemon had most of its leg through, and a hand emerged as well – if he could call it a hand. It perched at the end of what must be an arm and it had several of what could be fingers, but surely fingers did not writhe like maddened snakes, wriggling every which way? Surely fingers did not pulsate, widening and thinning along their length? Nor did they have barbs at the end, which widened into circular teeth-filled apertures that could only be called mouths? Nothing had hands like that, at least, nothing from this world.

Think rationally, Alaric told himself desperately, levering himself up on one arm and then getting one knee beneath him as well. Keep your mind focused on the small details. Do not let it overwhelm you.

The skin... that was something. He concentrated on the skin, what he could see of it. It was scaled, but not like a snake or a fish. More like – well, more like a shingled roof, each scale overlapping the one before it and protruding above it a bit. Except that these scales were sharp and curved outward, creating little hooks all up and down the creature's limbs. And the colour! His mind tried to rebel again, but he forced it back. That colour was like nothing he had ever seen, like nothing in this world. It was dark and his mind screamed red, but his eyes claimed black or perhaps green or sometimes brown. When he tried to name the colour he could think only of death and blood, and war and pain. That was the colour it bore.

One of the cultists behind him had collapsed, foaming at the mouth, at the creature's appearance, and as he reclaimed his rapier and stood, Alaric saw the one by the statue spinning in circles. For some reason the sight helped calm him. Is this what you expected, he wanted to ask them? Is this what you hoped for? You summoned this creature. Are you displeased with the results?

At least one cultist was not disappointed. 'My lord,' Kristoff moaned, clutching his chest, but still struggling to sit up. Alaric cursed – apparently his aim had been off. It was a good job his father and old Mardric were not here to see that. 'We welcome you in the name of Khorne! We salute you! We praise your strength and rejoice in your aid!'

'Oh shut up,' Alaric told him, kicking idly at Kristoff as he walked past him to approach the creature. It was still emerging from the strange dark-lit disk, moving as slowly as a large man manoeuvring his way through a tight doorway. The rest of the arm was visible now, up to the barbed shoulder and the strange overlapping plates across the shoulder and upper chest. Its lower chest was covered in thick hairs or perhaps they were tentacles since they waved about wildly, but at least it was not armoured. If the creature possessed vital organs then some of them would be in the hairy abdomen, Alaric hoped. Not letting himself think about what he was doing he stepped forward and lunged, his blade sliding between several of the squirming hairs and sinking deep into the daemon's flesh.

It shuddered, and then made a strange deep gasping sound, wet and raspy, that stabbed at Alaric's head. The sound came again and again, and Alaric felt his own blood run cold as he realised the creature was laughing at him. He had stabbed it, delivering what would have been a mortal blow for any man, and it laughed.

The hand swooped in, faster than Alaric could clearly see, and grasped his rapier a foot below the guard, just before the point where it entered the body. The hand turned suddenly, a sharp motion, and his sword snapped, leaving him holding a hilt with a foot of jagged metal above it. The other portion disappeared within the creature, sucked in as if the daemon was made of brackish black water and the sword tip had been tossed in from above.

'Yes!' Behind him Kristoff had managed to regain his feet and tottered forward, swaying, face still pale from blood loss. 'Display your strength, great one! Teach this unbeliever the folly of opposing you! With your power this city will fall and the Lord of Skulls will feast upon the blood we provide! He will know us as his favoured servants and – *urk!*'

Kristoff stopped suddenly, his words choked off as the daemon's hand lashed out for a second time, this time catching him by the throat. It lifted, raising him so his feet dangled above the ground, and then those wriggling fingers tightened. The trader-turned-cult leader gasped for

breath, his face going purple, both hands beating use-
lessly at those monstrous fingers. Then something long
and thick and sinuous – a tail? A tentacle? Alaric forced
his mind back to smaller details – whipped through the
portal and wrapped around Kristoff's waist. It tugged
down while the hand yanked up and as Alaric looked
away hastily the trader's head was torn from his body.
Blood fountained from his neck and the tentacle disappeared back through the portal, taking the body with it.
Alaric heard a loud throaty noise, punctuated by gulps,
and realised that the daemon was drinking Kristoff's
blood. The trader's head had fallen to the floor and rolled
up against the nearest wall, its eyes still wide with surprise. Perhaps, thought Alaric, this was not what he had
expected either.

The remaining cultists were certainly not thrilled at the
daemon's response to Kristoff's greeting. They fled, screaming and crying, and pleading for their lives, leaving only
Alaric and Dietz behind to watch as the daemon continued its advance. The tentacle had returned and part of
what would be considered a hip had emerged as well.

'What can we do?' Dietz shouted, running over to Alaric,
and for an instant Alaric wanted to hug the older man.
Dietz's face was pale, his eyes wide and he had been muttering something as he rushed over, but his voice was level
and his movements normal. He was keeping his sanity
tightly leashed as well.

'I don't know,' Alaric admitted, still unable to look away
from the horrid sight of the daemon's emergence. 'I
stabbed it–'

'I saw,' Dietz confirmed. 'Weapons won't work.'

'No they won't,' Alaric agreed, 'and we couldn't fight it
anyway. Look at the size of it! You saw what it did to
Kristoff.' He shuddered at the recent memory. Much as
Kristoff had deserved to die for his crimes no one deserved
that. 'It's too powerful for us,' he finished softly.

'We could get help,' Dietz pointed out, but Alaric shook
his head.

'No time,' he said. 'We'd have to navigate the tunnels again and then make our way back to the surface. Then we'd have to find someone who would believe us. Kleiber might, but by the time we found him and convinced him, and he marshalled some troops the daemon would have completed his entrance. Once he's fully in this world he'll be invincible.'

'Then we can't let him enter,' Dietz argued. Alaric started to laugh, and then stopped.

'It shouldn't take this long,' he said, not realising he had said it out loud until Dietz responded beside him.

'What, you'd hoped it would be faster?' He laughed, a short, bitter sound that was a relief from the madness nonetheless, and Alaric managed a weak chuckle in return.

'No, of course not,' he replied, 'but the process should have been much quicker. The gate opens and the daemon steps through. Why is it inching through one piece at a time?'

The daemon was now almost halfway through – the tentacle was revealed as sprouting from its shoulder just below the neck, and one powerful, bat-like wing had edged through as well, fluttering as if eager to take flight.

Dietz pointed to the statue where it lay on the floor. 'It fell over,' he said. 'Did that alter the gate?'

Alaric frowned as he thought about everything he'd learned about Chaos back in school and added in what he had deduced recently about the statues and their function. 'It shouldn't have,' he said finally. 'Not just laying it down. The portal would still open normally.' He studied the statue instead. Even with its strangely deformed edges and its partially melted base it was reassuringly solid and normal compared to the daemon it had summoned.

'It's the blood,' he decided after a moment. 'It only received blood along one side.' He gestured towards the statue and the markings they could now see carved upon it – the ones on the side against the floor were glowing with the same dark light as the portal itself. 'The portal is only partially open,' he told Dietz. 'That's why the daemon has to enter so slowly.'

'What if we smash it?' asked Dietz, reaching down to pick up a club that one of the cultists had dropped. He indicated the cracks across the statue's side. 'It's damaged already.'

'That might be slowing the process as well,' Alaric admitted. He thought about it and nodded. 'Yes, breaking the statue might close the gate, but we'll have to act quickly, before the daemon can stop us.' He frowned, glancing around. 'It would be best if we had a distraction.' Then his gaze fell upon the cultist still turning in circles. 'Right, leave that part to me.'

'What will you–?' Dietz started to ask, but Alaric pushed him away.

'No time,' he admonished, gripping his shattered rapier. 'Get ready!'

Dietz nodded and moved, walking quickly but quietly around the room to approach the far side of the statue. His lips were moving again and Alaric, catching the words 'Sigmar protect,' realised his friend was praying. Well, he'd never known Dietz to be religious, but this was certainly a good time to start. Perhaps that was how he'd held onto his sanity despite the daemon's presence. Alaric whispered a quick prayer to Sigmar himself, deciding it couldn't hurt. Then he waited until Dietz was halfway across, and strode forward, ruined blade in hand.

'Here, piggy, piggy,' he whispered to the cultist as he approached. This would be easier, he'd decided, if he thought of the creature before him as a pig rather than a human. Not that the cultist was able to understand what was about to happen.

Reaching the cultist, Alaric glanced up and then away again quickly. The daemon's head was starting to emerge from the portal, and even the brief glimpse he'd received had been enough to send his mind scurrying away in a panic. Think about something else, Alaric urged himself, anything else. He held his rapier desperately before him and studied its truncated length. Forged in the mountains, he told himself, by the dwarf smiths. It was my sixteenth birthday present from my father. 'You're a man now,' he'd said. 'You'll need a man's weapon.' Thinking about the blade and its history and the many times he'd used it, Alaric took another step. He was right beside the spinning cultist. Then in one swift motion he reached down, grabbed the cultist's hair near the front, and lifted. His other hand lashed out and the edge of his shortened rapier slid across the deranged man's throat, sending a spray of blood before him.

The cultist gasped, gurgling and choking on his own blood, as Alaric dropped his rapier and hauled the dying man up by the shoulders. 'Here, take him!' he shouted to the daemon, eyes tightly closed, and shoved the bleeding man forward. He felt a swoosh and knew the creature's tail or tentacle, or hand had darted forward to seize the cultist. Alaric himself stumbled back, crouching to present less of a target, eyes squinting open as he heard the same gulping sounds as before with Kristoff. The daemon had accepted the offering.

'Now,' Alaric whispered, but he needn't have bothered. Dietz had already crept forward and, with the daemon distracted, he raised his club and brought it down hard on the statue. The heavy wood struck with a loud thud and the cracks widened, sending flakes and chips of stone everywhere. Dietz struck again in the same spot and now a large rent appeared across the body, and another smaller gap above one shoulder.

The daemon had tossed aside the drained cultist and now it turned, seeking the source of the noise. Its eyes fixed upon Dietz, who refused to look up and struck the statue a third time. The daemon shrieked, realising what he intended, and struggled to pull itself the rest of the way through the portal, even as its tentacle flailed towards Dietz.

'Over here!' Alaric shouted, leaping out into the centre of the room and waving his arms. The daemon paused and then its head swivelled on its impossibly long neck, those glowing, glittering rows of eyes turned towards Alaric instead.

'That's right,' Alaric said loudly, keeping his gaze fixed on the daemon's broad chest instead and studying the pulsating red object erupting forth as if the creature's heart had burst through its skin. 'I am the one you want.' He tried to sound brave and tough, but his voice wavered. I have to keep going, he reminded himself, hearing another dull impact as Dietz struck the statue a fourth time. I have to give him enough time to break the statue and close the gate.

'I closed the other gates,' he called out. 'I shattered the other statues and stopped you from crossing.' The daemon roared, whether in rage or recognition or something else he did not know, but it was still fixated on him. He had to dance back several steps as that strange hand reached forward, the fingers snapping and biting only a foot from his face.

'I stabbed your high priest,' he continued, neglecting to point out that the daemon itself had been responsible for Kristoff's death. It did not seem to care much, however, and so he tried again. 'I defy you and your god!' he shouted, almost looking into those stacked eyes and stopping himself just in time. He knew somehow that if he met the daemon's gaze he would never look away again. It roared again, this time definitely in rage, and he forced himself to go on. 'I defy Khorne!'

That shattered the daemon's self-control and it lunged forward as best it could, a hand, a tentacle and a barbed tail all struggling to reach him. The creature's second wing was still trapped on the other side of the portal and caught as it thrashed, holding it back mere inches from its goal. Alaric, for his part, stood frozen, unable to move now that he had finally succeeded in earning the daemon's rage.

Fortunately Dietz had not been idle all this time. He had struck the statue again and again with his borrowed club, each time widening the cracks and loosing small shards. Finally, as the daemon twisted to free its second wing, he slammed the club down again and was rewarded with a deep splintering sound.

'Rrraargh!' If it was a word it was in no language Alaric had ever heard, but the rage and frustration was clear enough, and startled Alaric enough that he glanced up without thinking. His eyes locked with those of the daemon, sinking into its burning gaze, and he felt his mind being stripped away by layers. His feet moved without his control, first one stepping forward and then the other as he marched slowly but surely towards his own doom.

The daemon had little time to spare him. It whirled about, seeking Dietz and the statue, but far too late. Even as its hand whipped towards him the statue shattered at last, falling into several chunks upon the floor. Instantly the portal began to fade, its whorling darkness slowing and dimming.

The daemon screamed again, shrieking its denial. Its hand lashed out at Dietz, knocking him away from the statue, but already the damage was done. Its tentacles lashed out, not towards Dietz, but at Alaric, determined to claim at least one of the foes that had foiled it. But even as the tentacle's barbed tip flashed past his neck the daemon began to withdraw, its body sucked back into the narrowing disk.

'K'red'lach!' it wailed at Alaric and then it was gone, pulled back into its home dimension. The disk vanished, leaving a stink of burning flesh and spoiled milk. The torches, which had burned unnoticed on the wall, gave off ample light now that the dark-emanating disk had disappeared, and the flow of blood had stopped, leaving the grating to spill warm sunlight onto the floor below. The room was empty once more, save for Alaric and Dietz, and several bodies.

'Done?' Dietz asked, hauling himself back up from where the daemon had sent him sprawling and eyeing the rubble that had been the last statue.

'Done,' Alaric agreed, rubbing a weal on his neck absently. His mind still shuddered from the memory of the daemon's gaze and its final cry, but he forced it away, locking onto mundane details instead.

'We'll have to report this, of course,' he said, earning a groan from his friend. 'Someone will have to be told.'

'Who's going to believe it?' Dietz asked, dusting himself off and walking slowly over to his friend, skirting a fallen cultist along the way.

'Oh, they'll believe it,' Alaric replied, his gaze landing on something that lay off to one side. 'We'll bring them proof.' Reaching down he hefted Kristoff's head, raising it to show Dietz.

'I think they'll want to talk to him,' he said.

CHAPTER NINETEEN

'THAT WAS CERTAINLY interesting,' Alaric said, plucking a stray hair from his cloak.

'Humph,' was all Dietz said in reply.

They were descending the broad steps of the palace, the same steps they had been escorted up several months before. This time, however, they were alone, and leaving not as prisoners or even suspects, but as honoured citizens and favoured guests.

It had taken several days to straighten out matters to everyone's satisfaction. Dietz was not entirely satisfied, in fact – he felt there were still a few loose ends to consider. In particular he remembered Kristoff talking about his cult's demise during the siege. The trader had mentioned that he 'and one other' had survived and rebuilt the cult. Yet he had sneered at the other cultists in the chamber, saying they were nought but replacements. Did that mean one original member still existed and had not been present? Dietz thought so and even had his suspicions as to who it might be. Whoever it was must have some authority in

Middenheim to help arrange the statues' transportation so easily. That same person had known where they would be before setting out, allowing Kristoff to join them that first evening, and the individual would be placed highly enough so that he would still be at his post even during the attempted opening, in case anything went wrong.

After leaving the tunnels that morning Dietz and Alaric had walked resolutely towards the palace, a large leather satchel clasped in Dietz's hands. They had marched up the steps and into the entryway, where they had demanded to see their old friend Struber. When he had finally appeared the heavyset official seemed distracted.

'Yes, what?' he snapped at them as he descended an upper stair, adjusting his velvet cloak on his shoulders. 'Who are you and what do you want? I'm a very busy man.'

'This might interest you, Herr Struber,' Dietz said. He reached into the satchel and pulled out its contents.

Struber went chalk-white at the sight of Kristoff's head dangling before him. Several other courtiers and clerks were in the wide entryway and exclaimed as well. One of them fainted.

'Friend of yours?' Dietz asked innocently, shoving the head towards the official. The man's eyes widened and he started again, glaring at Dietz for an instant before regaining his composure.

'What? No, of course not – I've no idea who he is, but what is the meaning of this? What – happened to him?'

'He was part of a Chaos cult,' Alaric started to explain, pitching his voice so everyone nearby could hear. Realising that as well, Struber had quickly hustled them back upstairs, insisting that Dietz restore the head to its satchel for the time being. He had closeted them in a small meeting room and told them to wait there, and wait they had.

Dietz had worried that the official would gloss over their visit again, or, worse, find a way to make them seem the guilty parties. Either his fears were unfounded or too many people had seen the head, because after an hour or perhaps two they were escorted down another hall and to a room they had seen once before: The elector count's throne room. There, in the same seats they had occupied the last time, were the two most important men in Middenheim: Elector Count Boris Todbringer and Witch Hunter Captain Halmeinger.

Struber had not recognised Alaric the day before, but his superiors had no such difficulty – the minute they saw Alaric and Dietz they told Struber to shut the door, ordered all but a handful of guards outside, and demanded to know what had occurred. Dietz uncovered the head a second time and set it on the floor before him as Alaric explained the events of the previous night and this morning.

'Fastred Albers is dead, then?' Todbringer asked when they had finished. 'Good man, that. Damn shame.'

'No one else saw this fight but the two of you?' Halmeinger inquired, his eyes narrowed, 'and no one else survived the incident underground?'

'Some of the cultists may have survived,' Alaric corrected. 'They fled at the sight of the daemon.'

'Yet you stayed,' the witch hunter captain pointed out, his lips twisted into a superior smile.

'Someone had to close the gate,' Alaric replied, 'and there was no time to summon help.' He bowed to Halmeinger and Todbringer, making it clear that they would have been the first to be called upon, and Dietz once again admired his employer's skill. When Alaric wanted to he could be extremely diplomatic. Thank Ulric this was one of those times.

'We will need to examine this chamber,' Todbringer decided, stroking his chin.

'Of course,' Alaric replied, bowing again. 'We can guide your men there.' He straightened. 'Perhaps you will send Herr Struber along to coordinate? He has been so helpful already.'

Struber directed a quick, suspicious glance at Alaric, who merely smiled back. Dietz watched his employer as well. Did Alaric share his suspicions about the official? Or did he genuinely want Struber along?

Todbringer missed the exchange entirely. 'Go with them,' he ordered Struber. 'Study everything and report back to me.'

'I will send my witch hunters as well,' Halmeinger offered, receiving a grudging nod from Todbringer in response. 'You are already acquainted with Herr Kleiber, I believe?' he asked Alaric, and it was all Dietz could do not to show his relief. He had worried they would be saddled with a stranger and would have to prove their loyalties all over again.

'Certainly,' Alaric replied. 'Herr Kleiber accompanied us on our mission and proved invaluable in the destruction of the other statues.' He nodded his head politely towards Halmeinger. 'Thank you for assigning him to this matter.'

Todbringer was still frowning. 'We will have to tell Ar-Ulric,' he said finally.

'Why disturb his prayers,' the witch hunter captain objected, his face contorted in rage, but his voice silky smooth. 'Surely his devotions to Ulric are more important than this simple matter?'

The elector count shook his head, however, and met Halmeinger's sharp, dark gaze with his own ice-blue glare. 'This matter has gone beyond mere politics,' he stated. 'This creature is a foul abomination, a champion of Chaos, and it very nearly emerged within my city! The White Wolves are our spiritual defence against such creatures and the Ar-Ulric must be informed!'

The two men matched stares for a moment before Halmeinger looked away. 'Of course,' he said softly, conceding. 'We must include the Church in this matter. I had merely thought to spare him the complication.'

With that resolved, Todbringer launched into action. He sent Struber to fetch both Kleiber and a guard captain, and, in what may have been punishment for defying him, dispatched Halmeinger to personally request the Ar-Ulric's presence. That left Alaric and Dietz alone in the throne room with the elector count, a handful of his elite guards and a severed head.

'Now what shall we do with you?' Todbringer muttered, and Dietz was sure he was not referring to Kristoff's remains.

Fortunately Alaric was still in good form. 'You should clear us of all charges, first of all,' he replied smoothly. 'You should also pardon Rolf, the stonemason, of complicity. It will not restore his life, but at least his family will bear no shame.'

'Yes, of course,' Todbringer replied, leaning back and drumming his fingers on the arm of his throne. 'But truly, if this did occur as you say, we owe you a great debt, both of you, and I repay my debts.' He studied them for a moment. 'So, what can I do to show my gratitude?'

Alaric thought about that for a moment. 'Well,' he said at last. 'I do need a new sword…'

AFTER EMIL VALGEIR, the Ar-Ulric, had arrived and been told what had happened he had ordered a squad of his own Knights of the White Wolf to accompany them as well. No mention was made of the previous statues or of the mission to destroy them, but Dietz was sure he saw a spark of recognition when the high priest had looked at them. Valgeir was no one's fool.

Together with Captain Herrer – the same guard captain who had arrested them and Rolf – and his guard detail, plus Kleiber and several lesser witch hunters, Struber and the White Wolves, Alaric and Dietz had returned to the tunnels and retraced their steps. The chamber looked much the same as it had when they had left it. Bodies were still strewn about, the statue's remains were still scattered across the floor, and one of the cultists was still thrashing on the ground, foam still emerging from his tight-clenched lips. The daemon's footprints remained as well, gouged deep into the rock floor.

'Clearly it is as you said,' Kleiber announced after walking around the room. 'The daemon came forth just there and you destroyed the statue before it could fully emerge. The Empire is in your debt, gentlemen.' Kleiber had

already impressed them that morning; when he had
arrived and discovered the Ar-Ulric and his White Wolves,
the witch hunter had bowed low in what seemed genuine
respect. Halmeinger might not like the Ar-Ulric, but
Kleiber seemed to admire the man's devotion and he
treated the six White Wolves with them as fellow warriors.
Now his willingness to acknowledge what had happened
impressed them further, and Dietz was glad yet again that
Halmeinger had put Kleiber in charge instead of some
other member of their order.

The White Wolves had agreed with Kleiber's assessment
and, an hour later, they had all returned to the surface,
dragging the writhing cultist with them. The elector
count's guards removed the bodies as well, and workers
were sent to scrub away the blood. If anyone else realised
that the witch hunters' excesses had contributed to the
near disaster, no one mentioned it.

Rolf was posthumously exonerated, though Dietz suspected the money his widow received as recompense
meant more to her than the nicely worded apology. Dietz
and Alaric were cleared of all charges and formally
thanked for their assistance to Middenheim. They were
granted favoured status in the city, which meant they were
essentially minor nobles here, but without any lands,
monies, or titles. This meant little to Alaric, who was
already a noble by birth, but it mattered a great deal to
Dietz, whose family would share in his elevation. The
witch hunters had formally cleared them as well and pre-
sented them with a small note of thanks for their
assistance. The White Wolves had sent a similar note,
though it included a suggestion that they bring any such
future troubles directly to the Church, a subtle reprimand
for not involving them earlier.

'From outlaws to heroes,' Alaric commented after the last
of the recognition ceremonies. 'If we stay here much
longer we'll be running the place.'

Dietz nodded, but felt a pang. He had known they
would not stay, of course. Alaric had too much wanderlust

in him, and over the past year or more Dietz had acquired it as well. This matter was closed and it was time to move on, but that meant saying good-bye to his father yet again, and to Dagmar. Still, with the elector count's gratitude he could perhaps make their lives a little easier. Something Alaric had mentioned in passing, just before they had pursued Fastred, returned to Dietz and suggested another way to aid his sister in particular.

'You're in a good mood,' Alaric commented that evening. They were back at the Dancing Frog and Dietz had just entered their room, whistling. Glouste was wrapped around his neck as usual and purring like mad, sharing her master's mood.

'Indeed yes,' his friend replied, dropping into the other chair by the small table near the window. He grinned and stroked his pet, which nipped at his fingers affectionately.

'Care to explain why?' Alaric had been jotting down some notes in his journal, but set that aside now, curious. It was rare to see Dietz so visibly pleased with himself.

'Just taking care of my family,' was the reply, but Alaric stared until Dietz sighed and elaborated. Not that he seemed reticent – on the contrary, for once the tall man seemed eager to talk. 'Todbringer asked what we wanted,' he reminded Alaric, who simply nodded for him to continue. 'I asked for Kristoff's house.'

'A fine place, as I recall,' Alaric agreed, 'but what do you need with a house? Ah,' he said, seeing the look on his friend's face. 'It is not for you.'

'No.' Dietz looked smug. 'I gave it to Dracht.'

'Your brother?' Alaric frowned. 'I thought you two were not on the best of terms.'

Dietz shrugged. 'No, though this may help.' He leaned forward. 'But that was not why.'

Alaric contained his impatience. Clearly Dietz wanted to tell this story at his own pace. 'All right, why then?'

'It is much nicer than his old house,' Dietz explained, 'and much larger.' He grinned again. 'Large enough for Father to have his own room.'

'O-ho! Now I see.' Alaric admired his friend's deviousness – Dietz was normally a very straightforward man, but he could be extremely clever when he wanted to be. 'Dracht had claimed he couldn't care for your father because he lacked space for him. Now you've removed that argument.'

'He could hardly refuse,' Dietz agreed gleefully. 'The house is a definite improvement for him and much closer to the shop, and as the eldest son it is his duty.'

'Which leaves Dagmar free to pursue her own life,' Alaric agreed. He noticed that Dietz looked, if possible, even more smug now. 'What?'

'I've not been idle there either,' Dietz admitted. He laughed. 'I went to see Dagmar today, and I brought Hralir with me.' At Alaric's blank look he explained. 'Rolf's son?'

'Ah.' Alaric remembered the tall, fine-featured man in the stonemason's shop. 'I never got his name.'

'He and I were friends as youths,' Dietz said, his eyes trained upon the past. He smiled. 'Hralir is a good man and a fine carpenter, and he has always thought highly of Dagmar, and she of him.' He looked very pleased with himself. 'Now that she's free to choose her own life, and has the money Todbringer gave me as well, I suspect Hralir is even more interested.'

'Busy indeed,' Alaric agreed. 'Good for you.' Something bounced from the back of his mind, stirred by what Dietz had just said. 'Wait a second – Hralir!' He stood, crossed quickly to his chest of drawers and began rifling through it.

'What?'

'Rolf's son gave me something back at the shop,' Alaric explained, still digging through shirts and socks and razors and scarves. 'A small casket – ah!' He pulled the casket from the bottom drawer and carried it over to the table. 'Rolf wanted me to have it,' he explained as he sank back into his chair.

'What's in it?'

'The mask,' Alaric said, opening the casket and removing the mask to show Dietz. His friend did not seem entirely pleased to see the carved stone face again. 'Oh, calm yourself! It is only a carving, and a valuable one at that.' He looked into the casket again, 'but there's something more in here.' Setting the mask down carefully, he reached in and pulled out a worn-looking scroll. 'What's this?'

Dietz stood and moved aside as Alaric carried the scroll to his bed and carefully unrolled it. 'It's very old,' he told Dietz over his shoulder as he fingered the silk-smooth parchment. 'Look here, these markings. That style hasn't been used in centuries.' He frowned and rubbed his jaw, remembering something else. 'Rolf had said, when I showed him the mask, that he had some other items he thought would interest me. These must be them – he never got the chance to show me himself and so he left Hralir with instructions to give them to me.'

Dietz shook his head. 'Nice of the witch hunters to admit their mistake,' he said gruffly, 'but Rolf still died for nothing.'

'I know.' Trying not to think about it, Alaric returned to studying the scroll. 'Look at this!' He pointed to a strange figure, almost a glyph, and Dietz leaned closer to examine it over his shoulder. 'That mark was on the statues!'

'Are you sure?'

Alaric nodded. 'Positive. I even sketched it in my notes.' He fetched his journal from the table and flipped through it until he found the correct page. 'Here.' Held side by side the marks in the journal and on scroll were clearly identical.

'We should tell someone,' Dietz suggested, but Alaric shook his head.

'Not until we know more about it,' he argued. 'For all we know that could simply mean "power" or "wealth" or something else innocent and universal.'

His friend did not look convinced, so to distract him Alaric turned to the scroll again and began pointing out

other details. 'What is this here?' His fingers traced a set of
tiny triangular marks.

Dietz studied the pattern, frowning. 'Hills,' he said
finally.

Alaric stared at them again. 'You're right,' he admitted
after a moment, 'and this must be a river.' He tapped a long
wavy line. 'This is a map!'

'It is,' Dietz agreed, stepping back to squint at it. 'But of
where?'

Alaric looked in the casket again and pulled out a second
piece of parchment. This one was much smaller and not
nearly as old, the edges not yet worn smooth. 'Perhaps this
will say,' he said hopefully, unrolling it and scanning it
quickly. 'It's badly damaged,' he said after a moment. 'Little more than scraps left. It almost looks like someone
meant to destroy it, but I can still make out a bit.' He
squinted and traced the edge of a word near the top. 'Yes!
Listen: "...seems to be a map to an ancient tomb. I can't
quite make the name out... in the Borderlands... famed
for... treasures beyond imagining."' He glanced up at
Dietz. 'It's a map to a tomb in the Border Princes!'

'We don't know where,' Dietz pointed out. 'This scroll
only shows a small area. It could be anywhere.'

'It could be,' Alaric admitted sadly. He looked at the map
again. 'But wait, these scratchy marks appear to indicate
geographic features – rivers and mountains, probably. If
we compare this to a map of the region, and try to match
them up, we should be able to find where it is!'

Dietz scratched his chin. 'Might work,' he said after a
minute.

'We must find this tomb,' Alaric announced, hopping to
his feet and pulling his worn saddlebags from under the
bed. He started to toss them onto the bed, stopped, rolled
the scroll back up and set it aside, and then tossed them
down. 'Those markings from the statue – you're right, it
could be connected. We must make sure this tomb does
not contain a portal of its own, or some other daemonic
lure.'

Dietz groaned. 'Couldn't we send someone else?'

'Don't be foolish,' Alaric admonished, tugging clothes from his drawers and tossing them onto the saddlebags. 'Who else knows as much about this as we do?'

'Besides,' he said, feeling the smile stretching across his face as his mind began to race. 'Think of it! We could be the first to explore this tomb! The first to examine its mysteries! Just think of what we could find!'

Dietz groaned again and collapsed back into his chair. 'At least you've got a sword again,' he said finally, gesturing towards the rapier at Alaric's side.

'Hm? Oh, yes.' Alaric patted the new blade fondly. Todbringer had made good on his promise, presenting Alaric with a beautifully crafted rapier. It was even finer than his old blade, both sharper and stronger. 'I suppose it might prove useful.'

'You did say "tomb", didn't you?' Dietz asked after a moment.

'Yes, a tomb.' Alaric was trying to figure out how he had packed so many clothes into the saddlebags the last time. 'Why?'

'Tombs are underground,' his friend pointed out. 'Dark, tight spaces; your favourite.'

'Oh.' Alaric thought about that for a moment, and then shrugged. 'I'll manage. Besides,' he grinned at his companion, 'if it gets too scary I'll just send you.'

Dietz growled, causing Glouste to glance up. 'Never mind, Glouste,' he told his pet. 'You get used to him after a while... sort of.'

'Why wouldn't you?' Alaric asked, putting on an innocent expression. 'I am all charm and delight. Now get packing!'

ABOUT THE AUTHOR

Aaron Rosenberg has written role-playing games, educational books, magazine articles, short stories and novels for White Wolf and the *Star Trek: Starfleet Corps of Engineers* series. He also runs his own role-playing game publishing company. Aaron lives and works in New York City.